Days of Endless Night: Eschaton Cycle
Runeblade Saga Book 1
MATT LARKIN
Editors: Clark Chamberlain, Regina Dowling
Cover: Yocla Designs

Incandescent Phoenix Books
mattlarkinbooks.com

D1742391

CONTENTS

MIDGARD

THULE

NIDAVELLIR

LAPPMARKEN

SVIARLAND

JAMTLA

DALAR   UPSAL

NJARAR

OSTERGOTLAND

MORIMARUSA   NORREVISKE SKANE

CUMRIS   ARUS SJAELLAND BURSUNDAHOLMR

LAALAND

BRETLAND   REIDGOTALAND

RIJNLAND   MENZLIN

XANTEN

HUNALAND

BAIA

SWABIA   STYRIA

VALLAND

AQUISGRANA

IDAVOLLIR

OUTER MIKLAGARD

ANDALUS

KARJUBA

MIDDLE SEA

VANAHEIM   SERKLAND CALIPHATE

POHJOLA

KVENLAND

KALEVALA

SAMODIYTSIA

BJARMALAND

HOLMGARD

QAZAN

MIDGARD WALL

UTGARD

JARNVID

HALFHAUGR

AUJUM

KIOVIA

TARAZ

BLACK SEA

MIKLAGARD

MIKLAGARD

EXTRA RESOURCES

For full color, higher-res maps, character lists, location overviews, and glossaries, check out the bonus resources here:
https://tinyurl.com/y47j3gcj

PROLOGUE

*I*n ages past, the dvergar spread across Midgard and built four great cities at the corners of the Mortal Realm. Odin did not know exactly when each had fallen, but they had, abandoned even as the Old Kingdoms of men rose. And to barter peace with each of those kingdoms, the dvergar had wrought nine runeblades. Fell works, one given to each prince of an Old Kingdom.

Careful of his footing, Odin drifted amid trees in the marshes of Sviarland, waving a torch before him to dispel the mist. This land had embraced him, had embraced all the Aesir as their new gods. And as such, these people had many uses. Walking openly among them would have only confused them. No, Odin disguised himself as a simple vagrant on these long sojourns, and it well suited him. Men did not watch their words around old wanderers as they might among kings or gods. In illusion, one could catch bits of truth.

Odin had seen the effects of some few runeblades himself. The flaming sword Laevateinn, once the pride of the Lofdar, then wielded by mighty Frey. The perilous

Gramr, arm of the Niflungar, now given into the care of the Volsung clan. Most runeblades though had been lost in the ages since the Old Kingdoms themselves had fallen, eight hundred years ago.

But what was lost did not always remain so.

Beyond the marsh, in the kingdom of Dalar, a sorcerer-king slept. Gylfi. One of Odin's most useful servants. Very few among mortals were touched with the Sight. Those who were ... well, those few could be reached, influenced by the Otherworlds. Or by Odin, projecting himself beyond Midgard and thus able to walk in the dreams of the select few. Many did not even know he did this, that he used them so. Gylfi though, wise and schooled in the Art, would suspect the source of his visions.

And he would act, so eager to impress his god. So desirous to build his legacy.

Odin settled down on a dry mound, folded his legs beneath him, and closed his eyes.

Those runeblades had the power to change the course of a battle. And a great battle was coming, an end battle for this world. Before it came, Odin needed the runeblades back in play. He need not own them ... just make sure he could control those who did. All of it—moves on a tafl board, pieces—positioned to win the long game.

For naught else truly mattered.

And so ... Odin let his mind drift from Midgard and beyond, into the shadowy Astral Realm from which he might visit Gylfi. And offer a vision ... a lost city.

A great treasure.

And a chance at glory.

Men sought such petty things.

Odin offered whatever men sought. For his was a greater game.

PART I

Eleventh Moon
Year 26, Age of the Aesir

1

HERVOR

*A*n etheric light hovered over the hills, beckoning or forewarning, depending on the constitution of one's heart. Hervor's heart was cast from iron. No daughter of a great berserk feared to tread in any land, nor did ghost stories frighten her.

Her own crew had refused her, refused to even set upon this island after sunset. They had argued against even anchoring off shore, had wanted to return to other lands before dark. But Hervor—or Hervard as she called herself when she thought it best others mistake her for a man—had led this crew on more than one raid. They had bent to her will, even if she'd had to row ashore on her own.

She had left the rowboat behind and headed for those hills. The ever-present mist grew thicker in these lands, thicker than Hervor could explain, unless the ghosts themselves conjured it. It did not matter. She carried a torch to ward against the poison fumes and had several more in case of need. That ephemeral light meant her destination lay before her. Skalds called the light barrow fire, claiming the wakeful dead might sometimes cast it above their resting places.

The bravest of men would turn craven at the mere thought of beholding a ghost or draug. In this case, she was lucky enough not to be a man. Her errand here had waited long enough, her vengeance delayed for far too many years.

The damn mist seemed almost as thick as a wall of water, and she had to keep waving the torch back and forth to drive it back. Fire was the only true defense against it. Breathe in too much of the stuff and you went Mist-mad. She'd seen it happen. A raider with her had lost his torch and come wandering into camp, hollow look in his eyes. Hervor had cut him down. You let men like that go, they'd turn on you or run off into the wilds becoming Odin-alone knew what. Death was quicker, even if the mist drew the poor bastard down to Hel.

The snows had melted for the summer, and wiry grass had spread, covering the hills of Samsey. A flame flickered just before those hills—a real flame, not some etheric light. Fire meant people. Since when did people live on this haunted island? Had some trollfucking looter come here thinking to steal *her* plunder?

Even as her steps quickened, she jerked free the broadsword slung over her shoulder. No one would take what was hers. No one. She raced forward.

You couldn't see more than a few feet ahead in this cursed mist. But one torch probably meant only one ... she nigh to collided with a grazing sheep. The creature let out a mewling cry and scampered away, running off into the night.

"Dammit!" a voice shouted. "Who moves in this land?" The torch drifted closer, the light burning away mist and revealing a man. Despite the axe in his hand, he was no warrior. Stance was wrong, didn't have the bearing. And those simple clothes. A man grazing his sheep—brave to do so at night. "What mortal would dare these shores? Do you not know where you are? Find shelter quickly."

The shepherd glanced up at the moon, barely visible through the vapors blanketing the ground.

Hervor advanced on him but did not raise her sword. "I have never been one to flee, old man. These hills are barrows, aren't they?"

The man's eyes widened, and he fell back a step. "Do not ask such things." A slight sneer. "Have you gone Mist-mad? If you're some raider, you have come very far astray. This island belongs to an old people, one best not disturbed. To say naught of what lies buried in ..."

Odin's stones. This was just some frightened slave. Hervor sheathed her sword. "I do not scare easily. Stand aside. Something of mine lies here, and I will have it this very night."

The shepherd did step aside, shaking his head. "Any man who ventures onward is a fool." He scurried past her, chasing after the lost sheep, away from the hills.

Torch before her, Hervor pushed forward, upward. No path led over the hills, but neither were they too steep. The barrow fires glowed but produced no heat. Indeed, as she passed among them they seemed more like luminous mist than aught else. Except ... she swayed a little ... it made the hair on her neck stand on end. She shivered at a sudden chill, then swept the torch around in anger.

"I know you are here, dead ones. I do not fear you."

Far away yet somehow all around her, the mist seemed to laugh. She shook herself. Her own mind playing tricks and naught more. Instead, she wandered, embracing the chills and walking toward where they grew stronger.

When a faint shock ran along her fingers all at once, she paused. Turned. At the base of one hill lay a mound of stones. Behind one lay a crack revealing darkness. The entrance to a barrow. Hervor planted the torch in the ground then grasped the stone with both hands and heaved.

Dust and dirt cascaded around the stone. She pulled until her muscles felt ready to burst, but it did not pop free.

"Fucking Arrow's Point" she said, then spat. That murderer must have put this here. Or put it back. She wiped her brow, then climbed above the mound.

Back braced against the hill, she used both legs to push at the stone. Pain welled in her lower back. Her fingers dug into the dirt and scraped rock, and she grunted with the effort.

All at once, rocks beneath that stone shifted. The stone slipped free, tumbling away from the mound. Hervor fell forward and slammed against the remaining stones. Grimacing, she sat there a moment before gathering the strength to rise.

With the top stone removed, the barrow opening was large enough for a small man—or a well-muscled woman—to squeeze through. She reclaimed the torch then crawled forward on her belly, holding the light out in front of her. After a few feet, she dropped down into the barrow tunnel.

She was tall for a woman and had to stoop to avoid hitting her head on the roof. Years of dust caked the walls. With the torch, she batted at spider webs choking the whole passage. The webs ignited and sparked away. Skittering creatures retreated from the torchlight.

Odin's stones.

The air had grown stale, rank. Hard to breathe.

She pushed her way forward a dozen feet. The path delved down deeper into the hill before opening up into a triangular chamber just tall enough to allow her to stand properly. She cracked her neck side to side and flexed her shoulders. A stone slab lay here, with a body rotting on it. Hervor held the torch over it.

"Angantyr?"

The corpse did not respond. It had a sword clutched in one hand. Hervor brushed dust off it. Pattern wrought iron but otherwise unremarkable.

This wasn't it. It wasn't him.

The flickering torchlight should have spread farther than it seemed to. The mist had seeped down here, but it wasn't thick. Still, the tomb's shadows did not retreat from the light, not as much as they ought to have. Hervor paced the room. On each wall of the triangle, an opening led to another such chamber. Those in turn opened up into more tombs.

Scowling, she turned about. One tunnel led out, and if she lost track of it, she might wind up wandering this mound for hours. Not that she was frightened. She feared naught.

Still.

That stench of death had grown so thick. Not like the smell of blood and shit and piss that saturated a battlefield. No, the smell here was old. Flesh had rotted away to leave decaying bone. A smell of eternal damnation and unending despair. Like a stench escaping from the gates of Hel.

She might well search this whole place and not find what she sought. And were she to do so she might truly run out of torches. How much longer did this one have? An hour, at the most. Not even a brave woman should climb around barrows in darkness.

No.

She had come here for a purpose, one that demanded it

be fulfilled. Turning about, torch held high, she cleared her throat.

"Angantyr, wake now! The daughter of Svafa calls upon you. *Your* daughter, your only child. Wake, Father!"

Her voice echoed through the barrow, ringing from one tomb to the next and seeming to repeat too long. Hervor swallowed. Could she have the wrong barrow? No, this had to be the one her family lay in. Her father, her uncles, all entombed here to rot and writhe in restless sleep. Denied Valhalla or even the halls of Hel.

"Hervard! Hjorvard, Hrani, Angantyr!" She turned about again. "Berserkir wake! Have the children of Arngrim turned to mold and dust? Will not one speak to their kin?"

Unintelligible whispers seemed to carry on the mists, to stalk the shadows. All the hair on her body stood on end now, and fresh chills wracked her.

But no voice spoke that she could understand.

There were ghosts here, but they did not deign to speak with her. She had once heard a völva say there was another world, an invisible world. This Astral Realm was the true home of ghosts and vaettir and all beings not quite of Midgard. A barrier one could not see or touch separated the worlds, but sometimes, those on the other side could see this Mortal Realm. Could hear it.

In places like this, the barrier was thin. Or so the völva claimed.

"If you will not speak to me, then may it seem as though a mound of maggots wriggle through your ribs. Let your corpses mold and rot if you will not fetch for me the sword Dvalin made." She turned about again. A palpable anger had begun to creep into the air, one that felt like a stone beginning to compress around her heart and lungs. She grunted. Harder to speak now. "It does not become ghosts to hoard such valuable arms. What use have the dead for sacred blades?"

The pressure lightened, and she sucked in a deep breath, forced to steady herself on the wall. Her hand came away caked in mold and unidentifiable black slime. She scrubbed it on her trousers.

"Why do you hail me, Hervor, daughter?" The voice came from the opening to her right. She spun, torch forward. Naught there. "You tread swiftly toward your own doom. You walk in darkness." The voice was like a hollow whisper, as if spoken by the wind, from far away.

She pushed forward, slipped into the next tomb. No sign of aught.

"You have gone mad, your mind dark, when you think to wake the dead."

Hervor's jaw trembled. She wanted to deny him, to defy him. She was not scared. And she had come here to avenge *him*.

No words escaped her, though.

"Our father Arngrim did not lay us in these cairns, nor did any kin of ours. Our enemy placed us here, cursed us, and took from me Tyrfing. It is lost."

Hervor gasped, rubbed the back of her hand over her mouth. "You lie! By Odin, you lie! I have come here for my due, Father. I, your only child, demand my heirloom." The stories agreed with what the slave had told her—Arrow's Point had entombed Tyrfing with the brothers. It had to be here. And after all she had done, all she had risked, now she had found her father. And he was *lying* to her. She drew a dagger and sliced open her palm. The same völva had told her a blood offering could contact that invisible world ...

Hervor pressed her bloody palm onto the wall. "By the blood of the living I beseech you! Show yourself, ghost!"

A crack resounded through the entire barrow. The ground trembled, and dust and dirt fell from the roof. The whole mound was going to cave in. Before she could react, even try to run, etheric blue flame erupted from the next tomb and swept inward. Hervor threw herself against the wall and covered her head with her hands. She did not scream.

No heat reached her—if aught, the graven chill only deepened.

She dropped her hands.

Across the tomb drifted the image of a large warrior, writhed in blue flame, clad in a bearskin. He was translucent, his features hard to make out, save those piercing, flaming eyes. A great gap had been cleft through his skull, and yet the two pieces hovered together. "You willingly call open the gates of Hel and crack the barrows. This island is thick with ghosts, girl, all now blazing into grim wakefulness. Your ship shall burn around you, lest you reach it quick. If you still can, maiden!"

Hervor glanced back at the exit. No. Another lie. She swept the torch in front of her. "You cannot light any flame, ghost. Fire is the enemy of Hel and all her misty children. I am not afraid of you! Yes, I see you, blazing in the darkness, standing on the threshold between this world and the next. Is that your wish? To drag me down to meet Hel?"

Her father's form flickered, appearing closer to her, though the blaze had dwindled. He appeared almost lifelike, with just the barest hint of that ethereal fire. "I am trying to spare you, daughter. Hervor, heed my words. Tyrfing will be the ruin of all your family. Take the sword and your children shall wield it and suffer for it. The dvergar forged the runeblades for their own ends and for the hands of the Old Kingdoms. Their time has passed, and the blades ought to lie dead, in darkness, as their wielders."

Hervor squeezed her fist. "No! I make my own urd. And my kin lay entombed here, cursed and denied Valhalla because of the crimes of a living man. I too, remain human. And I will have the bane of Hjalmar before I leave this place."

The last flames around the ghost faded. The torchlight seemed to not set quite right upon him. He reached a hand to her cheek. It was not like being touched by a person. More like a feeling, a slight pressure without substance. At last his hand fell away, and he shook his head. "You are strong, daughter. And foolish. Beneath my back lies Hjalmar's bane, blazing, scorching me as was my curse."

Hervor grimaced. Arrow's Point had spared her father no agony.

"No woman would dare take up the runeblade," her father said.

"*I* will." She stepped around the ghost and trod into the next tomb. It must be this one. Another corpse rested upon the slab here. Its face had rotted, but it could have been the same man who stood beside her. She looked to the ghost.

A slight blaze had returned to his eyes.

"I will guard it well and use it to avenge the murders and the curse, both."

"Fool Hervor. I cannot refuse my own blood ... I warn you one more time—Tyrfing will bring ruination upon your line. It seeks blood and once freed, that bloodlust cannot be denied."

Hervor scowled at that and reached slowly toward the corpse. "My family lies here, dead and suffering. My father burning instead of feasting in Odin's halls. I have no sons. You do well to yield the sword to me. It is dearer in my quest than were I to rule all Sviarland." She pushed the corpse over.

The shade flickered as she did so, vanishing for a moment.

Beneath the body lay a sword, writhed in iridescent flames. Just more ethereal fire. It could not harm her. Her hand closed around the hilt. Flames surged up her arm, burning and searing. She collapsed to the floor screaming, clutching her flesh. The sword and her torch clattered down beside her.

Hervor gasped, trying to stifle her screams. Odin's stones! What the fuck?

The ghost watched her, saying naught. All the flames had gone out of him. Back into the sword. It was still there on the floor, glowing. Hot. It seemed the curse passed between Realms and allowed it to harm the living and dead both. Finally, he shook his head. "Do not touch the edges. The wounds they inflict will fester like poison and never heal."

She crawled over to where the runeblade lay. Pattern welded from a coppery metal, with a hilt of the brightest gold. And along the blade ran ancient dvergar runes that made it a weapon unmatched in the world of men.

"Nigh to twenty years you have lain here, burning in death," she said. "From today ... that suffering shall begin to rain on our enemies." Hervor snatched up the hilt again. Fresh jolts of agony seared through her flesh and seemed to melt her bone. She screamed in pain but did not drop the sword. Instead, she rose to her feet and only tightened her grip. "Tyrfing is ... mine."

The flames cooled. The sword stilled in her hand. Its blade shone with a white light that filled the tomb.

She turned, but her father's ghost had vanished.

BLOOD SEEPED between Hervor's fingers as she climbed from the barrow. The burns on her hand and forearm were all too real. Touching aught brought fresh agony. Bits of her skin had flaked off. Once free, she tumbled down the hill and lay there, beside her second torch. Had Odin seen what she had done? Faced down ghosts and withstood the burning of her own flesh to claim her family's legacy.

Yes, she should have the eyes of the gods on her now.

With a knife, she cut away a strip of her tunic. She had no völva's salve to apply, so she wrapped the strip around her arm and palm, teeth grit against the pain. Wrapping it hurt too, but it was better than constantly brushing it against things.

Tyrfing's weight over her shoulder was a comfort, a reminder of what her pain had bought. The first step toward vengeance. A great many men had wronged her family, and not one silver of weregild had ever reached her. No, her father and uncles had waited too long already for vengeance. Maybe, once Arrow's Point and his Yngling masters had fallen to her blade, maybe then her family's spirits could reach Valhalla.

And for that, she had to get off this damned island.

She pushed herself up, took up the torch, and stumbled on through the mist. She had raised a crew with some effort, though she could trust them. She even had led them raiding all around the Morimarusa, into Reidgotaland, Sviarland, Hunaland. And still they had not wanted to come here. Samsey was haunted, they claimed. Some ancient power dwelt here, restless and best left alone.

Men were given to such pointless superstitions.

The shepherd was long gone as, sadly, was his sheep. She could have used something to eat.

No matter, the crew would have something left of the night meal she could sate herself on. Blood seeped through her bandage. She forced herself to look elsewhere. Best to keep her eyes alert in any event, especially at night. *That* was more than superstition. Hervor did not much care for night, in fact. Daylight meant freedom, the ability to walk, run, raid. At night, men had to cower in front of flames not knowing what lurked in the darkness just beyond their sight. Naught tasted fouler than the impotence of that, of admitting to such weakness.

And the mist was always thickest at night. Legends claimed the mists came from Niflheim, from the World of Mist, domain of Hel. It seemed some skald's fancy to her.

Either way, Hervor would happily send a great many men to the gates of Hel very soon.

She passed out of the hills and down toward the shore. Thank Odin. Vengeance could wait a day or so. She needed a few mugs of mead, a hearty meal, and a long sleep. She paused a moment to check her helm and her mail. Most of the regular crew knew her for a woman. You couldn't conceal these things forever. They addressed her as Hervard though, because on a raid, men seemed more likely to fear a male leader. Men were stupid like that. Regardless, they had taken on some fresh bodies before coming here, and she saw no reason to let her secret slip needlessly.

By the shore, her steps stalled. Where the fuck was the ship? She was certain they had anchored here, in front of the rock face. Hervor paced around, past the rock, waving the torch to dispel the mist. What was going on? Where would they ... was that the light of a fire? Way out, over the sea and fading quickly. It was. A ship sailing away, vanishing into mist.

Hervor stood there, mouth open, not quite able to form a sentence. Her crew. Her trollfucking crew! They had *left* her here. Odin's stones! They must have seen the earthquake and ... and panicked like some untested boys. Those craven bastards!

"Get back here!" she shouted after them.

No way her voice would carry.

Samsey was haunted. That's what they claimed. Just about everywhere people didn't congregate and build large fires was haunted. But they had feared this place enough to leave their own captain behind. She worked her jaw. Her fingers twitched, eager to draw Tyrfing and spill their blood. It wanted to punish them. She knew it did.

Any sign of that flame was gone. And her own torch was dwindling. Sure, she had a few more. Maybe enough to get through the night. But she had no supplies, no food. There were woods here. She could gather tinder for a fire. That would be a start.

But without a bow, she couldn't hunt.

So how was she supposed to survive? Where would she get ...? The shepherd. If there was a shepherd, there would be other people. Locals, somewhere. She just needed to find them. There had to be some way off this island.

ॐ

THE RUMBLES of Hervor's stomach had begun to grow louder even than the waves lapping on the shore. A numb heaviness had replaced the burning in her right hand. Even flexing her fingers felt like it was tearing off her skin.

Following the shore meant she'd find fishermen sooner

or later. Or so she'd thought. It was a damned large island, and already the daylight was waning. It did not help that she'd slept beneath an ash tree for Odin-knew how long. But then, she'd felt ready to collapse not long after sunrise.

In daylight, the mist thinned, and you could almost allow yourself to breathe.

All the walking had worn her new boots in. She'd taken them off a man she'd killed the past moon but only just bothered to try them on right before coming to Samsey. Luckily, they had strong soles. What with her walking the shore all fucking night and day. When she caught those craven, traitorous crewmen, she'd have each and every one of them flayed and cursed down to Niflheim. A skald once claimed that, in the depths of the World of Mist, a dragon gnawed upon the helpless corpses of murderers, rapists, and oath-breakers. Her crew had already managed to fall into the first two of those categories, and now they'd earned themselves the third. The worst of all crimes, many would say.

The dark dragon would suck the marrow from their bones, and they would feel every instant of it. For the dead were dead already and could find no respite from their suffering.

Hervor, however, was not going to break her oath. She had sworn vengeance on the House of Yngling and upon its champion Arrow's Point.

Her steps on the sand had become shuffling, graceless. A long time more she walked, trying not to think too much. Just keep moving. Do not consider that her throat had grown so dry it felt on fire. Do not think about drinking seawater. It would not help.

There had been a shepherd. He had gone somewhere. Obviously, she had picked the wrong direction to walk. But if she turned around now she'd lose another day. There had to be someone living here, some way off this cursed island.

As twilight neared, the peak of a longhouse came into view, praise Odin. Hervor increased her pace. The wind howled, as if welcoming in the fresh reinforcements of the mist. Had she inherited her father's berserk nature she might have welcomed the night and rejoiced in the moonlight. She had not gotten it, however. As a mere human, the night was strange, alien to her. And if it did not embrace her, why should she not scorn it in return?

She almost collided with the wall surrounding the house. It only rose up to her chest. Easy enough to vault were she not bone tired. She shook her head. These people were not here for her to plunder in any event. Their presence had like as not saved her life. She edged along the fence until she reached the gate. Out on the water, lay a dock. A small sailing boat, probably for fishing. Small but probably big enough to get to Sjaelland. From there, she could make her way back to Sviarland.

Hervor glanced back to the house. She was starving. Smoke rose from the chimney. Fire meant people, warmth, and food. Dammit. Vengeance would wait, at least for an hour.

She swung open the gate and ambled toward the house. Shuffling sounded inside. They had heard her. No one opened the door. She groaned. Obviously hospitality was not the highest virtue among these people. Perhaps they thought aught wandering alone during sunset was a vaettr or other force of ill.

"I am human." Her voice sounded harsh, cracked from too long with naught to drink. She rapped on the door. "I am a traveller in need. Open up, and let me in."

Whispers she could not catch sounded on the other side. Quickly stifled.

Frightened fishermen too stupid to know ghosts and trolls would not ask for permission to enter. Hervor shouldered the door. It creaked on its hinges but held as though a solid mass bound it. Had they barricaded it? Hel damn the peasants anyway. She was too hungry, too thirsty, and too fucking tired for this. She drew Tyrfing. As it left its scabbard, it emanated light like a torch but whiter, more intense in radiance.

"Open the door! I just want food and ale!"

Holding the sword filled her with renewed strength, much as it hurt in her cracked and bleeding palm. Perhaps it was just the refreshing feel of a blade in hand once again. Such a thing was nigh to a part of her.

Her heart was pounding, throbbing, beating through her like a drum. The whole World was beating with it.

Thump thump.

"Open the fucking door before I hack it down!"

Thump thump.

Her palm was sweating. The sun had already set. Grown chill. The mist was creeping in.

Thump thump.

She just wanted food. Well, and their damned boat. They were forcing her hand, after all.

THUMP THUMP THUMP.

She couldn't hear aught over that pounding, ringing in her ears. Were they mocking her inside? Did they think those ash wood planks protected them? With a war cry she could barely hear over the pounding, she chopped at the door. The blade sliced through ash planks as though they had the strength of wool. Hervor hacked again and again, grunting with effort.

Great chunks of the wood flew free.

The pounding had stopped. A woman was screaming.

Hervor fell still. Blood dripped off Tyrfing's blade. Odin's stones. Bastard had tried bracing the door with his own body, hadn't he? She kicked what remained of the door. Boards cracked and it swung inward, partially obstructed by the eviscerated man on the floor.

A woman had thrown her arms around two small children, shielding them with her body. She was shrieking in some language Hervor couldn't make out. Perhaps Old Northern? Studies had never been much of her interest.

Hervor shook her head at the mother. "I just wanted a damn meal."

The woman kept sputtering, but Hervor caught one word she recognized, repeated on several occasions: Hel. Whether the fisherman's wife was damning Hervor to the icy goddess or actually beseeching her for aid, Hervor could not say.

Either way, Hervor sheathed Tyrfing and stormed over to where the family had a steaming halibut sitting on a piece of wood near the fire. She snatched the plate up, grabbed a drinking horn filled with water—best thing under the circumstances—and stormed back to the threshold.

Fuck.

Hervor looked back at the family. She hadn't intended to kill anyone. She was desperate and ... and ...

She set down the fish and fumbled with a silver arm ring. What was the weregild for a fisherman anyway? Who knew? Instead of breaking off a piece of the silver, she tossed the whole arm ring at the woman. It was all she could do for them. Besides, she was still stealing their boat.

She drained the drinking horn in several great gulps, then tossed it back into the house.

The woman was staring daggers at her.

Hervor shrugged. "Maybe I'll meet Hel, maybe I'll dine with Odin in Valhalla. The only difference this made is now it'll take a bit longer first."

The widow gave no acknowledgement of understanding.

Hervor shook her head and walked away. She hadn't wanted to kill anyone here.

She hadn't.

2

STARKAD

The Kingdom of Upsal lay centered on the Fyrisvellir by the River Fyris above the marsh. It was one of seven petty kingdoms throughout Sviarland but a strong one, ruled by what had once been the strongest of dynasties. The Ynglings claimed descent from the Vanr, Frey, who wielded the flaming runeblade Laevateinn in countless battles against the jotunnar and other forces of chaos. Not that Starkad had ever seen Frey, nor was he like to now.

No, Odin and his fellow Aesir had cast down all the Vanir and banished them beyond the edges of Midgard. What exactly that meant, Starkad could not say, nor did he truly care. Such things had naught to do with him anymore.

Men called him a wanderer, and there was truth enough in that. He never stayed over long in one place. It didn't sit well on him, trying, like something began to eat away at his heart. Besides, a man did not grow rich by resting on past accomplishments.

Starkad had spent long years in service to the Yngling Dynasty, off and on. His path carried him far afield, beyond even the North Realms. He had seen things these petty kings could not imagine. And now they called him back. Word had spread through Sviarland that they sought his aid once again.

They knew it did not come cheaply.

Starkad made his way over the marshy plain, Afzal trailing a few steps. Countless treks here had taught him the safest way to pass. These wolds were haunted by the ghosts of innumerable warriors who had lost themselves in the mist, sunken into the peat. They watched him now, the dead. They did not show themselves, but a man could feel it as they neared, the chill in the air, the hair on his arms standing on end. The dead hated the living, envied them for the life so cruelly snatched from their grasp. Starkad had many enemies among the dead, many he had sent screaming into the next world. Those ghosts would lead him astray if he let them.

Afzal was pointing at a ghost light over the bog.

Starkad grabbed the Serklander with a hand on each cheek and spun him around, forcing the man to look into his eyes. "Do not look at the lights. They shall be the last thing you see with living eyes."

Will-o'-the-wisps, mere trickery of the dead, but those lights had drawn many a man to his death. So like life-preserving flame a man naturally looked at them, stared deeply, and so became intoxicated with the luminous flames. A man would follow them right off into a pit of peat and drown, still trying to clutch flames he could never hold. Starkad had seen it happen. It was not the worst death he had ever seen, but neither is there much honor in choking on muck.

Afzal blinked, then nodded. "How many times over should I owe my life to you?"

Starkad released him, then spit into the bog. "You are

free to leave any time you wish. I have not asked for your service."

"You have it, nonetheless."

Starkad smiled, just a little. Careful not to look too closely at the wisps himself, he pushed onward. The Serklander had not left his side in ... was it nine winters now? Not since Starkad had saved him when the foreigner was but a boy. It was good to have someone to talk to, anyway.

The Yngling hall lay by the river. Though built by modern men, it had stone foundations dating back at least to the time of the Old Kingdoms. Maybe even before. Maybe Frey himself had truly helped build the place, as the Ynglings claimed.

A stone wall protected each house in the town, the great hall included. Those gates were thrown wide, though with evening drawing nigh, they would no doubt soon shut. Now though, the Ynglings welcomed warriors from far abroad into their hall. Shouting and raucous laughter rang from inside. Starkad nodded at the guards at the door.

"Who the fuck needs two swords?" one whispered to the other as he passed.

Starkad stiffened. This oaf did not even know who he was. Did not know why he wore a sword on either shoulder. His fingers twitched idly.

"Not worth it," Afzal whispered in his ear.

"Dolt," the other guard said. "That's Starkad Eightarms."

The first guard uttered a satisfying hiss of surprise and perhaps self-admonishment. Enough so that Starkad need not personally introduce himself. He continued on instead.

He waded among the throng, accepting the drinking horn as it was passed to him. He took a long swig of it. The Ynglings still had the best mead; he'd give them that. He handed it off to some shieldmaiden without looking at her. She was not worth his time.

Women never were.

She tried to talk to him, but he ignored her and pushed onward.

"Orvar!"

Orvar was a tall man, well muscled though at an age most men never reached. Not that Starkad was one to talk. Still, Orvar showed his age more than Starkad. Most men would have thought Starkad not much more than twenty winters, despite his thick beard and scraggly hair. In truth, he was less than a decade shy of Orvar, who had to be pushing fifty winters now.

They had fought together many times, most often on the same side, though Starkad had once crossed swords with the man at the other's behest. It had been a short contest, though Orvar remained among the finest Starkad had ever faced. Still, the fastest man was the only one who mattered.

And Starkad was very, *very* fast with a blade.

"Odin's spear, man," Orvar said. "Time does not seem to touch you at all. If I didn't know better I'd think you one of the Aesir!"

Starkad barely stopped himself from spitting. "I am not one of them." The man had embraced the new gods and would not take kindly to any insult to them. "I was not certain to find you here. Not after—"

Orvar held up a hand. "Let's not speak of her."

"They are always more trouble than they are worth."

His friend snorted. "Not sure I agree on that one. At any rate, how goes it with you? I heard you made for the Midgard Wall."

"I wanted to see it for myself."

"And did you?"

Starkad grunted in assent. Stories claimed the Vanr sorcerer Mundilfari had raised the wall to enclose Midgard, protect it from the forces of Utgard. On occasion, a jotunn or such creature made it past, but the worst of them remained outside the Realms of men. Of course, it also cut Mankind off from the fabled treasures of Utgard. A trade, he supposed.

Orvar had seen the far side of the wall, had claimed there were breaches. One day, Starkad would find those and see Jotunheim for himself.

Orvar looked now to Afzal, who was trying to wrangle water from the slaves, much to everyone's chagrin. "Is that the same Serkland boy from before? He still follows you?"

He shrugged. "Yngvi is here?"

"Alf as well, yes, and the sons of both brothers too. Everyone gathers for this." Orvar beckoned to a seat on the benches.

Indeed, both brothers sat side by side on thrones. As their own father—Alrik—had shared kingship with his brother, so too they had divided the kingdom between them. Most like they hoped to avoid hostilities within the family— more than enough hardship had plagued the Ynglings already. Starkad could not see how fracturing the kingdom would end well, though. Whose sons would inherit? Or would the kingdom be yet further divided?

Starkad had served the two kings' father for a winter or so before tragedy had struck. Alrik and Eirik had killed one another, an urd Yngvi and Alf wanted to avoid. Time would tell.

All men had their own curses to face.

Slaves brought out great hunks of reindeer as well as roasted carrots and chard. A feast worthy of great kings, certainly. And kings who wanted something. Starkad dug in, pausing only to direct Afzal to a seat nearby. The Serklander did not drink ale or mead—despite the insult of continuously refusing the drinking horn. It was one habit Starkad had never managed to break him of. Shame, too. Instead of getting drunk, the foreigner preferred to smoke his strange herbs. Starkad had tried them once and found his stomach roiling like a stormy sea. Never again.

Orvar pointed to another table. Starkad almost choked on his mead. Old Bragi Bluefoot. The skald had to have had a decade still on Orvar, and here he was still, boasting like a young man and slinging insults at warriors half his age. Some things never changed.

"Friends!" King Yngvi shouted, as he stood and strode forward. The hall did not exactly grow still, but the noise fell to the point Starkad could at least hear their host. "Friends, welcome! The solstice approaches, and we will soon greet a new year."

Men shouted, raising their mugs or drinking horns or even reindeer bones in salute.

Yngvi lifted his hands for quiet. "And this solstice I have word from our friend King Gylfi."

Starkad snorted. Friend was probably a stretch. None of the kings of Sviarland much trusted one another and for good reason. Borders shifted often, and little wars soon grew into bitter feuds. Sviarland had been a divisive and war-torn Realm since the fall of the Old Kingdoms, and that was not like to change.

Still, Gylfi was a decent king, well respected. He'd ruled the lands of Dalar a long time. A sorcerer, though, and thus a man Starkad avoided.

"King Gylfi has had a vision sent by Odin."

And that was part of the reason he'd ruled so long. Odin had a penchant for reaching out in dreams to a chosen few, Gylfi among them. As was Starkad, much to his chagrin.

"The great Ás king has commanded his people in Sviarland to go forth and claim the World, to spread across all the lands and bring his name and cause to all peoples." This was not news. After overthrowing the Vanir, Odin had revealed himself to Gylfi, claiming godhood and ordering the Sviarlanders to spread his fame. It would never have been enough for the Ás king. If every land in Midgard turned to his worship, the Aesir would no doubt next try to convert the fucking jotunnar themselves.

"Odin has revealed the location of a land lost long ago, an island we thought but a myth. The lost island of Thule."

Now Starkad sat straighter. Gylfi often claimed to have visions sent by Odin, but the aged king probably invented half those visions to enhance his own fame in association with the god's. But if he had the location of a lost land, maybe Odin truly had spoken to him. Naught good ever came from Odin's mouth, but then, lost lands meant treasures of the Old Kingdoms. Wealth beyond measure for men in these times. And new places, new challenges. Places not seen by men in centuries. Such places held a call of their own, more powerful than the command of even an Ás king.

Starkad's fingers fair itched with the thought of it.

"And so my brother and I," Yngvi said, "we have agreed to partner with Gylfi for an expedition. We seek a crew of the bravest, strongest men in the North Realms. Ones who will seek out Thule and tame it such that a colony might be established there. And to do this, the crew must be able to pass the winter on the island."

A great many of the men exchanged glances. Summer raids were common enough, but Yngvi proposed something else entirely. An expedition not to steal from Kvenlanders but to tame a land gone wild. What dangers, what fell challenges might lurk on an island not walked by men in ages? What *glory* to those first men who took that land.

"To this end, I have called back my old friend, Orvar-Oddr!"

Starkad's friend stood now, spread his arms, and looked at all the gathered warriors. He'd known. The trollfucker had known why they were here and not told Starkad. Indeed, Orvar now spared him the merest glance.

Starkad slammed his fist on the table and stood. "No such expedition will leave without me!"

Afzal groaned, then stood. Starkad nodded at him.

One by one, others stood as well. There, Rolf Quicktongue. At another table, the man everyone called the Axe. And old Bragi Bluefoot too, claiming they would need a skald to take note of their deeds and turn them to song.

And what a journey this would be, what a tale. They would find this lost island, plunder its ancient riches, and win this new Realm for the Sviarlanders.

And Odin could sit and scheme in Asgard until the end of time for all Starkad cared.

3

HERVOR

*T*he mist had grown thicker than it ought to, almost enough that it seemed to slow Hervor's boat, as though the water created a little too much drag. Already the wind had died and forced her to take to oars. Now, approaching Sjaelland with sweat streaming down her face and back, every stroke felt like pulling against snow instead of water.

Hervor grunted with the effort. She'd wanted to skirt the coast until she found a town where she could buy food, maybe find some straw to sleep on. But at this point, she'd take land anyway she could have it.

Hel's frozen underworld. When would dawn break? It was too long coming.

Even her calloused left hand felt raw from the oars. And the right one, the burns ... best not to even consider that. Felt like she'd worn it down to the bone.

Heaving, she gave over as soon as the waters seemed shallow. Three dozen feet offshore but she'd fucking swim if she had to. This boat was faulty somehow; it had to be. She dropped the oars and leapt over the side. The water was cold, even in summer, and deeper than she'd thought. It rushed over her head and tugged at her mail. Hervor surged upward, sucked down a breath, and swam under the surface until her feet scraped sand. Finally, she waded toward shore.

This night—every night since she'd gone to Samsey—had not gone to her liking. When she found her traitorous crewmen, she'd—

A sudden undercurrent swept her feet out from beneath her. She pitched forward into the water. It yanked her back, pulling her toward the depths. Her fingers pulled through sand underwater, then caught on a rock. She couldn't see a damn thing. Felt like some eel had wrapped itself around her legs and was tugging on them. With her right hand, she swatted at them.

Naught there. Just water.

Already her lungs wanted to burst. What was it? *Where* was it?

She was *not* going to drown twenty feet offshore. Her grip on the rock began to slip. With her free hand, she grabbed Tyrfing's hilt. She had to twist around to free the sword. Once it leapt from its sheath a radiant light exploded from it, illuminating the depths. Fish darted away from the sudden brightness reflecting in all directions. Naught at all had held her. And it had let go.

She stood, gasping, panting. Barely able to keep her feet while she sucked down precious air. Was this the sword's curse? That nature and urd itself should turn against her? No. No! She refused to believe that.

Still coughing, trying to breathe, Hervor stumbled toward shore.

Shivers had built deep in her chest by the time she fell to the beach. Her hand remained clasped around Tyrfing, at least. Its glow had dimmed. She rolled over onto her back.

The mist had thickened across the shore. And her torches were now sopping wet. Dawn could not come soon enough. This night seemed crafted by Hel herself.

And her head was *pounding*.

Hervor froze. The mist was actually swirling, moving around her in what seemed a maelstrom. Odin's stones. Nature had turned on her. She rolled over and rose to her knees, holding the sword out before her.

It wasn't just her head pounding. Her heart seemed to beat in her temples.

Thump thump.

She jerked her head from side to side. Water flew free. She'd lost her helm underwater, hadn't noticed before.

Thump thump.

This was not nature. Not at all. "Who's there?"

No one answered. The mist continued to thicken, until she could not see a foot through it. And that maelstrom was closing in on her. She swung with Tyrfing but met only vapor.

Thump thump.

"Show yourself!"

Something unseen slammed into her back and threw her from her feet. She tumbled end over end, tearing her cheeks along the sand. Luck alone let her maintain her grasp on her sword. The World was spinning, reeling out of control. She rose and swung the sword wildly. The effort cost her balance, and she pitched over sideways.

Thump thump thump thump.

The heartbeat suffused the mist, echoing in her head like a gong threatening to beat her brains out of her skull. From the inside. She couldn't hear aught else. Couldn't see past the growing pain, the beating that deadened all other senses.

She pushed herself to her knees. "What are you!"

"Old death ... rising ..." The whisper came from all around her, somehow breaking through the sound of the heartbeat, if barely.

"Face me!"

THUMP THUMP!

Another unseen force rammed her shoulder and sent her crashing onto her back again. She kept her hold on Tyrfing and slashed through the mist again. It parted around the glowing sword but reformed almost immediately.

Hervor screamed. Her vision had taken on a red tint. Like blood. The mist had become blood, swirling, coursing. No—pulsing. With each beat of the heart.

THUMP THUMP THUMP!

Pounding toward the sword. It would have blood. It would take life. It must have life. It must have life.

And if there was no foe to bleed then ...

Hervor stared at her hands. She had begun to turn the sword backward, twist its point to her own chest. What was she doing?

No.

Stop.

"Don't ..." her mouth wasn't working right.

THUMP THUMP THUMP THUMP THUMP!

No. No, no, no. What was she doing? This could not end like this. Just drop the damn sword. Let it go. Her hand would not open, would not obey.

She had turned the blade fully around, pressed the point just over her heart. The pounding must be stilled. It must be stilled. It must drink, feast, and bring the silence. She had to end it. End it.

From the corner of her eye, she saw a man's face in the

mist, watching her open-mouthed. As shocked at her actions as she was. A vaettr? A sorcerer?

The pounding heart was coming from him, too. The moment she focused on him, her muscles responded. In one motion, she reversed the sword and lunged upward. The blade bit through the man's chest even easier than it had cleaved through the wooden door. At once, the pounding stopped, and her vision returned to normal.

The man—and he was flesh and blood, no spirit— looked down at the blade, then at her. And then he fell. The swirling mist parted, eased.

Hervor jerked the blade free and stared at it. The pounding in her head had abated, though her own pulse was racing. She tossed Tyrfing aside with a stifled scream.

It landed in the sand and lay still. Blood seeped from the blade, staining the beach. She had almost killed herself with that. She had intended to run it through her own heart. She had ...

She slunk to her knees, hand to her mouth. The sorcerer's blood had coated her hand, her arm. She stared at her hand not quite certain what she was seeing. The bandage yes, some of the blood her own. Some the dried blood of a fisherman. Some that of a sorcerer. Her hand ached from the burns but not so bad as it had been a few days ago. And she had almost impaled herself using that hand. That was less than ideal.

The sorcerer had bewitched her, tried to get her to send her own soul to Hel.

Except ... he'd looked shocked at her actions. Shocked enough to reveal himself. So no sorcery of his had possessed her. That meant ...

What had her father's ghost said of Tyrfing?

That it sought blood.

That once freed, the bloodlust could not be denied. Hervor stared at the sword, lying still on the sand. Its glow had faded now, and it seemed like any other bloody, discarded weapon. The hunger was its own, as was the pounding heartbeat when she held it. Once drawn, the runeblade would not be sheathed again until it had stilled a heartbeat.

Hervor crawled to the evil blade. Her father was right. It was cursed. But then, she had a great many heartbeats she needed to still.

So ... urd must have intended Tyrfing for her hand, after all.

4

STARKAD

The smoke of a half dozen braziers clogged the Upsal hall, flavoring the mead and lending the whole place an air of lethargy. Starkad wished he could enjoy it, but even his relaxed pose—leaning back in a chair, legs splayed—it was a ruse. A front to conceal the nervous energy almost bubbling to the surface in him. What was it about the thought of treasure and death? Why did he feel so damned drawn to it?

Much as Starkad wanted to blame Odin or Tyr or the other Aesir, maybe it had always been inside him. This wanderlust ... this need to claim ... fucking everything.

Afzal sat in the shadows beside him, puffing on that Serklander pipe, eyes glazed over from those herbs he liked. The Serklander leaned forward, bleary eyed as a drunk and yet, somehow he tended to remain insightful while in such moods.

"What is it?" Starkad demanded.

"You have that look again."

With a snort, Starkad waved that away. Such was his curse, and Afzal knew it well enough.

Across the hall, King Yngvi broke into raucous laughter, raising the drinking horn in Bera's direction. His brother's wife sputtered and snickered herself, almost choking on her own mead. The hour had grown late, and many men had retired, but Yngvi always liked to feast well into the evening. Starkad had business best discussed with few ears to overhear. Besides … night and sleep did not favor him. Dreams showed him more than one thing he preferred not to see.

"Did you see aught of note?" Starkad asked.

Afzal breathed out a long sigh, blowing discolored smoke in a stream. "Darkness. Long nights and skies aflame …"

The boy insisted those herbs let him see visions like a fucking völva. Thing was, Starkad had heard enough insight from him not to totally dismiss those claims, however unmanly they seemed.

"And knowing you," Afzal said with another drawn out breath, "such thoughts only drive you onward. You do not seek the good things in life, Master."

"Such as?"

"A wife? A family?"

Starkad snorted. No. Such things were not for him. Never. He patted the boy on the arm and rose from the chair to make his way toward Orvar. His old friend was busy wooing a shieldmaiden—waste of time, of course, and naught Starkad minded interrupting. Orvar shooed him away with his eyes, but Starkad ignored the hint and sat down beside the Nidavelliran.

"We have things to talk on, you and I."

"Not this night, I think," Orvar said without really even looking his direction.

"Run along, girl," Starkad said to the shieldmaiden.

"The old man's cock has shriveled up and dropped off long ago."

The woman sneered at him hard enough she seemed ready to take a swing in his direction. Wouldn't that have been amusing. Briefly. Then she rose and stumbled away, drunker than even Orvar.

"Wait," Orvar called after her. "Eightarms speaks of his own manhood, girl. I assure you mine is ..." He fumbled with his trousers but gave it over when she didn't glance back. Then he cast a weary glare at Starkad. "Just because you don't appreciate a woman's charms doesn't mean the rest of us shouldn't."

"Naught wrong with plowing a trench if the urge is powerful enough. It's everything before and after I find objectionable. The ... lies ... the false promises leading to inevitable betrayals. All of it. Men and women were never meant to have long-term relations. Fire and ice."

Orvar glowered, took another swig from the horn, and cast it aside. "I see you have become no less tedious in the past few years, Eightarms. So tell me, what do—"

"Because the hour is late!" Alf snapped at his wife, who still sat drinking by Yngvi.

Starkad glanced at the pair. Bera, Alf's wife, sneered at him, slurring her speech. "You never take time to enjoy the merits of this hall. Always off to bed."

"I have a kingdom to run in the morning, wife."

"Oh brother," Yngvi said. "Surely Upsal can manage a few hours without us—"

"Stay out of this!"

Starkad chuckled and pointed at the trio who were all now shouting. "You see what good comes from women, yes?"

"You speak harshly to your brother," Bera said, "when he

is no doubt a much better companion for a woman than you!"

Alf spat at her feet and stormed out of the hall, followed by Yngvi's chuckles.

Starkad spread his hands to take in the whole of this debacle. "Behold the loyalty of women, my friend."

Orvar groaned. "Alf is an abrasive trollfucker, and it surprises you his wife does not much care for it?" He threw up his hands. "You did not come over here to talk to me of women, I think. Nor, I pray, simply to ruin my evening."

"No. I didn't." Starkad sucked his teeth. "You ought to name me your second on this mission."

"Really? Here I sit, without my lady friend for the night —stones thick to bursting, in case you wish to know—"

"I truly do not."

"—And no one to blame save you, and you think I ought to bestow honors upon you? Pray tell, Eightarms. Amuse me."

Starkad pressed his palms onto the table and leaned forward. "You ever seen a man faster with a blade than I?"

Orvar drummed his fingers on the tabletop. "No denying that. Probably no man in all the North Realms has as much blood on his blades. Still, I cannot say you're much in my good graces this night."

Starkad sniffed. One move always remained open to him, loathe though he was to ever make it. Still, when losing the tafl match, sometimes a desperate gambit became necessary. Finally, he groaned. "He sent me ... dreams of this mission."

"Who did *what* now?"

"You know who I mean."

Orvar's eyes widened, and he stroked his beard a moment. "You would not jest over such a thing?"

Starkad scoffed. Given the choice, he would not bring up the Aesir at all.

Finally, Orvar nodded. "It seems a higher authority than even Yngvi wishes you along. Very well, I will name you second."

"And ... you're going to tell me the truth about what we're seeking on Thule, Orvar. All of it."

The Nidavelliran hesitated, looking like he might try to deny his omissions. In the end, though, he just nodded.

5
___

HERVOR

*T*he forest around the Yngling town was thick, dense, not unlike woods Hervor had once stalked as a bandit, save for the danger of sinking in peat. That she could have done without.

Arrow's Point was here, talk in nearby towns had confirmed it. A great many men had gathered at Upsal, heeding some call or other from Kings Yngvi and Alf. She would need to settle with the two kings of Upsal, as well, one day. Because of Yngvi and his Hel-cursed daughter, all of Hervor's kin were dead.

Hervor was the last descendant of Bolmso, and it fell to her to avenge them. Arrow's Point, however, and his friend Hjalmar had been the ones to strike the blows. Her father had felled Hjalmar, but Arrow's Point had somehow escaped the berserk brothers. Nigh unto twenty winters they had lain in restless torment in that barrow.

And now, Tyrfing had come back again, eager for the blood of its enemies, of her enemies. But she could not well storm Upsal and face Arrow's Point and all Yngvi and Alf's men at once. So Hervor kept to the woods and waited. They would leave eventually. Arrow's Point was a famed wanderer, never lingering in one place too long. It would be his undoing. She could track him through the wilds ... catch him alone.

And in the last, he would know who had come for him and why. That she promised her father.

Ravens in the trees took flight. Something had scared them off. It was daylight, so that probably meant men. Hervor ducked behind a tree. A tenuous footpath ran through the edge of the wold all the way to the two kings' shared hall. More men were following it, coming to partake of Yngling hospitality. Coming to dine at the table of her enemy, to praise him, maybe join him. Whatever the Ynglings wanted, she would deny them. Take from them everything, as everything had been taken from her own family.

Three men passed by, speaking of some glorious adventure ahead. After they passed, Hervor stepped out from behind the tree and slid Tyrfing free of its sheath. It was hungry. She didn't need to fear that hunger, though. Not when it could be so easily sated.

One of the men spun at her approach, clutching an axe. "Eh? What's this?"

"Throw your wealth down, and run for your lives," she said.

The other turned, and one laughed. "It's one man on three."

She shrugged. Good, they still took her for a man. Besides, she wouldn't know what to do if they *did* surrender. She *had* to kill at least one of them. Tyrfing demanded blood. "Not for long."

She surged forward, driving the closest man back. He raised his axe to block. She feinted left, then jerked her sword back across his face. The man fell, howling and clutching his split jaw.

The other two were not laughing now. One drew his own sword and charged her. Hervor fell back a few steps, turned, and stuck out her leg. The man's foot tangled on her ankle, and he pitched forward. She hewed a gash into his back as he fell, then turned on the last man.

She whipped her sword around in arc, flinging the blood from it. In daylight, its gleam was not as intense, but he'd seen it. He must have, for he was staring now at the runeblade.

"Who are you?"

She shrugged. "You would not have heard of me."

"A man who attacks others without even giving his name is a murderer."

So spoke a man serving the Ynglings. She had been called worse. She had *done* worse. "Tonight ... you will not dine with Yngvi or Alf. You may, however, dine with Odin. Ask him—I think he will know my name."

The man with the split face was rising, flailing about with his axe despite the blood blinding him. Hervor stepped around him, advancing on the final man.

"You have no name," the man said. "Murderers freeze in the deepest pits of Niflheim."

Hervor lunged at him. He parried, though clearly unaccustomed to using his sword like that. He wanted to reach for his shield on his back. You could see it on his face. Just like he knew she'd gut him if he tried. He fell back under her assault, ever farther from the path. Hervor batted his sword aside, then kicked him in the gut. The man fell on his arse, splashing down in the peat. He sputtered, tried to scramble forward. Hervor cleft in his helm as he neared, and he dropped dead before her, sinking back into the peat.

The axeman roared, charging forward. Hervor stepped back, let him swing wildly, and then knocked the axe from his hand.

"Why has Yngvi called so many men to his hall?" she asked.

The man spit blood and pulled his hand away from his face enough for her to see the raw, red ruin of it. A long gash tore open his brow, nose, and cheek down to his jaw. The bone itself looked sliced, and a flap of skin was hanging loose.

The sight of it turned her stomach.

"Why would I tell you a damn thing, bandit?"

Hervor kicked his axe off into the peat, then allowed Tyrfing's point to rest on the ground. "Tell me what I want to know, and I won't run you through."

The man spit again. "Fine. King Yngvi has called all his thegns and jarls, all men seeking glory and fame." The man panted and grimaced as he touched a hand to his wounds. "He mounts an expedition to a far-off island, one said to hold great riches and the chance to win Odin's favor."

"Who is going?"

"*We* were going. The king has called upon the famed Orvar-Oddr to lead the voyage. Yngvi seeks the strongest, bravest men in the North Realms."

Hervor snorted. "Obviously not you lot."

"Go fuck a troll. I will still go. The skalds will sing of this journey for centuries."

She shook her head. "No. You'll be dead." The man opened his mouth to object. "I said I wouldn't run you through, yes. But the wound on your face will fester and sap your strength until you wither and die. You will not see nightfall. But I will offer you mercy and a quick death."

Disbelief and anger warred on his face. Trying to decide

if she spoke the truth, probably. He must have decided, for his muscles tensed. With a predictable lunge, he threw himself at her. She jerked Tyrfing up, slicing open the man's gut. He stumbled forward and fell to his knees as shit and blood poured out into the dirt, slipping between his grasping fingers.

She had promised him mercy. Hervor stepped behind the kneeling man. Then she cleaved his head from his shoulders.

THE KINGS' hall lay several days walk from the sea and, when the party had left, Hervor had trailed behind them. A great many hard-looking men, all pent up, ready for plunder. One of those men had earned the name Arrow's Point. Nigh to twenty years ago that man had slain her kin.

The sword hated him, too. Or maybe it felt her hatred. Either way, it wanted to be free, to feast upon blood and send his soul screaming down to Hel. But. This was also a man who had defeated a small army of berserkir in single combat. He was a force out of legend, and she would not be so prideful as to rush headlong into a fight she wasn't certain to win. No, her father had wielded Tyrfing as well and still died fighting Arrow's Point and Hjalmar.

She needed the right opportunity to face him, a chance to catch him unawares and certainly not while surrounded by other warriors, many who had fastened names of their own.

They made their way across the country, Hervor careful to stay just enough behind so as not to attract attention with her torch.

The answer seemed obvious enough. They wanted men

for their little adventure, men who could fight and more, men who did not fear to tread into the unknown. And once on that crew, she'd be able to get close to Arrow's Point, very close. Sooner or later, opportunity came around to those who prepared themselves for it. It was like laying an ambush in the woods. You didn't have to chase after prey— you waited for them to come to you.

Just a matter of time.

❦

In the town, the raiding party spread out, probably gathering supplies for the journey. Their leader, Orvar-Oddr, and the scraggly haired man with him went to a longship at the harbor, one no doubt prepared for this purpose. The Yngling dynasty had grown either bold or desperate if they were funding such a voyage. In either case, it would be a pitching point, where the house could restore itself to glory or founder in ignominy. Hervor needed only make sure it was the latter. A weak house became an easier target.

The pair had paused as a third member of their crew was accosted by some woman clutching her bulging belly. "You ought to do your duty is what!"

The crewman smirked. "My dear, my duty looks well done, already."

The stupid woman seemed to think the raider would stop and marry her. Or that she'd be happy if he did so. Men were men. Only a fool woman wanted them to behave any other way.

Hervor's heart pounded against her ribs as she strode for the party. One of these men would surely know what she was about the moment he laid eyes on her. Distracted by the other woman or not, they'd see through Hervor's feigned enthusiasm to join the crew, know her for a foe.

One of those people might even be Arrow's Point. And if he realized her intent ...

No.

Fuck that.

Confidence, Hervor. Confidence was everything. She had not lost many fights in her life. That was because she knew how to pick them and was too damn stubborn to accept defeat in either case.

"You're bound for the lost island," she said. She'd had a lot of practice pitching her voice lower, like a man's. At least a young man's. It had become second nature now, really.

The scraggly haired man turned on her, looked her up and down. "We already have a crew."

"You can make room for one more."

The man scowled a little—just a slight narrowing of his blue eyes. But mistrust was there, she was certain. He spread his hands. "Maybe we could. Why should we?"

The other woman slapped the crewman for whatever he'd said next.

Hervor sneered. The poor bastard was in the wrong place at the right time. "Did this man do wrong by you?" Hervor asked the woman.

The man snickered. "I'd say I did right by her. Repeatedly." The man bore a golden arm ring, one carved like a dragon. She had mistaken him for a common warrior, but only a noble or a man of renown would own such a treasure. It actually made him a better target.

With a shrug, Hervor looked back at the woman. "Did he now?" Her right hook caught the man in the gut. He doubled over, lining him up for an easy cross to the face. He stumbled back under her blows. Hervor grabbed him by the arms and flung him outward. He collided with the ship's hull and then pitched forward into the sea.

The man sputtered and flailed a moment before getting ahold of the dock and climbing back up. He spit water, fuming. "Thor's thundering cock of a misfit. This boy-loving, troll-faced son of a donkey's shit hole—"

"Shut up, Rolf," the scraggly haired man said.

Orvar nodded at Hervor, then guided the drenched man away.

"This is the type of man you keep on your crew? Gets a woman thick with child and runs out on her? Can't even fight?"

The man folded his arms. "I'm Starkad. Who are you?"

Starkad ... "The one they call Eightarms?"

He nodded.

That gave her pause. According to the tales, Starkad Eightarms was the finest swordsman in the North Realms, if not all Midgard. Some claimed Tyr himself must have trained the man. He'd fastened the name to himself when a man claimed he moved so fast that fighting him was like fighting a foe with eight arms. A man like that could have been Arrow's Point—great warriors sometimes earned more than one name.

"I ..." her voice sounded a bit high there. "I'm Hervard."

"Well, you've got stones, Hervard. Taking on Rolf Quick-tongue like that. Have you had a name fastened to you?"

She shook her head.

"Be careful then. Act like that you're like to get stuck Hervard Rockstones. I don't care what went on between Rolf and some bitch. But I salute your courage. You wish to come with us to the very ends of Midgard and beyond?"

The ends of Midgard? *Beyond*? Odin's stones, where was this expedition bound? She nodded lest he have time to spot her fear or hesitation. She needed to be on that boat when it left if she was to have any chance of felling Arrow's Point. Especially if they were bound so far away. Odin alone knew when she might again have a chance at the man.

Hervor nodded.

Starkad cracked his neck. "Very well then. This ship will leave at dawn. If you're here, we'll take you with us. Prepare yourself—you won't see this place again for quite some time."

Hervor grunted in assent and turned to go.

"One more thing. You may have made your point—but you probably won't have a friend in Rolf."

She shrugged. "Doesn't seem someone good to be friends with. Rich, though."

"Oh, the arm ring? Claims some Reidgotaland princess gave it to him as a token of love."

"Claims? You don't believe him?"

Starkad scratched his head. "One story claims he raped and murdered the princess. And if he did, he probably convinced himself he was doing her a favor. Ask Bragi about it some time—when Rolf isn't in earshot. He'll tell the tale that Rolf next asked the bitch's father to pay him for his services."

Hervor scowled. This Starkad seemed not to care much for women. Or for Rolf. He bore watching. A man with a reputation for killing and one not tempted by flesh could be dangerous. Whether or not he was Arrow's Point, Eightarms had his own reputation.

Hervor would need to watch him—and watch herself. One slip up among this crew and she'd find herself worse than marooned on a haunted island. Maybe Starkad was right about Rolf, too. Maybe she should not have injured and humiliated him. Sooner or later, shamed men came looking for revenge.

But then, she had learned a great deal about violence. Sometimes, it was just the easiest path forward.

Other times, it was the only damned way forward.

6

STARKAD

*Y*ngvi had constructed a ship that could handle long days and nights at sea, yet still, they sailed the coast. Each night, they made camp upon land. It suited them all well enough, Starkad included. At night, the mist thickened, and men preferred the radiant flame of a bonfire to the small comfort of shipboard torches. By day, they passed the kingdoms of Sviarland through the Gandvik Sea and now were already moving into the Morimarusa.

Starkad had heard the sea here earned its name for the dead waters giving rise to unnatural stillness on the surface. That stillness was an illusion though. The depths hid unfathomable secrets, dangers not even Starkad deluded himself into thinking he understood. There were clans of mer, some in service to the dire queen Rán, who ruled the ocean alongside her husband Aegir. There were great serpents hidden in the depths, said to rise only in the most wrathful of storms. And worse, older benthic creatures slumbering, waiting to wake and consume the World.

The kraken, skalds called one such monster. And a sick

part of Starkad longed to look upon the monstrosity lurking beneath these dead waters ... to see it with his own eyes.

Still, monsters of the deep concerned Starkad less than what ancient evils laired upon the islands of Reidgotaland. True, in the past two generations, a strong kingdom had risen and begun uniting many of the islands. Some said the king, Healfdene, had done so bearing a runeblade of all things. But Healfdene was dead, and his son Hrothgar seemed not a fraction of the king the great man had been.

Starkad had known them both in his wanderings.

The men of Reidgotaland had much in common with Sviarlanders and so, often found interaction, both peaceful and otherwise. But Healfdene's faltering kingdom did not concern Starkad. Older civilizations had retreated to uninhabited islands in the Morimarusa, retreated and slept away centuries until at last wakened. Stirred by the changing of the World. For all he knew, Odin himself had woken the ancient powers, whether intentionally or by blunder as the so-called god so oft stumbled blindly in the dark.

At the ship's bow, staring into mist of uncanny thickness, Starkad did not suppose it mattered how they had wakened. Only that they had, and that now, the mist seemed intent upon them. It blinded them, obscured their course. They oft could not make out the sun in the day or the stars at night. And it was pursuing them, chasing after their vessel like a dire wolf pack stalking them, waiting for a moment of weakness.

Starkad spit into those dead waters. What was worse, the unknown horrors of the deep or the terror he knew too well lurking on the land all around them?

With a grunt, he turned away and threaded his way toward the stern, where Orvar sat, head in his hand. They had grown becalmed as soon as they passed out of the

Gandvik, a day ago, but so far, the men had not complained. Working the oars tired them, no doubt, but it also distracted them. They did not know what Starkad knew, did not know *what* was amiss here. But they would feel it, the slight foulness in the air, the chill on their skin that never passed.

Starkad knelt beside Orvar and placed a hand on the back of his head, whispering so none of the others might overhear. "We cannot make land here."

Orvar looked up, eyes wary.

"A great many years ago I warned you about these islands, and you did not listen. We are nearing Samsey, and it is not the only place *they* lair. They have been spreading, slowly, over the decades."

"I have never seen these sorcerers you so fear, Starkad, though I have witnessed wonders enough."

Starkad tightened his grip. "I have faced down a jotunn, Orvar. I have fought trolls, draugar, and a great many men. And still I would not willingly fight these Niflungar. They are perilous and treacherous, and I have a strong sense they are aware of us, following us even. Have you noticed the silent mist, ever chasing us? If we make land on these shores, I do not think we will ever leave them."

"I have sailed these waters many times. I have never had trouble with aught save storms and men."

Starkad released Orvar but did not back away. "I am asking you to trust me now. Push on, as hard the crew can take it."

"The men will be unhappy."

"Better unhappy upon the sea than unhappy waiting at the gates of Hel."

Orvar rolled his eyes, then pushed Starkad away. He rose. "Men—we will not camp on shore this night. We push onward, rowing in shifts until we sight the northeastern shores of Sviarland. Then we rest, follow the coast up and along Nidavellir."

As Orvar had predicted, a collective grumble ran through the crew.

"What the cock-beetle man?" Ivar the Loud shouted. "You won't camp at Reidgotaland, but you're willing to do so at Nidavellir? And pay tribute to the stone-cocked dvergar, I suppose? Maybe trade one of us off as a slave to the little rock-fucking bastards, too!"

Orvar jerked the man up from his oars and cuffed him on the side of the head. "You know me better than that, I hope. I'm not giving the dvergar so much as a hair off my arse. We'll land in the wilds, do some hunting, and be gone with the dawn."

Ivar shoved Orvar away and sat sullenly at his oars.

"Look now," Orvar said, turning about to address the full crew. "Nidavellir is the last place we can stop before trying for the Faeroerne islands. And from there, we sail into unknown waters. None of us favor angering the dvergar, but we need to get supplies while we can. We don't know how many days—or moons—we may be at sea before we find this Thule. And every single one of you knew the danger of this voyage before you first sat your arse on your sea trunk. So man the damned oars, and let us push on as best we may."

Starkad tapped Bragi Bluefoot on the shoulder, then took his place at the oars. The steady work would keep his mind from growing too busy. At least eventually, once his body tired. Now though, all he could think was *why*? Why would the Niflungar care about them or their mission to Thule? They were a people ruled by the Raven Lord, King Gjuki. The birds acted as his spies across the North Realms, ferrying whispers and secrets back. Perhaps they told the sorcerer king of this quest.

But that did not explain why the Niflungar would bother to interfere.

They knew what really lay on Thule, for certain. Perhaps they wanted to stop men from claiming it. Or ... they wanted to stop Odin's allies from attaining those treasures. The Ás king had made enemies of the ancient people, and now King Odin and King Gjuki seemed to be playing tafl on a grand scale, moving pieces in a slow game to control the North Realms. Perhaps all of Midgard. And Starkad did not like the thought of being a pawn.

He liked the thought of dining with Hel even less.

7

HERVOR

*T*he towering mountain peaks scratched at the sky above, rising almost straight out of the sea and disappearing into the mist. Hervor had seen mountains, true, but these were like something from another world. And indeed, Nidavellir was the famed Realm of the dvergar who lived beneath these mountains, demanding tribute in treasure and slaves. Oh, and all lands paid that tribute. Her grandfather paid—every five years, he sent a ship to these shores, laden down with captured booty and women and boys.

Once, Hervor had gone on a raid to claim the tribute. The women had pled with her, back before she'd taken to disguising herself as a man. Pled, as though she would spare them their urd, serving the needs of perverse vaettir in the faraway land. Better them than her.

The crew sat huddled around a bonfire in the valley of wooded foothills beneath those mountains. Mostly evergreens sprouted here, and game was no doubt light, though Orvar and the Axe had gone out hunting, bidding everyone else remain at camp and keep quiet.

The scant fire barely illuminated beyond a few feet into the woods, the darkness leaving Hervor on edge. And with winter approaching, nights would only grow longer. This was a fell place, ill suited for Mankind and best left to the dvergar. Unfortunately, their quest would take them farther still abroad from the lands of men. And unless she acted soon, she'd be stuck with these fools for a long haul.

Bragi Bluefoot, self-styled skald, was wagging his tongue again, this time carrying on about tales of Healfdene the Mighty. "See, stories tell, he had the blade from his sister, the princess. And with it, he held back the mist and conquered island after island, until all men feared to stand before him in battle."

Rolf Quicktongue snorted. "I could stand to hear a bit more about this Reidgotalander princess. I may have known one or two of those in my time."

The biggest of their companions—oddly named Tiny—folded his arms. "I heard you raped and murdered the woman."

"I ... I did no such thing! Why this," Rolf said, patting the golden armband, "was a gift and promise of her eternal love."

Tiny glowered. "So why did you not marry the woman then and live as a prince?" King Gylfi had sent Tiny along as his own emissary on the trek, a towering mountain of an emissary, perhaps to keep the rest of them reminded of his interests in this quest. Since Tiny didn't actually work for the Ynglings, Hervor had no real quarrel with him, but he was like to prove a problem when she did finally strike against Arrow's Point.

"Well," Rolf said, drawing out the word long enough to grate on Hervor's nerves, "alas she was pledged to another and could not break that bond. In recompense, she gave me this armband."

Hervor sneered. "You just said she gave it to you for love."

"Right. Loving recompense."

"Full of troll shit," Hervor mumbled under her breath.

Ivar the Loud, sitting beside her, bust out laughing.

"What?" Rolf said. "What did he say?"

"He said," Ivar offered, "that you're full of beetle-cocking troll shit, Quicktongue."

Rolf scowled, then rose, stomping over toward Hervor. "I've had just about enough out of a *boy* who hasn't even fastened a trollfucking name to himself yet. What do you think? Troll shit … should we call him Hervard Trollshitter? Hervard Shitsniffer? Or maybe … Hervard Nostones?"

That the last was actually accurate had no bearing. You couldn't take that kind of talk from your crew. If you did, you were like to wind up with a blade in your gut when it came time to divide up the booty. Hervor would know. She'd planted a blade or two in men's guts. She rose, hand going to Tyrfing's hilt. Already, the runeblade seemed to be purring to her. Seeking blood. Needing to still a heartbeat.

All she had to do was draw the blade and … and she would not be able to sheath it without killing this sorry excuse for a person.

"Sit down, both of you!" Starkad snapped. "We have enough trouble in these lands without bickering over a gods-damned woman none of the rest of us have even met. What Quicktongue did with the bitch is between him and her father."

"Right," Rolf said. "Naturally, that's why he gave me this armband. As proof there were no—"

Hervor's hand twitched. That Starkad was right made it

no better. She dearly wanted to end Rolf and not just because of some Reidgotaland princess that may or may not have existed. He was a colossal arse, and she'd be doing the World a favor. It was not the place, though.

Instead, she forced a smile and sank back down to the fire. "How about a different tale, Bragi?"

"Oh yes, of course. Any requests?"

"Hmm," Hervor said. "The legend of Arrow's Point, I think."

Starkad groaned, ever so slightly.

"Oh ho ho," Bragi said. "A good one. Apt, I suppose, and you being so young you'd not have heard about our illustrious companion." Bragi settled back onto his haunches and snapped his fingers, at which Starkad passed him a skin of mead. The skald took a long swig before passing it on. "It began with a prophecy, you see. A völva foretold he would die by his own horse, near the same place he was born.

"Now Arrow's Point, being a brave man, he didn't fear death. But he wasn't keen on dying to a horse, so he killed the beast and buried it deep. Then he set out, planning to leave his homeland behind. His father—that was Grim Shaggy-Cheeks, of course, a legend himself—granted him a fine bow and gave him seven magic arrows—"

"Nine," Starkad said. "It's always nine ... the number has ... significance."

How did Starkad know that? Was he Arrow's Point?

"Eh?" Bragi scratched his beard. "Nine, then. Nine magic arrows. One he used to kill a jotunn, earning him the name Arrow's Point. Who knows how many he has left now? Not many, I'd wager, given all the other tales about him."

Hervor fixed Starkad with a heavy glare, though he wasn't looking at her. In fact, he had his eyes closed. "What tales?" Hervor asked.

"Oh, Odin's beard. Roaming and raiding into Bjarma-land where he helped defend Holmgard. Some say he even went to Jotunheim, though I find that hard to credit. Then there was the fight with the berserkir of Bolmso."

Yes. "Tell me about that," she said.

"A dozen berserkir, if you can believe that. A dozen of them, faced down by two men. Only one man left Samsey that day. None else alive witnessed the battle, but it must have been glorious. Shame to have missed that."

Indeed.

"A lot of men went to Valhalla that day," Tiny said. "Not sure I'd have liked to have seen it all, though."

A lot of men died. Hervor's father. Her uncles. They hadn't seen Valhalla, though.

Finally, she lay down beside the fire. And she ran her fingers over the golden hilt of Tyrfing.

8

STARKAD

A bitter wind swept across the sea as their ship drew nigh to the Faeroerne islands. Starkad was the first over the side of the ship, boots splashing down into freezing water and then scrambling ashore for all he was worth. Some few of the crew might have balked at such discomfort, but Starkad cared naught for these concerns. This was the edge of the known world. Here, Midgard all but ended.

Even the Faeroernes remained sparsely populated—at least by man—and one could see the wild, the Realms of chaotic nature at the fringes. You could almost feel the vaettir, hidden just out of sight, watching Mankind trespass upon their domain. It all left his heart racing, pulse pounding. It left him *alive*.

"We spend only one day here," Orvar shouted. "Then we make sail north."

Of course, they needed to push hard. Winter was settling upon them, and with it came fell storms apt to capsize even the largest of ships. They needed to make Thule before that, and no man knew how far this mythic island lay. It was almost perfect.

Beyond the shore, a small village sat on a small patch of level ground. Most of the island rose up steeply to a plateau where tales claimed other villages lay, though none could be spied through the mist. Indeed, it was so thick, Starkad could make out little beyond a few dozen feet. The unknown did not concern him, but the mist, that held dangers all too familiar.

Torch out before him, he made his way into the village. The locals watched him with wary eyes. Most like, these people saw strangers only once every few years, if that. In their isolation, they'd mistrust anyone not known, perhaps even suspect them of being vaettir. Starkad paused before an old man in the center of the village, leaning on a walking stick and watching. An elder.

"You speak the North tongue?"

"Yes." The man's word came out slow, slurred like it tasted funny on his tongue.

The North tongue was spoken throughout the North Realms, but dialects varied. Bragi Bluefoot had once claimed the tongue came down to them from the Old Kingdoms, but it changed over time. People changed it.

"We want to trade," Starkad said. He pulled a pouch from his belt and dumped a handful of Miklagardian silver coins into his hand. "We need food, fresh water, mead, wood for fires, whale oil ..."

The old man shambled closer, then leaned in to examine the coins. He picked up one between two fingers, rubbed it, and shrugged. "Very ... shiny."

Starkad nodded. "Yes. Melt them into jewelry or do as you will with them. You understand what we need?"

The elder nodded, then barked something to a nearby boy, speaking a barely intelligible dialect. The boy scampered off, apparently to fetch all Starkad had asked for. With a nod, Starkad dropped the coins into the man's hand. It wasn't like these villagers would try to steal from them—the men on the ship would clearly take whatever they wanted if that happened. Hel, that seemed to be happening now.

Rolf was leaning in on some fisherman, the man backed against his house. Rolf was barely looking at the man though, instead, leering at someone inside the house. A wife, a daughter, who knew?

Starkad frowned and shook his head. He'd known too many men like Quicktongue.

Feet shuffled up behind him as he watched, and Starkad turned. Afzal struggled, arms awkwardly wrapped around an empty water barrel. Beside him, the Axe more easily carried one that had housed mead, sadly now run dry. The older veteran took in the sight of Rolf and shook his head.

"Bastard starts in with the locals, and we're not like to find pleasant shelter here again."

Starkad nodded.

The Axe dropped the barrel at his feet. "Should I remind Quicktongue?"

"Do that."

The Axe grunted, then trotted off to berate Quicktongue. Like as not, it would do little good. But if the Axe wanted to try ...

"Master?" Afzal asked.

Starkad grabbed the barrel from the young man. "Give me that." He carried it back to the village center and deposited it by the locals, Afzal shadowing behind him. "Fill it with water," Starkad said to a villager.

"Have you been here before, Master?" Afzal asked.

Starkad shook his head. "I had always planned to, it is famed, but until now ..." Well, there had been no reason to come. Naught lay out here save the edge of the World and perhaps the tail of Jörmungandr, or so skalds claimed. But Odin knew otherwise.

Afzal cleared his throat. "We will stay here tonight?"

"Yes."

"Then I will arrange a place with some locals for us."

"You're a good friend."

"Yes, Master. You deserve a full night's sleep for once."

Starkad snorted. He wasn't certain he'd had a full night's sleep in years. Not since Ogn.

No, before that. Not since Vikar died.

Or maybe he could lay his troubles at the feet of the Aesir, of Odin, of Tyr.

Or, more like than not, he ought to most blame himself.

"Afzal," Starkad called after the Serklander.

"Yes, Master?"

"Stop calling me that." Starkad scratched his beard. "You … look to your own rest. Tomorrow we sail beyond the edge of this world, and even I know not what we shall find."

Afzal blanched.

Funny, Starkad had meant the words to garner excitement. It was easy to forget few other men saw things his way.

PART II

Fourth Moon
Year 27, Age of the Aesir

9

STARKAD

They were too long at sea, too long in the bitter cold, and now on the cusp of winter. Starkad was certain their course remained true. The islanders had called them Mist-mad for sailing farther north.

To the north, they said, lay only the endless sea enclosed by the tail of Jörmungandr, the great World Serpent. But Gylfi had said Odin told him otherwise, that the Ás king had blessed this voyage.

Starkad's trust in Odin had limits. Severe limits. Word of his so-called miracles had spread across the North Realms in the past few decades. Where the Vanir had taken no hand in the world of men, Odin wandered—in disguise, true— but he walked among men. He offered advice, sometimes even wove sorceries to aid men in their endeavors.

The Aesir had brought strong harvests, even cured the sick. Odin's son Thor had slain trolls to preserve towns. Most of the crew believed with their whole hearts in the new gods.

But then, they had not been there at the beginning.

As a boy, Starkad had marched with Odin across

Midgard, had seen him cast down the Vanir and claim godhood. Whether true or not, the man was indeed a mighty king. Besides, Starkad owed the Ás.

Whether he liked it or not.

But the ocean went on and on. And the days grew very short—a few hours of light and then darkness would fall again, as it had now. Those iridescent lights had filled the sky again, like great clouds of color. One saw such things at the northernmost reaches of Nidavellir. When wandering Kvenland, Starkad had heard those lights were born from molten flame, beaten on anvils by the dvergar.

Some of the crew claimed it was a sign from Thor or Odin, guiding their passage. Telling them to remain true to their course. Of course, those lights had existed long before Thor was born.

"Such a wonder," Afzal murmured behind Starkad.

Starkad nodded. "The further reaches of the World hold many."

"And are they enough to replace the comforts you always leave behind?"

Starkad snorted. The Serklander thought far too oft of marriage and children, as if it were the very purpose of life. And yet, Afzal refused to leave Starkad's side and claim such things for himself, saying he must repay the debt he owed.

"Look! Look!" Ivar shouted before Starkad could form an answer.

On the horizon, rising out of the mist. Great peaks of ice, mountains.

Half the crew leapt up, straining their eyes to gaze land at long last. To see hope.

Or the beginning of their true mission.

OUT HERE, even the mist was not so thick. Those lights in the sky seemed the palest blue fires, dancing as the ship neared the frozen shore. They dared not run aground, nor did anyone seem eager to leap into the freezing sea. So they dragged the rowboat forward and ferried over to the shore in small groups.

Orvar insisted on being in the first group, and Starkad went with him.

"And still no sun," Afzal complained from the back of the boat.

Starkad heaved at the oars without responding. The others, Tiny, Ivar, and Hervard, all stared transfixed at the island.

They wondered what dangers and glories they'd find on Thule. As did he. One more tale to add to his own legend. And when it was done ... he'd be off to the next and the next again.

Such was Starkad's urd.

The rowboat scraped ice. A half dozen seals barked and scrambled away at their approach, diving into the freezing waters.

Orvar tested the ice with one foot before putting his full weight on the sheet. He nodded at the others.

"Tiny," Orvar said. "Take the boat back, and ferry the others. Trade off until everyone is ashore."

Orvar himself strode forward, taking the lead.

The island was large enough a man could not easily judge its full extent. At its heart rose towering mountains, with the hint of evergreens in the valleys. Very little other foliage seemed apparent, and snow and ice covered the greater portion of all Starkad could see.

"How the fuck are we supposed to build a camp without wood to burn?" Ivar complained.

It was a good question, if an obvious one. Ivar had earned the name "the Loud" for obvious questions, among other things.

"We'll have to fell one of those trees," Orvar said as he started off toward one of those evergreens.

"You want to haul wood from all the way—"

"I want to have fire, Loud. And you're coming with me."

"Travel to the ends of Midgard so I can be a fucking lumberjack." Ivar patted the axe at his side. "It's for chopping necks you know."

Orvar shrugged, and they started off.

"Help set the camp," Starkad told Afzal, then started after Orvar and Ivar.

They all walked in silence for a short time. Ivar seemed awestruck by the ice-covered landscape and unexplored peaks. "Remind you of any place?" Orvar asked.

"Yeah. The north of Nidavellir and the cock-beetling dvergar mountains."

"Mmm hmmm. Not sure that's a coincidence, either."

"Wait, what?" Ivar stumbled. "Are you saying there's cock-beetling dvergar on this island? It was supposed to be uninhabited! Uninhabited means no cock-stomping dvergar!"

Starkad snorted at the comment, though it lacked any real humor. Orvar and Ivar had both come from Nidavellir, under the ever-present yoke of dvergar masters. But while Orvar had been the son of a great man, Ivar had been a common raider in service to the dvergar. He'd raided and pillaged across the North Realms until one such expedition in Sviarland went bad and left the rest of his crew dead. And then he'd turned bandit on his own, right up until Yngvi had asked Orvar to put an end to him. Instead of killing his countryman, Orvar had recruited him. Ivar was loud. Ivar was an imbecile. Ivar was also very good at cleaving things in half with his axe, a pursuit he seemed to like quite well.

Starkad had a measure of respect for him. A small measure but a measure.

"I see a beetle-cocked dvergar, I'm gonna chop it in half!"

Orvar grunted, waving his torch to dispel the mist. "The dvergar or his cock?"

Ivar grunted, then worked his tongue over his teeth. "Both of 'em."

That drew a snort from Orvar and an actual laugh from Starkad.

After a chuckle, Starkad shook his head. "I don't think dvergar still live here."

Ivar glanced back at him. "Then what, man? Can we claim their gold? Gods above. If I could bring my girl dverg gold ..."

Orvar should never have brought it up. He may have shared kinship with Ivar, but then men did still call him Ivar the Loud for a reason. Best not tell the man aught they didn't want everyone from here to Miklagard knowing.

Starkad frowned. "All I can say is, Odin didn't send us to this island looking for farmland. There is something here, something of value, and we will take it."

"I *like* taking things." Another reason Ivar was an ideal raider.

10

HERVOR

*H*ervor pounded a tent stake into the frozen ground, grunting and panting with the effort of it.

Nearby, Bragi Bluefoot was humming while tying off ropes. The skald rarely fell silent. It seemed if he had naught to say, he'd fill the air with songs or poems. Failing that, he sometimes made clucking noises with his tongue.

Hervor paused a moment, wiped her brow, and caught her breath. She looked to Bragi. "You don't like the quiet?"

"Hmm? Oh!" Bragi chuckled. "Oh, not so much I suppose. In the woods, time things get all quiet is like to be when a predator is about, stalking you."

"Huh." Hervor slammed the stake down with a mallet again. "And you think humming is like to make the wolves vanish, then?"

"It's its own kind of magic, now."

"What magic?"

Bragi chuckled. "Self-delusion."

Hervor smiled. Despite herself, it was hard not to smile

on occasion at the skald's foolery. She hoped her vengeance would allow her to spare the man.

On the long voyage, she'd been careful. Asking questions but not too often. Naught that would give away who she was or her true purpose on this quest.

Bragi had proved the most useful, of course. His love of talk meant he needed very little prompting to carry on, telling tales of not only his own adventures but the rest of the crew. Most everyone on this expedition had fastened a name to themselves, and that meant they all had tales.

Murdering bastards, every one of them.

Like Hervor herself.

Orvar and Starkad were the most famed, of course, wanderers and mercenaries who had—according to Bragi—travelled the whole of the North Realms and beyond. But the others had their own stories, too.

The way the skald told it, the Axe had fought in more wars than any man alive. He'd hired out with Healfdene in the final conquests of Reidgotaland. He'd fought for Siggeir Wolfsblood in border struggles against Ostergotland, and again, when the king sacked Rijnland. Hel, there was even tale of him raiding Kvenland in a failed attempt to claim some beautiful wife from the frozen wastes there.

Of Tiny, Bragi knew less, but still, the man had fought great battles on behalf of Gylfi. By now, the Dalar King had all but ceased his wars, but not so many years ago, he'd roamed far and wide, spreading faith in the Aesir by word or sword point. Apparently, Tiny had been a thegn to him even back then, if a young one, and had put to the sword more than one village that refused to turn from the Vanir. Hervor remembered tale of a few such holdouts being razed when she was a small girl. She remembered thinking when she was grown, she'd do such work as well, striking down those who refused to honor Odin's name.

Ivar the Loud had run as a bandit in a crew not unlike one Hervor had once joined, and Hel alone knew how much blood lay on his hands. But for a few miles difference in territory, Hervor might have worked at his side.

And of Rolf Quicktongue, the tales were as black as pitch, though he would have cast himself as a hero in every single one.

In the end, Hervor was pretty certain she knew who Arrow's Point was.

A crowded ship had offered her no chance to strike down the man without detection. But this island was vast, and they planned to explore it all in search of plunder and a good place to plant a settlement. During such times, men spread out far.

An opportunity would come and sooner rather than later.

When it did, Hervor would be ready.

As would Tyrfing.

11

DAYS GONE

Two Years Ago

*B*ow-in-hand, Hervor crept through the woods. Summer had broken, and that meant trade, with merchants trying to travel between towns in Ostergotland. Merchants tended to be overburdened with goods, silver, and food. All things her little band could use.

Beside her, Red-Eye moved with the grace of a boar. The so-called King of Deeppine lacked subtlety, lacked finesse, and wasn't half so stealthy as a bandit leader ought to be. On the other hand, he was good with a bow, great with an axe, and roughly the size of a snow bear. It did tend to intimidate men.

Not Hervor. She was pretty certain she could beat him if she had to. Size counted. Speed counted more. And she was fast with a sword. Her grandfather's thegn had trained her as a shieldmaiden.

She motioned for Red-Eye to hold in place. The bandit king scowled at her and looked ready to spit. She turned away and slunk forward, toward the path. Deeppine covered so much of Ostergotland you couldn't really cross the Realm without passing through it. And that meant taking one of two paths. Those heading to Jarl Bjalmar's lands took this one.

Men's voices rang out from down the path. Coming this way. And not quiet about it. These folk either hadn't heard of Red-Eye's Boys, or they were just fools. Red-Eye knew what he was about. He was the one who had insisted she disguise herself as a man. She could fight as well as any man —better than most—he'd granted that. But merchants tended to be more afraid of young men than they were of girls of seventeen winters. So he'd told her to wear a helm, bind her breasts tight under her mail, and keep up the illusion.

And he'd been right. More merchants surrendered without a struggle when facing an armed man than an armed woman. Men were fools, after all.

Hervor signaled back to the chief. He, in turn, let fly an arrow into the depths of the woods. A signal. Ahead, the Boys would be converging, blocking the trail.

One of the merchants had started singing. She and Red-Eye exchanged open-mouthed stares. "Fucking imbeciles," he mouthed.

She nodded.

Yes. The long trail was lonely, boring. Still. Even if you didn't believe in trolls or other such things, attracting undue attention like that invited trouble. Most like, these were foreigners, maybe from Skane or one of the other kingdoms in Sviarland. Anyone native to Ostergotland would know better. They'd have to know better.

A pair of well-laden carts drawn by mules appeared around the bend, each protected by a pair of guards walking beside it. The singer was the driver of the first cart, who kept casting glances at the bundle-wrapped woman sitting in the back. Trying to impress his wife. How adorable.

The singing stopped when one of the guards fell, Red-Eye's arrow in his neck.

Hervor loosed as well, her own shot catching the opposite guard in the chest. Their prey was shouting, the remaining guards drawing weapons.

The Boys let out a whoop and rushed forward. Six of them, and she and Red-Eye made eight. Eight on two guards, plus the cart drivers and merchants. Good odds. And good fun. She slung the bow and drew her sword, making her way forward.

One of the guards had already fallen, but the other was holding his own against three of the Boys. Trained, experienced. Maybe even a former raider or soldier. No wasted movement. An efficiency that made a man seem faster, able to face more than one foe at a time.

He should have surrendered though. One of the merchants already had. Red-Eye had taught her something else too. If a man fights, you kill him. If not, you let him go. It encourages others not to fight.

Then again, she liked the fighting.

As she closed in, the blanket covering the back wagon fell away. Two more men jumped out, these armored in full chain. One rushed against the remaining Boys. The other glanced around a mere moment before settling on her.

His eyes locked on hers.

Gunther.

Hervor fell short as he closed in. Her former trainer moved in with deliberate confidence, sword and shield in hand. And she had left her shield behind a tree. She dared not take her eyes off him to check. Instead, she fell back a few steps at a time, keeping her sword in front.

"What in Hel's frozen arse is this, Gunther?"

"You never did learn to guard your tongue, girl."

She spit at his feet. He grimaced but did not slow.

She could make a break for it. Maybe lose him in the woods. Or at least make it to her shield.

Bellowing, Red-Eye charged forward at Gunther. The aging thegn pivoted, shield catching the King of Deeppine's descending axe even as his sword swung low. It slashed into Red-Eye's unarmored knees, and the bandit king toppled over.

Hervor used the chance to rush Gunther. He twisted around but couldn't get his shield back into position. Her sword scraped off his mail, tearing a gash in his side. With a groan, he fell back. She pushed her advantage, slashing again. This time he caught the blow on the edge of his shield. Splinters of it flew loose. The impact jarred her for an instant.

Enough time for Gunther to fall back into a proper stance. "You can still surrender now. Come with me, and answer for what you've done."

"You're outnumbered."

Gunther shook his head but did not bother to look at the rest of the Boys. "Not for long."

She did look. Those guards were Gunther's men, and they'd already downed four of the Boys. Not even counting Red-Eye, who was stumbling, trying to rise. He'd probably never walk right again. Red-Eye was an evil bastard, but he'd been good to her and had given her a place among the Boys. Damn Gunther.

With a grimace, she twirled her sword. "I'm going to gut you and leave you in the mist."

Rather than frightened, he seemed sad, shaking his head. "Hervor ..."

"It's Hervard!" She rushed forward and swung, a feint to get him to move the damn shield.

He did, but not to block. He thrust the shield forward, impacting her sword and driving her off balance. He leapt forward into her and slammed the shield forward again. It hit her square in the chest and sent her sprawling. Her back connected with a root. A flash of red pain blinded her.

She blinked it away. Her legs wouldn't respond. Arm was twitching. Odin's stones, that hurt.

Groaning, she rolled over, tried to stand. Gunther had stepped away. He kicked Red-Eye in the face. The bandit king fell over backward and hit his head, then lay still.

"No!" Hervor's voice sounded more like a croak. "Don't kill him ..."

Gunther glanced in her direction, then moved in to help his remaining soldiers. They cut through the Boys in a few moments.

Her arms gave out beneath her twice before she managed to rise to her knees. By then it was over.

Gunther had returned and bent to snatch her sword before she could even reach for it. She spit at him again. She could just throw herself at him, try to bear him down and claw his eyes out. All that would earn her would probably be a blow to the head and maybe tied hands. Still damn tempting though.

Red-Eye was alive, and guards were already binding his hands.

"Release him," she demanded.

"The jarl's orders override yours, girl," Gunther said. "He'll decide the *king's* urd." Some of the others snickered at the title. "Here's a new lesson for you. Before you throw your lot in with a king, make sure he has more than a dozen subjects. Otherwise he's not a king, just a self-important arse. One who only managed to draw the jarl's attention when word reached him of your activities."

"I have naught to say to him."

Gunther shrugged. "Well, your grandfather has more than a few things to say to you, girl." He motioned to two of his men. "Double bind her. She's a slippery one."

They dragged her hands behind her back and tied them.

Red-Eye was staring at her the whole time. "Jarl Bjalmar is your *grandfather*?" he demanded once the soldiers had begun to march them down the trail.

Hervor tried not to look at him. The jarl would surely hang the man for his crimes. And if Gunther spoke true, her grandfather had only even known about the Boys because of her.

Because of her, they would all die.

No. She could not look at Red-Eye, could not face him.

12

STARKAD

*M*en died, they fell before him in droves. As was his gift, his blessing, perhaps his curse. They screamed, erupted in fountains of blood. They fell to his swords; they fell to his words. They fell to his urd.

A friend, a brother, becalmed and desperate. Looking at him.

Starkad groaned, tried not to see it. Not again. He just wanted to sleep, he just wanted ...

Vikar.

His little brother—half-brother. Hanging from a tree, body twisting, writhing in the windless night. Eyes bulging. Tongue lolling to the side.

And they called Starkad a criminal, a kinslayer.

Starkad moaned, rolled over on the icy ground. The crackling bonfire nearby provided the only warmth. He pushed himself up, blinking against the firelight. It was always like this, nigh to every night. More fool him, trying to sleep without being dead drunk.

Groaning, he rose and strapped his swords over his

shoulders. His sword. And Vikar's. There was another, smaller fire down by the shore. Starkad wandered down there. Bragi Bluefoot sat, staring out over the waves. The ocean was rough, much rougher than the dead waters of the Morimarusa, churned as though by the heaving of Jörmungandr.

Starkad lowered himself down by the old skald, who passed him a skin of mead without him even having to ask.

"Not so much left."

Starkad took a deep swig and passed it back without answer.

"You may have to learn to sleep without it."

Starkad grunted. It was not that he could not sleep without drink. It was that he did not *want* to sleep without it. The mind played tricks, twisting fear and memory upon themselves until a man was left with naught but painful truths and nowhere to run from them. He had committed a great many crimes in his life, and, perhaps there would be more still to come. His fame in the North Realms only barely outpaced his infamy, and one day, he would like as not find himself chased from all civilized lands.

But his dreams cared naught for fame.

Starkad rubbed his face. "You never told me how your name got fastened to you."

Bragi laughed. "Gods boy, don't you know that?"

"Do not call me boy. I've seen more than forty winters now."

"And still I have you beat. Oh, and it was a cold winter earned me that name. Otwin was young, but already King of Njarar then, back where I was raised. There was still fighting with the Ás tribes, back before we knew gods walked among them. Fighting on a frozen lake, and damn my luck but I stepped on a crack and shoved my foot through. Got it stuck halfway up to my knee and I swear to Odin I couldn't pull the damned thing loose. So there I was, thrusting with my spear and trying to keep barbarians from cleaving in my head while my foot is stuck in freezing water." Bragi took another swig from the skin before returning it to Starkad. "So I figured I was good as dead anyway, and I start mocking the Aesir. Never was too wise, you know."

Starkad forced himself to chuckle, though thinking of Bragi's situation held little humor despite the skald's smile. Much less knowing what Starkad knew of the Aesir.

"So I got this Ás berserk so mad he seized me by the shoulders and yanked me right out of the ice, planning to throttle me with his bare hands. Then I put my spear right through his neck. Hehe. Should have seen it, Eightarms. So yeah, the battle over, the völva comes to treat me. My whole foot is blue with frostbite, and I'm shaking with deathchill. She got me warm, saved my life. Lost a few toes, though. But Hel, I got a name fastened to me, even if it wouldn't have been my first choice."

Starkad drained the last of the mead. Bragi was right enough. He would have to sleep without the comfort of it soon. This place had no people to trade with, and certainly no bees where he could harvest honey. "So." Starkad pointed to the slumbering form of their largest member. "Tell me about this Tiny. Who is he really?"

Bragi snorted. "Claims to be from the Waegmundings. Says they call him Tiny because he's the smallest member of his family, the runt if you can imagine that."

Given the man was nigh to a foot taller than anyone else on this quest, Starkad found it hard to believe.

"Maybe he's got jotunn blood," Bragi said. "Or troll blood."

"Neither one of those things is a laughing matter."

"Who's laughing?" Bragi snorted, then vainly tried to squeeze one more drop out of the skin. "This island is colder than the fortress of Hel. It stays night twenty hours a day, and we're supposed to pass the winter here. And we're running out of mead. Not much to laugh about." Despite his words, he continued to snort.

"Drunk old man."

Bragi thumped Starkad on the chest with one finger. "People don't mind a drunk old man. What they hate is a useless old man. Not me. I'm not gonna wither away and die in my bed. When I go out, it'll be with a blade in my hand, a full belly, and empty stones. And hopefully drunk."

Starkad grinned. "This island has no food, no drink, and no women."

"Then I'm not gonna die here, am I, boy?"

"Don't call me *boy*."

Bragi winked and stretched, then stared at the glowing sky for a time. "You know why we're really here don't you?"

Starkad said naught. Orvar and he had agreed to conceal the truth until absolutely necessary. Truth like that could make men rash, greedy or fearful, or both. Rash men made poor choices. Starkad would know.

"Uh huh," Bragi said. "So Odin, King of the Gods, sends us to the ends of Midgard to establish a colony ... just to see if we can. Spread the word to the locals." Bragi waved his hand at a pod of seals laying on rocks down the beach. "Get him some new worshippers, maybe. Does he answer prayers of fish?"

"Seals aren't fish."

"And I don't have mollusks between my ears, boy."

"We wouldn't be able to trust you to make this a fine tale if you did."

Bragi snorted again. "Have it your way. Keep your secrets. Truth always comes out in the end, though. Nowhere to run from it in a place like this."

Starkad opened his mouth to reply.

The brief scream of a man in agony cut him off.

13

HERVOR

*H*ervor jerked awake at the cry. She lay in a small tent near the fire. The scream had come from outside. Tyrfing slung over her shoulder, she darted out. The mist had thickened. She couldn't see more than a few feet in front of her save right by the fire. And those cries had come from out in the mist.

Even those strange lights in the sky had vanished, leaving them in profound, stifling darkness. All about the camp, men were scrambling, drawing weapons, fumbling around and searching for attackers.

Hel.

Her hand closed around Tyrfing's golden hilt. It wanted her to draw it. To shed light in the darkness, to drive back the mist and slay her foes. But what foes were those? Instead, she snatched a burning branch from the fire and stalked into the mist, waving the flame before her. Mist skittered away from the smoldering branch only to reform behind her.

That was unnatural, even for the fell mists of Niflheim.

Her foot snagged, and she pitched forward, toppling

over on something soft and warm and wet. The torch hit the snow and flickered out. Hervor scrambled up off the … body. What was … Hard to make out in the darkness. She leaned in close. A crewman lay dead there, his face and neck gnawed off by some beast. Bile scorched her throat.

She'd seen a lot of death, but this was sick. She was soaked in his blood.

She pushed forward—or backward, she'd gotten turned around. She needed her damned torch. She was breathing too fast, sucking mist deep into her lungs. She knew she was but couldn't stop herself. Fear had coiled around her gut and was clenching it like a serpent, squeezing ever tighter, blinding her. She waved her hands in the mist. It was too thick, too solid even.

Pulling her away, driving her into the darkness.

Her foot brushed over another body, and she knelt. Hakon. His arm was bitten off at the elbow, a mask of agony on his face. Must have been his scream she'd heard.

Ghostly whispers rang through the mist around her, like the hiss of a fell wind, seeping out of Niflheim. This place was thick with dire spirits or vile beasts. Either way, she was not prey. She was the fucking hunter. She jerked Tyrfing free.

Immediately it flared to life, radiating blue white flame that reflected off of the mist and nigh to blinded her. The mist did not retreat from the sword's light like it would a normal flame. Hervor panted, grasping her blade in both hands. She should have grabbed her shield from the tent before she left. The scream had so caught her off guard she'd not even thought.

"Who is there?" she shouted.

Other voices rang in the mist, echoing unnaturally. Vaettir distorting the sounds, separating the party?

"Hervard," someone shouted. She couldn't identify the voice.

She spun one way and another, searching out whatever creature had done this. Tyrfing had burned her father's ghost. That meant the runeblade extended into the Otherworlds could harm creatures not from Midgard. She needed but find the source of these murders, and she would make it pay. And once dead, perhaps the mist would disperse, and she could find the other explorers.

She took very slow steps, turning about after each, careful to keep an eye in all directions. Some presence, some unearthly being was toying with them.

"Starkad!" she shouted. "Tiny! Ivar!"

Voices rang out in answer, but they all sounded far away, on the edge of some great abyss. Something brushed her shoulder. Hervor spun, sweeping Tyrfing through the mist. It parted before the blade but reformed almost immediately.

Another scream echoed, resounding over and over.

"What are you!" she said through gritted teeth. "*Where* are you?"

She turned again, and her heel brushed something. She looked down. A severed hand trailing blood. She kicked the morbid thing away.

Heartbeats had begun to ring out through the mist. Maybe she could track her foes like that, though those heartbeats echoed in her head. Pounded at her temples.

Not again.

Thump thump.

"Where are you!"

Thump thump.

There was a fire here. If she could just find her way back to it, she would be safe. Most vaettir would not draw within a fire's near radius. Certainly not spirits of the mist, cloaking themselves in frost.

Thump thump.

A wind blew at the back of her neck, tickling her hair beneath her helm. She twisted, slashing with Tyrfing. Again, it cut through mist and naught else. She screamed in frustration. Maybe the blade could harm a vaettr, but only if she could see the damn entity.

Thump thump thump.

She screamed again but could not even hear her own voice over the pounding in her skull. The flickering light, the half-flame of the sword revealed shadows dancing around her. Naught more. No answers, no salvation, no truth.

Swinging wildly, she stumbled around. It was close to her, that much was certain. Toying with her, driving her to madness. Laughing as if it knew she would soon turn her cursed sword on herself. If it stayed away from her ... she had relied on a dark blade for safety. A blade that saved none.

THUMP THUMP THUMP.

Roaring in agony, she swiped the blade backward. It cleaved through something half-solid and came away bloody. Ha! "Die trollfucking vaettr!" she shrieked. Again and again she swung, hewing through flesh. A form fell beside her.

Hervor drove Tyrfing's point into the body, then knelt beside it. Three great gashes had carved him up, but this had been a man.

Rolf Quicktongue ...

He had earned his name for his way of spinning stories to make himself the hero. On the moons they had sailed together, Rolf constantly spoke of all the women he had bedded. Raped, really, as he explained they had not known how much they wanted him until he showed them. He also explained how he'd helped a man find out his true nature by torturing him half to death. Showed the man who he really was.

If any man on this ship deserved to die, it was Rolf. Certainly more than poor Hakon.

But Rolf had not gnawed Hakon's arm off.

Something else had.

And it was still out there.

14

DAYS GONE

Two Years Ago

*G*unther and his men marched Red-Eye, Hervor, and the last of the surviving Boys—Big Spear Harold they called him—into town just before nightfall. Her grandfather stood there watching, as did her mother, although the latter stared at her feet rather than meet Hervor's gaze. No one spoke.

Not even her grandfather. The jarl pointed to the gnarled oak on the west side of town. Gunther grabbed her shoulder and dragged her along while his men marched Red-Eye and Big Spear Harold to the tree. They threw thick ropes around the branches, and men began to tie nooses. Those nooses were placed around the Boys' necks. Gunther's hand on her shoulder tightened, warning her against trying aught.

"Stories claim Odin hung himself for wisdom," her grandfather said. "Sacrificed himself, to himself. These criminals I sacrifice to Odin in the hopes we may all learn wisdom."

Bastard meant her. He wanted her to learn from her mistake.

The jarl waved his hand, and men yanked on the ropes, yanking the Boys off their feet. Hervor forced herself not to look away. She owed the Boys that much respect. One did not reach Valhalla with deaths like these, but still. Even if they were bound for the gates of Hel, she owed them. More than she could repay.

The two men struggled, kicking, a long time choking to death. Finally, her grandfather's men dropped their bodies to the ground.

"Burn them. We need no draugar haunting these woods." He turned, ostensibly addressing the gathered crowd. But he was talking to her. "King Gylfi had it from Odin himself that the corpses of oath breakers and the worst criminals are food to the vilest of serpents in Niflheim. Let these disgraceful savages thus feed the dragon Nidhogg and his spawn. Speak of them no more."

Hervor clenched her jaw.

The sun had set, but numerous torch poles and bonfires lit the town. Rather than build a proper pyre, men hurled the bodies of her friends on those bonfires. As that awful stench reached her, Gunther ushered her away, back into the jarl's hall.

Her grandfather received her there alone. No sign of her mother.

Gunther unbound her hands and let her stand free in the middle of the hall.

Her grandfather drummed his fingers on an armrest. "I indulged you too much, Hervor. You refused to learn womanly arts, sought always to fight, to hunt, to ride. And I let you!" He rose from his throne, slapping the armrests with both hands. "I had Gunther teach you to use shield, sword, bow. Let you go on raids. Aught you wished, you had, and never did I force you to learn weaving or to manage the household. Despite your mother's wishes. And now this. *This* is how you repay me. By taking up arms against my own people. By throwing in with criminals and thieves and for what!" He spread his hands as if expecting some answer. "Surely you did not want for coin, for jewelry? What was my hall so lacking, girl? Speak!"

Hervor scoffed. "You indulged me, Grandfather? Did you? Did you let me go on the raids last summer, when the men went out on the Morimarusa? Or did you insist I stay here and meet suitors from your allies and enemies? I seem to recall one pompous arse after another offering you silver for my trench. How much would you have sold that for, by the way, had I been here?"

Gunther's sudden intake of breath was her only answer.

Jarl Bjalmar trembled as he lowered himself back onto his throne. He shut his eyes a moment more before answering. "And did you let those ... *dogs* touch you?"

Now she smiled, couldn't quite stop from laughing. "You mean did old Red-Eye plow my trench?" She pressed her palms to her eyes, still grinning. Odin's stones, was that what he cared most about? That his precious commodity might be sullied? It wasn't as if a man wouldn't trade for her if she wasn't a virgin. She raised her hands in mock timidity. "Oh, Grandfather, it was *awful*. Those big strong men held me down. I tried to stop them, but they did things to me. Dirty things." She pretended to shiver, then grinned. "And I *liked* it!"

"You are a disgrace, Hervor."

"Then you should not have forced me to return, Grandfather."

The jarl looked to Gunther. "Get her out of my sight. She is forbidden from leaving this hall without guard."

The thegn grabbed her arm and pulled her into the side rooms. Her mother stood in one, face ashen. Damn. She had not expected her to hear that. Hervor opened her mouth, but no explanation or apology seemed sufficient.

"They didn't really touch—" she started to say.

Her mother turned away and stormed out.

Hervor looked to Gunther, who shook his head. He didn't want to hear aught she had to say either. The thegn left her there in the hall before her old room.

The door just stood there, inviting her. Mocking her. Just like the slaves, sitting on the outskirts, staring at her, judging her.

"What?" she demanded.

Two of the men looked away, but the other met her gaze. Now *he* was judging her? A slave daring to think himself fit to decide what she ought to have done. Hervor ran her tongue over her teeth. No. Not this motherless slave. Not today.

She strode purposely toward the slave, who finally looked away. Too late little man. Hervor grabbed him by the tunic and shoved him against the wall. The other two slaves rose from the bench but were smart enough not to interfere.

"What is it? You have something you want to say?" She edged in closer, giving the man nowhere to move, though he glanced to one side and the other. "Come on!" She shoved him again, and he collided with the wall. "Come on, slave."

"Naught, my lady."

She stepped back. "Good. Then next time shut your mouth and your fucking eyes." She punched him in the right eye to emphasize her point. Her knuckles stung from it, but his head collided with the wall. After a heartbeat, he slid down it, groaning.

Hervor wrung her aching hand. A slave who didn't know his own place had no business judging her for stepping out of hers.

"We should have expected no better from you," one of the others mumbled.

Hervor spun on that man. "What did you just say?"

Now this man stood, defiant, glaring at her. Red-Eye had told her once, the best way to get cooperation was to let someone know how far you'd go right from the start. He almost always killed someone before making his first threat. Hervor wasn't going to kill anyone.

Not quite. She grabbed the speaker by the scruff of his neck and pulled his face close. "You have a death wish, slave?"

The man refused to look away. "The jarl forbids us to speak of it, Hervor. It shames him for you to know. You, who disdain us slaves. When your own mother lay with the basest of our kind."

"How dare you?" She could barely form the words.

"Oh, Lady Svafa had the ache real bad between those thighs of hers." The other slave gasped, mumbling for the speaker to quiet.

Hervor squeezed his neck closer. Drew the man in until she could smell his fetid breath on her face.

"You liked it in the woods with bandits, did you? No surprise. Mama couldn't get a jarl's son to take her so she ordered her slaves to it, I hear. One by one, until she was good and finished. Fuck, but Odin alone knows whose you are, girl."

Hervor slammed her forehead into his nose. Cartilage cracked, and blood splattered his face. He screamed for an instant before she head-butted him again. She rained blows upon his ribs and gut until she was gasping for breath. Then and only then did she let the slave drop. He fell in a bloody pulp.

His fellows, even the one she'd banged up before, rushed over to help him.

Her hands were trembling. Knuckles split open, blood dripping between the fingers. Shaking like a child.

She stumbled as she tried to walk away. Why would a slave tell such a lie?

No. No, her father had been a visiting noble who had died raiding. Her mother never talked of him, but she'd said she could not speak of her sorrows. That was all.

The slave lied.

He'd lied.

15

STARKAD

*S*words in hand, Starkad plodded through the mist, with Afzal a few steps behind him. The Serklander wielded a curved sword that had belonged to his father. Shamshirs, the Serklanders called them. Afzal could hold his own, but Starkad wasn't about to send him wandering out in the mist by himself. Not with whatever had done that to the bodies.

"Ghuls ..." Afzal mumbled.

Starkad turned, slowly, counting the tiny flames of other torches moving through the mist. Afzal held their only torch since Starkad could not well wield two swords and carry one. "What are ghuls?"

"Like draugar, I suppose. But they eat the dead."

Another glance at Hakon, his arm gnawed off. "More like the work of varulfur." Not that he thought varulfur still lived on this island. Hel, maybe Afzal was right. Maybe these ghuls of his did lurk in the mist.

"Stay close."

A fell gleam lit the night ahead, but not one of any torch. Starkad pushed forward, past Tiny, who was inspecting another body. The big man shook his head at Starkad's approach. No idea what hunted them.

The strange light had vanished, but a torch ahead called him on in that direction.

Hervard knelt beside a body hacked to pieces. Afzal moved closer, holding the torch out before them.

Rolf Quicktongue.

The two men had been at each other from the first day of this voyage. Small wonder, as Hervard had first beaten Rolf bloody, and then—probably worse in Rolf's mind— poked holes in Rolf's tales of self-styled heroism.

"What have you done?" Starkad tried to keep from shouting.

Already, other torches were heading this way. Bragi stepped out of the mist and stared at the corpse, shaking his head.

"What have you done?" Starkad repeated.

Hervard rose, challenge in his eyes. "Something came upon me in the mist, attacked me. I didn't know it was Rolf —I defended myself." He turned about, looking at each of the gathering party. "As would any of you!"

Starkad lowered his swords but did not sheath them. "You murdered a member of the crew."

Hervard spit. "It was not murder; it was an accident. And I'll pay weregild to his kin."

Orvar cleared his throat. "Everyone draw in, close to the bonfire. No man by himself. Now!"

The murderer glared at Starkad before moving toward the flame as Orvar had commanded. Starkad lingered, though he sheathed his swords and ushered Afzal back toward the fire.

"Well?" Orvar asked. "You believe Hervard?"

Starkad glanced down at Rolf's body. Hervard had

hacked the man repeatedly and impaled him. "Rolf may well have crept up on him. Maybe meant to murder Hervard, I don't know. Quicktongue was treacherous as a snake and about as pleasant as a troll's arse. But still."

"Still—how does a man accidentally strike another so many times?"

"Yes. And I'd have sworn I saw a strange gleam from this direction."

Orvar's face grew even darker, if that were possible. "I thought I saw the same. We have bigger problems before us, though. Something lives on this island, something that ought not to be here."

"Stumbling around in the night is not like to get us far."

Orvar shook his head. "It's all night here, Starkad."

Indeed.

By the bonfire, Afzal had lit his smoking pipe. He burned those rank herbs, sucked them down through a tube. All of it inherited from his father, Hakim. The man had come as a trade emissary all the way from Serkland. His mission might have had more success had raiders not set upon him. When Starkad found Afzal, the boy was the last survivor, a child desperately clutching his father's dead hand.

When they had finally left the scene, Afzal Ibn Hakim had taken the few of his father's possessions the raiders had left behind. A sword and a smoking pipe. Some foreign herbs, the boy claimed, let his father pierce the veil between worlds.

Not certain why, Starkad had helped Afzal get revenge on those raiders.

"Times like these call for drink, not cocking smoke," Ivar said, staring at Afzal.

The Serklander ignored him, continued puffing away, and stared off into the mist as though he saw something there. Perhaps he had. Starkad could never be certain.

There was a story—spreading among völvur and skalds now—a story that Odin had hung himself from the World Tree. Sacrificed himself to gain wisdom from beyond this world. To see into the secret Realms. Some völvur had tried to repeat this miracle. They were dead now. Afzal's way seemed more effective.

The young man blew out a long, shuddering breath as Starkad slunk down beside him. Starkad focused on Hervard. The man sat by himself, unsurprisingly shunned by the others. He'd always been a loner, but after tonight, who would trust him? Once the immediate threat—be it ghuls, draugar, varulfur, or some other vaettir—was dealt with, he would need to see to Hervard. Rolf got what was coming to him, but ... they could not have men in their small party murdering one another. Their numbers were too few for petty rivalries to end in blood.

Starkad spit on the snow. This island was cold as Niflheim, and the wind had begun to howl, grating on his mind. Still, he did not wish to leave. Not before they saw all Thule had to offer, uncovered its secrets and plundered its treasures. The so-called colony would not last the whole winter, he had no doubt. But long enough to explore the island and find Nordri. That much, they would manage.

"What do you see?" he asked Afzal.

The Serklander sniffed, coughed, and rubbed his eyes. "Shadows."

"We all see shadows. Night has a death grip around this land, squeezing it dry. There must be more than that."

Afzal coughed again and wrapped his arms around himself. "Shadows stalking us, converging on us from all sides. This place is accursed, abandoned by all goodly folk and by the gods themselves. You want to know what I see, Starkad?" Afzal turned to the bonfire. "I see a day when all warmth fades and all fires dwindle. And I see it growing cold for us, ever colder. And shadows are circling us, looking for a way in."

Starkad groaned. They definitely needed more mead.

16

HERVOR

*T*he sun had risen, bright in the sky. It reflected off the ice and drove back the mist, nigh to blinding Hervor as she looked across the frozen island. The sheer size of this place was striking. They would indeed need a full winter to explore the whole of it, especially with but a few hours of daylight at a time. And as they drew closer to the winter solstice, the daylight would grow ever shorter.

But then, Hervor had not actually come here to explore some forgotten island. She needed to draw Arrow's Point off alone and face him down. The unfortunate incident last night with Rolf would make the others suspicious of her, especially if she killed another of their group. She would need to make certain they could never trace his death back to her. That meant waiting for exactly the right moment.

Orvar-Oddr beckoned all the crew together now and held up his arms. "We all know something is hunting us in the night. We also know nights are far too long and will be upon us again in a few scant hours. We are left with but two choices. We return to the ship and sail for home as cowards and failures ..."

"Like a beetle-cocking troll's arse we will!" Ivar shouted.

"Or else we become the hunters. We use those few hours of daylight to find what stalks us and end them."

"You did not really think that a choice?" the Axe said.

A few of the men laughed. Hervor folded her arms.

"Fine," Orvar said. "We still have to watch the boat. Starkad and I will go, take the Axe, Bluefoot, Tiny, and Loud with us and scout the way."

Hervor stepped forward. "I didn't come here to be left behind."

"No one did," Starkad said. He looked back at the crew, worked his jaw, then spit. "Fine though, Hervard. You seem far too eager with your sword. I'd rather have you where I can keep an eye on you."

"Master?" the Serklander said.

Starkad waved a dismissive hand. "Of course you're coming, Afzal. The rest of you, gather as much wood as you can in the daylight then build a perimeter of fire. And for the gods' sakes, let naught damage our ship. None of us want to spend the rest of our lives on this frozen, Hel-cursed island."

With that, they set out, climbing the icy slopes. Like the others, Hervor had fitted crampons to her feet, making the climb easier. Not *easy*, though. Everything not snow and ice was rock, rising at dramatic angles that oft had her using her hands to balance herself, even climbing directly with them.

Starkad led the way, pushing them ever deeper, toward the heart of the island. Maybe he was following tracks, maybe he was just assuming their foe must lie beyond the shores of Thule. Either way, he paused only rarely, glancing around before adjusting their course.

The old man, Bragi Bluefoot, was lagging behind, last in their party. Orvar-Oddr was a fool to bring him along at all, much less on their attempt to hunt for whatever fell creature had attacked them. The man wanted a skald along to sing their praises when all was said and done. But that would not happen if the skald dropped dead on some nameless mountain.

The man uttered yet another grunt as he tried to pull himself over an icicle-crusted ridge. Fuck it all. Hervor turned back and knelt on the ridge, offering the old man a hand. He took it, pulling himself up, then lying on his back panting.

"Don't worry ... just enjoying the scenery. The gods make wonders you know."

"Starkad is pushing too hard," Hervor said.

Bragi chuckled. "Starkad always pushes hard. It's his nature ... his curse, you might say."

"His curse?" Hervor helped Bragi back to his feet. "We don't want to fall too far behind."

"That's damned true." The old man stared at the ice face above them. They'd have to climb almost straight up or else lose time searching for a way around. Lose time and they'd not find the others again before nightfall. Already, the sun seemed to be waning.

"We can't get caught out in the open like this," she said.

Bragi winked. "You don't say?" He hefted himself upward, digging his crampons into the ice, then climbing with surprising grace. Not quite a useless old man after all.

Hervor followed after him, not looking straight up as he kept sending showers of ice down on her. "So what *is* Starkad's curse, then?"

"Oh, the tales about that one. He doesn't talk about himself overmuch, makes it hard to say what's true and what's not. Tales say he's killed more men than any save maybe the Aesir themselves."

Hervor frowned. Yes ... the slaughter of many men. Brothers, fathers ... more blood on his hands than most could imagine.

Bragi panted. "There's a story though, tale was, he killed a jotunn."

"Troll shit." Stories claimed Odin had slain a jotunn. Gods might do so. Mortals did not.

"That's the story anyway. And with his dying breath, the jotunn cursed Starkad with eternal wanderlust." Bragi grunted, pulling himself upward more, panting. "Some also say there was more to it ... that ... well, that he would always hurt those dearest to him. Not sure on that one."

"Well, you're his friend. Has he hurt you?"

"Not yet. I—fuck!" Ice shrieked, cracked, and fell, sending Bragi crashing down atop her. She tried to catch him, but he raced past her. One of his crampons caught in her mail. The spikes punched through the armor and dug into her back before his weight ripped them free.

Hervor screamed, clutching the side of the mountain for all she was worth. Bragi had wrapped his arms around her waist. His weight was bearing them both down, threatening to send them tumbling below. They'd like as not shatter bones on the ice.

She glanced down at the old man. Her blood was smeared over his face. "Do not let go, you old fool."

If she moved even a foot, they'd fall. Nor could she support them both forever. Slowly, muscles aching, she slid her arm over a wide rock. She needed a proper grip. Odin's stones, the wound in her back was on fire. She ought to just let the clumsy trollfucker fall. Except he seemed like a decent man.

Panting, getting so hard to hold on.

"You have to climb up my back. Can you grab my shoulder?"

Bragi shifted, his bloody face pressed into the small of her back. With one arm, he tightened his grip around her waist; and with the other, he grabbed a fistful of her blood-soaked mail. That he used to heave himself upward to her shoulder. From there, he reached for the rock himself. His crampons scratched her arse, and she had to grit her teeth to keep from screaming.

"You fall down, Bluefoot?" Tiny shouted from above. Hervor glanced up as the big man tossed a rope down to the skald.

Bragi grabbed the rope. "You wouldn't think you'd miss a few toes so very much."

She was going to kill them both.

Bragi climbed the rope enough to get above her, then Tiny hauled him up. Hervor lay against the cliff side, panting, trying not to think about the pain. The bleeding, the cold.

The fucking *pain*.

Finally, she pushed away and began to haul herself upward as well. Hand over hand. Crampons dug into the fucking ice and not someone else's back and arse. Imagine that. What a way to use climbing tools. And who the fuck tried climbing with crampons if he was missing toes?

At the top, she rolled over. They were standing atop one of the lower mountains. Across a valley pitched an enormously tall waterfall. Though thin, it fell so far and with such force, it had not frozen over, at least not this early in winter. The water pitched into a lake far below them.

She rose to her knees and stared at it, breathless, and not just from the climb. Never had she seen a sight like this. The land stretched out beyond the waterfall in an endless plateau, shrouded by mist, as was the valley. But it was deep, wide, and within it, beyond the rocks, grew a small wood.

"It'll be dark very soon," Orvar-Oddr said.

Starkad nodded. "We cannot stay here. The valley beneath the fall will offer shelter and fresh firewood."

"So." Bragi cleared his throat. "What you mean to say is, you want us to now climb back down. In the dark. Into the mist. And the dark."

Starkad offered no answer, save to start walking in that direction.

Hervor stifled a groan. Killed a jotunn had he? Well, that was fucking amazing. And now he was king of Midgard. And telling her to march on, to climb on, never mind the holes in her back.

The worst of it was, he was right. There was no shelter up on the mountain, not from the howling wind, not from the icy chill it brought. And not from any foes who might be hunting them come sunset.

Bragi suddenly grabbed her and pulled her to her feet. "We have to get a fire going before full dark sets in. And that means we'd best do as he says. Can you walk?"

Hervor sneered. "Just don't fall on me again, old man."

"Eh. Well, I'll just go first this time." And he did.

17

DAYS GONE

Two Years Ago

*J*arl Bjalmar had no völva of his own, and so a simple healer, a woman from the town, treated the slave Hervor had beaten. For three days, the man had lain abed, and the healer could not say whether he would live or die. Hervor had peeked in on him twice, each time greeted by the disdainful stares of the healer and the other slaves who had come to visit their friend.

Three moons she had spent among Red-Eye's Boys, and with them she had killed many men. Not like this, though. Not someone she had seen every day, even if she did not know his name. She had not intended to cripple him. She didn't know what she'd intended. His words had enraged her beyond all withstanding. And she was within her rights to kill a slave for speaking to her thus—for any reason at all, she supposed, though it would mean she'd owe her grandfather the man's worth in silver.

But it wasn't what she'd meant to do.

What she'd intended mattered little, in the end. Not after the man died from the injuries she inflicted.

She'd paced the jarl's hall since then, never able to settle her mind nor her stomach. To think her mother would lie with such men left her nauseated. She needed a sword in her hand and a foe before her to kill. Someone to punish. For the lie. It had to be a lie.

But then, she had not been able to confront her mother about it, and the slave would never talk of it—or aught else —again. And so Hervor found herself waiting outside her mother's door once again, unable to knock, unable to ask a question she so dreaded the answer to. Men did that kind of thing—fucked slaves to sate their lust. But women, especially noblewomen, were meant to have self-control.

Did this so matter?

She'd lied to her mother, too, when she'd tried to claim Red-Eye hadn't fucked her. Of course he had, though he certainly had not shared her with the Boys as she'd said to her grandfather. The old man was just too tempting to humble, to shame. Like how she now felt shamed to know of her true parentage. A child born to a slave belonged to the mother's owner. So what if the mother was a noble?

Well then, at least her mother would have no more right to judge *Hervor's* excesses. She was about to knock when the door opened. Her mother jerked back to see her standing there, then stared at her a long time.

"What do you wish now?"

"To speak with you."

"I'll hear no more lies."

Hervor folded her arms over her chest. "I just want the truth."

At that her mother pursed her lips, then sighed, and motioned for Hervor to come in. She had rarely visited her mother's room. It was well decorated with tapestries, some of which she had probably woven herself on the loom in the corner. A small brazier kept the room warm and well lit.

Her mother sat in a chair beside that brazier and beckoned Hervor join her in the other chair. "I had given up inviting you in here."

Hervor tried not to sneer. Her mother meant to say she had given up on Hervor completely. "Who is my father?"

With a sigh, her mother shook her head. "I thought we were past this. I do not wish to speak of—"

"I'm sure you don't. The slaves told me, though."

"They *what*?" Very real concern marked her face.

"So it's true. You forbade them speak of it. You lay with so many men you don't even know who my father is."

"W-what?" Her mother stood so swiftly her chair toppled over. "Who speaks such lies? *Who!*"

"A deadman, as of this afternoon."

Her mother groaned, then began to pace the room.

"So now I know." And neither her mother nor grandfather had any right to complain about *any* of her actions.

"You know naught, spiteful child!"

Hervor froze, looked to where her mother stood by a shuttered window.

"Your father was a jarl's son, Hervor. And we were properly wed, though yes, he died before you were born. Angantyr, son of Jarl Arngrim, who gave him a perilous sword to wield in a duel."

Now it was Hervor's turn to stammer, unable to wrap her mind around what she was hearing. "My father was a hero?"

Her mother wrung her hands, then looked back to the window again. "He was famous, yes. The most famous of his band. Twelve brothers, all berserkir. It was said they took no one else into battle with them, so mighty were they.

Angantyr was the eldest, the most famed and most powerful. He had eyes like furnaces and arms thick as a real bear's.
And he ...

"There's another kingdom here in Sviarland, to the
north. Back then, King Yngvi had a daughter famed for her
beauty. And Angantyr's brother, the next after him—Hjorvard—he swore to marry her. But he was challenged for her
hand by a housecarl, if you can believe that. A mere servant
to the king thought to marry the beautiful princess."

That took some temerity. Hervor drifted to her mother's
side and put a hand on her shoulder. "And what happened?"

"They arranged a duel, on the island of Samsey, in the
Morimarusa. And before they went to the duel, the brothers
wanted to seek their father's blessing. They passed through
here and father gave them all shelter, feasted them for a few
nights and they ... Angantyr and I met. Angantyr told me he
thought me fairer even than Princess Ingibjorg, and he
asked my father for my hand. Father agreed and we were
wed, feasted. It lasted only one night since they were in a
hurry to reach Samsey."

"I was conceived the night of the wedding feast?" Hervor
could barely hear her own voice over the crackle of the fire.
"And the duel?"

"I was not there."

"But you know what happened. Tell me." Part of her did
not want to know. There was only one possibility after all.
Clearly, her father had not returned.

"The housecarl took with him a crew and a champion,
Arrow's Point, skalds call him. No one knows exactly what
happened on Samsey. But Arrow's Point was the only one to
leave that island."

Hervor's hand on her mother's shoulder tightened. "My
uncles?"

"He killed them all. Your father, his eleven brothers. All lay, unblessed by any prayers, perhaps never even burned on the pyre. All I can say is now Samsey is called a haunted place, and no one will go there."

No. This Arrow's Point had destroyed not only her father but all his kin. Her kin. "*I* will go."

"Do not be a fool."

"A fool! Did Arrow's Point come here and pay us weregild for our losses? Did he pay Jarl Arngrim for the death of his sons?"

"One does not pay weregild for an agreed-upon duel, Hervor."

"A duel ends with a man dead. When it ends with *twelve* men dead, I call that something fouler! They were murdered, probably set upon unawares and killed. And you tell me he may have left them to rot?"

Her mother shook her by the shoulders then. "Listen to me, child—"

Hervor batted her mother's arms off. "No! No, I will have vengeance for my father. This I swear. I will avenge him and my uncles both, and I will do it with father's own sword." She stormed off toward the door.

"You are but a girl!"

Hervor froze. "I am my father's only heir. And I will not break this oath. No matter how long it takes, I will avenge him."

18

HERVOR

*D*aylight had faded, giving way to those strange lights in the sky once again. And the mist. Always the damned mist. One more reason to hate the night. Still they climbed down, torches in hand. The slope had grown level enough to allow that much, at least. Far ahead, the crash of water echoed through the valley, almost allowing Hervor to forget what a horrible place this truly was. Almost but not quite. An island without proper day, where beasts fed upon men in the night. Truly, it seemed a landscape dreamed up by Hel.

"You seem very deep in thought," Bragi said. The old skald walked beside her as they brought up the rear of the party.

If she was quiet, perhaps it was because blood continued to seep out of her wounds, freezing against her mail. The wounds were not as deep as they might have been, but still, she would probably have to stitch them. Already weakness had begun to slow her steps. And you never let men see weakness, especially not men who might be enemies.

Better then, to keep him distracted. And skalds love to talk. "Where do you hail from, Bluefoot?"

"Originally? From Njarar. When I was born, Old King Nidud reigned over the kingdom."

"I know that name." She couldn't quite place it, but she had heard of Nidud.

"I should think so. His tale has become quite famed—or infamous, perhaps, much as the king himself. I was just a boy, mind, so I didn't hear the tale until years later. You see, we lived in a small town below the mountain where Nidud reigned. The old king was fabulously wealthy since his ancestors had stolen a dverg hoard."

Hervor chuckled. "You expect me to believe a man stole from dvergar and got away with it?"

Bragi put his hand over his heart as if offended. "Would a skald lie?"

"Only while breathing."

Bragi shrugged in acknowledgment. "Never mind that. However much gold he had, it wasn't enough for him. He spread war in Sviarland and in Aujum. The Aesir lived there in those days, before we knew they were gods. And Nidud wanted weapons to challenge them and their mighty warriors. So he abducted the most famed smith in the North Realms—Volund. Well, Volund didn't want to work for cruel Nidud, so what did the king do? He hamstrung the smith so he could never leave the forge."

She *had* heard this tale. Of the cruel revenge of the dark smith. "And Volund repaid him by killing his sons," she said. It was getting harder to speak. Her breath felt short, and her back seemed on fire.

"Oh yes, that's the short of it. More properly, you might say Volund ruined Nidud's line. The king killed himself and left the throne to his last son, Otwin."

The rest of the group had gathered in the valley before the waterfall. The fall pitched down into a wall a dozen feet below the level where they stood. Down there, seals lay upon the banks, so the river must lead to the sea at some point. Had they known, maybe they could have sailed the ship up this far.

Orvar-Oddr stood in the center of the party, pointing at the woods. "Everyone go in pairs, get firewood. Do not go far. We camp here and wait for better light."

Starkad took his Serklander friend, Orvar went with Ivar the Loud, and Tiny and the Axe went off chatting, leaving her with Bragi. Orvar had ordered them not to go alone. But then she did not care much for orders from him or anyone else.

"Go on," she told Bragi. "I'll catch up."

"Orvar said—"

"Orvar didn't know a clumsy skald put a crampon spike through my back."

"Ah, you can't well patch yourself up. Here, let me see it. I'm a fair hand with a needle, and I even know a thing or two about völva poultices."

Hervor sneered. She wasn't about to take off her armor, much less her shirt, in front of the old man. Might be a tad difficult to maintain her disguise at that. And she had gone to extraordinary lengths to conceal her gender while at sea, so she wasn't going to let on now. "I can see to myself. Go get the damn wood."

Bragi shrugged and trotted off toward the trees, mumbling under his breath. Hervor plodded around the proposed campsite until she found a slope leading down to the water, one that put a number of large rocks between her and the rest of the group.

There she slumped down with a groan. Chills wracked

her. Blood loss? Or just the fact it was fucking freezing this far north? She set Tyrfing down. This would not be enjoyable. Gingerly, she tried to remove the chain. Blood had dried against the mail, making it stick. Worse, links of chain had wedged into her skin, even through her leather jerkin. The crampon had torn through metal, leather, and flesh like a weapon.

Teeth grit against the pain, she peeled those links from her back. A grunt of pain escaped her as iron tore flesh. She slumped against the rock, panting as the last links broke free. She hated this place. She fucking *hated* this whole damned island. And the whole Yngling dynasty for forcing her to come here—as if she did not have enough reasons to gut them all.

Still short of breath, she pulled the mail over her shoulders and tossed it aside. That would need some serious repair, too, and she was not like to find a smith here on Thule. Well, there was no help for that. She unlaced the jerkin then tossed it aside so she could pull up her tunic.

Twisting around, she could see the bloody mess on her back and her flesh already looking sallow. There was no way she'd ever reach that to stitch it though. Damn Bragi. She stretched, reaching around, even knowing it was helpless.

"Fuck," she groaned. If she didn't get this patched, she'd not see another day. "Frigg ... I could much use your help here."

The goddess did not answer.

She let her tunic drop back into place. Beneath that, she'd used linen strips to bind her breasts as close as she could. But without the jerkin and armor, someone would notice. More so if she had to remove the tunic. Bragi had made this mess of her back. Maybe the old man was the one who could help her now.

She pushed herself up, then stumbled back along the path until she could spot men returning from the woods.

"Bragi!" she spat when the old skald came wandering back with an armful of firewood.

He looked around.

"Bragi!"

The man nodded in her direction now and trotted over after depositing the wood at the campsite. "Come to your senses, boy? I've seen a lot of fool things in my time. Never saw a man stitch up his own back before. Though I imagine it might have made a fine tale had you managed it."

Hel take the smug old man. Hervor spit in the snow. "You going to help or not?"

"Yes. Of course I'm going to help you. Take off the tunic."

Hervor glared at him a moment. Then she turned around to face the river, sat, and pulled her tunic up over her head.

"Huh." Looking at the linens.

"Another old injury," she said.

"Uh huh." He sat down behind her.

She glanced back, and he was heating his needle on his torch.

"What the fuck?"

Bragi chuckled. "A völva once told me fire spirits help seal out infection from the mist."

After a moment, he pressed calloused hands against her back. Then he set to work.

Hervor grit her teeth and tried not to complain.

19

STARKAD

*W*hatever vaettir dwelt on Thule, Starkad was going to be prepared for them this time. Much as he wanted to blame Hervard for Rolf's death, the man *might* have made a real mistake. Either way, some dangerous beasts lurked here, and the best way to prepare for beasts and vaettir alike was with flame. Flame and spears.

"I want small bonfires ringing the main one. There, there, over there by the rocks."

Tiny grumbled about how much wood it was going to take, but the Axe laughed.

"Remember that battle against the men in Reidgotaland?" the old veteran asked.

Starkad nodded. A pair of jarls had tried rising up against Healfdene, who'd hired Starkad, the Axe, and others to make an example of them.

The Axe rubbed his beard. "We put those giant wooden spikes all around the camp thinking they might attack in the night. Had those big burning torch poles too."

Starkad snorted. "Cowards took one look at the defenses

and refused to attack, started building their own fortifications." It almost made him smile. "I remember. Not sure that's like to happen tonight."

The Axe shrugged and waved in the general direction of the island. "I'd much rather be on the offense, but best to have the defenses in place."

Tiny dropped a massive armful of wood in front of the Axe. "Then you can make those defenses. I'd rather hunt our foes down."

The veteran chuckled. "And we did, despite the locals raving about it being dragon country." He snorted. "Didn't see any fucking dragons. Just men and blood and screaming." He turned, as if examining the campsite. "This place, though. This place looks like it ought to house a dragon or two. A refuge for old, wily serpents. A place not meant for men at all."

Starkad had begun setting the woodpile, preparing the bonfire, but he looked up at the Axe's words and slowly took in the woods, the icy slopes, untouched by man in countless long winters. He had seen a great many monstrosities in his day, but dragons were not among them.

"I'd like to see a dragon," Tiny said. "Imagine the fame of it, to slay such a creature. I hear Odin slew a dragon once."

Starkad spit. "You wouldn't like to see a dragon, Tiny. Even the jotunnar avoid the serpents."

"Besides," the Axe said, "such talk can anger the gods. Careful lest they grant your request."

Tiny grunted, then fell silent.

Starkad rose. "Get those fires going. All of them. Dragons or not, we don't know what might lair here on Thule." With that, he made his way back to where the rest of the group sat.

They had gathered around the central bonfire, most gnawing on what remained of salted fish.

Ivar spit out a bone as Starkad sank down by the fire. "One good thing about the sea—fresh beetle-cocking fish. We're going to have to hunt if we're to winter here."

Starkad grunted. "Saw some tracks in the snow. Looked like fox."

"Wonderful," Ivar said. "A fox ought to feed the eight of us for maybe an hour. Assuming Tiny doesn't inhale the beast whole."

Orvar grunted. "There are seals down there. It means fish in the river."

Ivar flung another bone into the fire. "Troll cock on fish. Let's hunt the beetle-cocking seals."

At that, their leader snorted. "As much noise as you make, the seals would be halfway back to Sviarland before you got close enough." He shook his head. "No, I'll take my bow and shoot one. Then we'll all have fresh meat."

"All right," Starkad said. "Be careful, though."

Orvar rose. "I reached manhood in Nidavellir. I know how to hunt a damn seal and not one of you is as good a shot as I. Just try not to make too much noise over here. Don't want to scare them off." With that, he trod off, down toward the river.

Afzal had melted snow in a pot, and now he dipped a drinking horn in it. The Serklander took a long drink, then passed it to Starkad, who also drank. Warm water was no substitute for mead, but he supposed it would keep him alive.

Though, he did not look forward to trying to sleep.

Vikar waited for him in dreams. And on the nights where his brother's ghost left him be, there was always Ogn's. And hers was maybe the worse of the two; she slipped in and out of his mind like a mara—a nightmare spirit. Maybe that was what she had become. Maybe he had made her into it.

"Oh, now you'll take the cocking drinking horn," Ivar said. "You Serkland men seem a lot like little girls to me. Can't hold your mead, won't taste the ale. A sip or two might put some hair on your stones, boy."

"It seems to me," Hervard said, where he sat wrapped in a blanket, "you have cocks on your tongue a great deal, Ivar."

Starkad spit water laughing.

Ivar scowled. "Yeah, well what the troll cock ... what's a ghul anyway? I hear you're all saying that's what's preying on us."

Afzal shook his head. "Unclean spirits. But I don't know if that's what we face. Could be though. Where I come from, the caliphs banish the mists from the cities by binding spirits of flame. We call them jinn. But some men—sorcerers—use ghuls to prey on their enemies. Tales to scare children, maybe."

Ivar's eyes widened at that. "Thor's thundering cock! Your own rulers are wizards, it sounds to me."

Afzal stared into the flame and did not answer.

Bragi, who Starkad would have expected to jump at the chance to hear of lands so far off, was watching Afzal but said naught. When the skald fell silent, trouble was amiss. That was one thing Starkad could count on.

"What is it, Bragi?" Starkad asked.

The old skald looked to him, then shook his head.

Starkad scowled, then cocked his head off toward one of the fires Tiny and the Axe had finished building. He rose and waited for Bragi to do the same and follow him. The skald did, amidst hard looks from the others, especially

Hervard. They might not like secret talks, but Starkad and Orvar had agreed to be careful not to reveal too much. The men were on edge enough already.

"Speak, old man," Starkad said when they reached the perimeter fire.

"We should not have come here, I think."

Starkad groaned and cracked his neck. "Bit late to think of that now. And I doubt that's what so troubles you, so out with it."

Bragi sighed, rubbed his arms. "We've seen a lot, you and I."

Starkad shrugged. "Wars and raids and more than one vaettr, yes. What are you on about?"

The skald warmed his hands by the fire. "All men have secrets, Starkad. You should know."

So that's what he meant. Bragi had been around long enough to have heard tales about Starkad, stories he had shared with few men besides Afzal. The old man almost certainly knew about Vikar, the self-made king, slain by his own brother. The worst of Starkad's crimes, though neither the first nor the last of them.

Starkad too warmed his fingers. This place was cold as Niflheim. But it was wondrous, too, strange and unknown. How could a man deny the call of such a place? To uncover its secrets, unearth its long buried treasures. He did not know why the dvergar had left this island, but he would find out. He would have it all, until Thule had no hidden places left. And then he would move on. Such had become his way. Maybe one day he would even travel to Serkland, beyond the Midgard Wall. Afzal did not ask to go home, seemed almost as wary of his homeland as men like Ivar were. And yet ... what strangeness must lie there, in a land where men ruled spirits of flame?

"I do not ask you to share all your secrets," he said at last. "But if something threatens us, I need to know it."

"Eh. Threatens? No, I think not. But sooner or later you'd learn of it, and I'm worried what would happen if it came at the wrong time."

Starkad spread his hands, awaiting some explanation.

Bragi sighed. "Hervard—well, it seems he is not a *he*."

"What?"

"*She* has been concealing herself from us. Damned well too. I'm not one to miss noticing a woman often."

Starkad knew his mouth hung open, but he couldn't quite think of a worthy response. Ivar would have. Something involving trolls and cocks, no doubt. And Bragi was right—if Hervard, or whatever her name was—was a woman, she had hidden it well. She had lied to them for moons.

No surprise. All women lied. They had treachery woven into their very souls.

Starkad ran his fingers over the hilts of his swords.

"She is not Ogn," Bragi said.

The warning in the skald's voice grated on his nerves. It did not matter. They were all the same.

Starkad stormed back toward the main bonfire, even as Tiny and the Axe were heading that way.

"Starkad, wait," Bragi called after him.

He did not.

Hervard rose as he drew nigh to her and held up her hands in warding. He grabbed her by the tunic and yanked her to her feet. She tried to bat his hands away. He knocked hers aside. She pushed at him, and he punched her in the gut. She doubled over, and he grabbed her chest. Definitely a breast.

Starkad flung her to the ground. "You lying bitch."

She grimaced, groaning in pain. Blood had seeped through the back of her tunic. She rose, fists balled.

"No more lies, woman. Who are you?"

"Woman!" Ivar shouted.

Several of the others had risen, too.

The woman spat at his feet. "I'm Hervor. What of it?"

Starkad toyed with the idea of hitting her again. "Besides the obvious? You lied to us all about who you were."

"Because you men think with your fucking cocks! To say naught of your kind oft not placing enough trust in shield-maidens."

"Hard to trust liars."

Her hand went to the golden sword hilt on her shoulder. Fingers closed around it. Her eyes shone with murder.

"You want to see who's faster with a blade?"

"Starkad!" Bragi grabbed his shoulder. "Whoever she is, she saved my life on the cliff."

Hervor charged forward then, swinging not with her sword but with her fist. Starkad shoved Bragi aside, blocked her punch on one arm. With the other, he landed a hook on her ribs. She buckled under it. He snapped his other fist into her gut, and as she doubled over again, slammed an uppercut into her chin.

The woman pitched back and landed in the snow.

"Not fast enough," Starkad said.

Bragi had grabbed him again and was pulling him away. This time, the Axe helped. The two men pulled him aside until he shrugged them off.

"Having a trench instead of a cock isn't a crime," the Axe said. "We've fought with maidens on a shield wall."

Starkad spit, then pushed away from them. He paused only to grab a burning branch from a perimeter fire, then stalked away from the camp. He didn't need them, not right now. Could they seriously be taking her side after so many moons of deception? Hervor was right—they were thinking with their cocks. The only woman on the whole damned island and maybe they both wanted to bed her. Well, let them. Let them fuck her all damned night if they wanted. It was the only use for a woman.

He didn't need her, and he didn't need them.

No, he had trusted a woman once. He had loved Ogn, had fought a fucking jotunn for her. And she had betrayed him, fallen for the monster instead of the man. Such was the way of women, traitors, and unworthy of faith. And her ghost would haunt him for all his nights.

Even now it lurked somewhere out of sight. Waiting for him to shut his eyes so she could wrap her fingers around his heart and squeeze. Ogn was his mara, but Hervor wasn't going to be one. Her death would not be on his head; it would be on her own. There would never be another Ogn.

Never.

20

HERVOR

*H*and to her bloody lip, Hervor climbed down toward the river. She ought to have drawn Tyrfing and fought Starkad. She was so close. It wanted to taste his blood. But if she drew it ... it would have to taste someone's blood. And Starkad Eightarms did not lose a sword fight. With his fists alone, he'd thrashed her before she knew what had happened.

What then? She was good, but she'd be a fool to think herself a match for Starkad under any circumstances. Or Orvar-Oddr, if he expected a fight. The two of them were like legends.

Right now, though, Orvar was alone, hunting seals in the mist. Alone on an island where they knew some vaettr or beast stalked them. It was the best chance she was like to get, and she would not waste it. No, and she knew enough of stalking silently to creep up on him. He would not see her coming. She'd run him through, dump his body in the river, and sneak back to camp. No one would know what she'd done—they'd think the beast had taken him.

Even if Starkad had more blood on his hands, Orvar-

Oddr was the Arrow's Point. Of that, she had little doubt remaining. He had murdered her family in service to the Ynglings.

And he would not be the last to die for that crime.

Hervor had paused in camp only to grab her mail. No sense in facing Arrow's Point without her armor, damaged though it may be.

Starkad would still be a problem. She could run him through while he slept, but the others would kill her. He was a bastard, a son of a troll. But she would have to find a way to keep him from turning on her. By Odin's spear, what was his problem with her?

So she had pretended to be a man. It was only sense to do so.

She braced herself on a rock as she descended. Her ribs felt like she'd been kicked by a donkey. Naught seemed broken though, Frigg be praised.

Damn Starkad.

The barks of seals echoed out even over the roar of the waterfall. They sounded near. Strange that Orvar had not felled one and returned yet. Or maybe he had. The creatures were no doubt heavy. What a way for the great Orvar Arrow-Oddr to die—a sword through his back while dragging a seal carcass up a slope. Shame no one would know or tell that tale. It would prove a fitting end for the slayer of her kin.

She struggled to contain her grunts of pain. He'd never hear her coming, not over the water and seals. Still, best to keep silent. Stick to the shadows. She had not brought a torch, of course. It was dangerous to wander in the mists without one, very dangerous. Even if she didn't go Mist-mad, vaettir could creep up on her.

But without flame, she could also creep up on a man.

Advancing in a half crouch, she scurried from one rock pile to the next, right up to the river's edge. She ought to have seen Orvar's own flame by now. Even if he had left it somewhere, it should have been visible.

Why wasn't—

On the ice near the river, the man's bow and quiver lay. What in Hel's frozen underworld? She near leapt to her feet, hand on Tyrfing's hilt, barely suppressing the urge to draw it. Not until she was certain.

That lesson she had learned with Rolf.

Orvar must be here now, waiting for her. He had seen her coming. Must have.

She turned in place, slowly, not releasing her grip on the sword. Where was he?

There.

A man stood a dozen feet away, on the riverbank. Hervor advanced.

The man was not Orvar.

In fact, he was naked. How had he not caught the deathchill like that? As she drew nigh, several other naked men and women came into view. One among them, a woman, had Orvar slung over her shoulder like a fresh kill. Was he dead already?

No. He stirred, ever so slightly.

Hervor froze in place. These people had not seen her yet. And they were taking Arrow's Point. If they killed him, was her vengeance satisfied?

No.

No, she had promised her father's ghost *she* would kill the man. She had sworn an oath on Tyrfing. He must die by her hand.

Were these strange, naked people the ghuls Afzal had spoken of? It did not matter. She'd have to kill them to get to

Arrow's Point. She had taken only a single step forward when her foe's captors began to walk into the river.

Hervor almost tripped. They just stepped into the current and dove under, dragging her prey with them. The cold might not affect them, but it would surely kill Orvar before long.

"Oh damn it." She started to run, fighting through the pain in her ribs and back. Damn it!

The man's captors moved quickly in the water, vanishing into the mist over the river in a few breaths. It was so thick down here and growing thicker, almost like wading through water.

"Stop!" she shouted. "To arms!"

Her voice might echo, might carry to the camp above. Might not, too.

Grunting, she ran on, racing along the riverbank. She had to catch them and fast. Or her chance at vengeance would be lost forever.

STRUGGLING, panting Hervor ran. Firelight appeared ahead, and she stumbled toward it, then fell short when the torch-bearer turned on her.

Starkad.

He glared at her. "There was someone in the river."

"They took Orvar." Her lungs hurt. She was sucking down great gasps of mist, too. She drew closer to the protection of his torch.

Starkad grimaced. "Water vaettir, most like. Nixies, maybe. We have to find them. What are you doing down here?"

"I ... needed to treat my injuries. Wanted to be alone."

"Then stay here if you wish. I'm going to find Orvar." He spun and began to run down the riverbank.

With her injuries, it took all she had to even keep him in sight. She needed a torch, flame, light. Gods, she needed some damned rest.

Someone else was climbing down the slope, bearing another torch.

"Get down here!" she shouted. "Hurry—"

Solid mist hit her with enough force to lift her off her feet and fling her onto the ice. She landed hard and skidded toward the river's edge. Her mail sheared through the ice. The impact sent fresh jolts through her injured back, and she struggled to breathe, to even see straight.

"What?" she managed to groan.

"Little girl ..." The voice seemed to whisper from the mist, coming from all around her. "You have trespassed against an ancient power."

Hervor rolled over and rose to her knees. *Everything* hurt now. But she had heard mist whisper such things before. "Another sorcerer?" She slung Tyrfing off her shoulder but did not draw it. Still in the scabbard, she pushed the point against the ground and used it to steady herself. "How many of you people do I have to kill?"

A shadowed form coalesced out of the mist, taking on the shape of a man with ashen hair. He bore a blade in his hand, which he pointed at her. "I do not know how you bested one of us, but if you think to face a Niflung blade master, then come. I shall send you swiftly to Hel. There is none greater."

Hervor groaned. She had no idea what he was talking about, except that he seemed to actually worship Hel like some Mist-mad abomination. That being the case, he wasn't like to allow her a respite to recover from her injuries.

She rose, swaying slightly on her feet. And she drew Tyrfing. It gleamed like a ray of sunlight, reflecting off the mist and casting the river in ethereal colors like a dream.

Or a nightmare born beyond the gates of Hel.

"Hervor!" Afzal shouted from the slope.

"Fool child," the sorcerer said. "You truly bear that blade. It was not wrought for you, not for any of your child-like people. And bearing such a treasure you tread *here*, upon these ancient shores. You have no idea what evils lay buried beneath Thule. My killing you is a mercy." The sorcerer glanced at Afzal who was running toward them, then turned back to her. "You are strong to have taken the sword and favored to have slain a Niflung. Kill the foreigner and give the sword to me. I will spare you, take you away from this cursed island."

Hervor grit her teeth. She was in no shape to fight this monster. But she sure as Hel was not going to kill Afzal, not like this. Besides, Arrow's Point was still out there. Waiting to die on Tyrfing's edge. In answer, she advanced slowly, struggling to remain on her feet.

The sorcerer chuckled and shook his head. "You shall find no peace, even in death."

Torch in one hand, curved sword in the other, Afzal bellowed and rushed the sorcerer. Hervor pushed forward as fast as she could, but the Serklander reached the Niflung first. The sorcerer spun, hand trailing mist like a whip. It wrapped around Afzal's legs and swept them out from under him, sending him tumbling to the ground.

The Niflung leaned in to impale Afzal, but Hervor lunged forward and knocked his sword aside.

As Afzal struggled to rise, the Niflung spun, sweeping his sword in tight arcs that drove her backward. The sorcerer twisted, struck at Afzal, who barely got his sword up to block.

The Niflung moved just fast enough to keep her crew-mate from being able to attain his feet. Afzal gave over trying and swept his sword at the sorcerer's legs. The sorcerer responded by whipping mist around into a disk that froze like ice and blocked the attack, even as he struck at Hervor with his blade.

She parried on Tyrfing, falling back.

At full strength, she could have fought him, maybe.

He didn't try to block Tyrfing with the mist. Maybe his magic could not turn a runeblade. It had pinned Afzal though.

"Use the torch!" she shouted at him.

Afzal did, swinging the flame. It dispersed the mist shield, forcing the sorcerer back a step. Hervor pressed forward, hewing with Tyrfing with all the strength she had. Her enemy fell back farther, finally allowing Afzal to rise.

It was a brief respite. A wave of the Niflung's hand sent a wall of mist surging at them. Hervor cleaved at it, and it broke apart before Tyrfing. Afzal, however, hurtled backward. His torch skittered along the ice before falling into the river.

The sorcerer laughed. "You should have taken my offer when I made it. But I offer you one more time, little girl. Kill the boy and give me the sword."

"Go to Hel."

The man shrugged and advanced on her. "The only thing your companions will find of you is your head. I will leave it for them."

Lacking a retort, Hervor settled for a glare.

Beyond the sorcerer, a torch burned through mist. He jerked his head in that direction, as if drawn by the burning vapors. Then the Niflung turned back to Hervor with a sneer. "Just one more of your friends who will die for you, girl."

That torch touched the ground, and a line of flame erupted, surging out in an arc that ran all the way to the river. Mist recoiled and leapt away, almost seeming to shriek in pain. The flame illuminated Starkad, who was drawing his second sword and advancing.

The Niflung spun on him.

"I'm not like the others," Starkad said. "I know what you are, sorcerer."

Now the sorcerer waggled a finger at Hervor, who stood panting. The promise of a return. Then he turned back to Starkad and jerked his free hand forward. From it flew an icicle the size of an arrow.

It shot for Starkad like a flung spear.

Starkad cleaved it aside with one sword and continued advancing.

The sorcerer flung another shard of ice and another, a barrage of them. Starkad leapt over one and cut aside others, ever closing in.

Impossibly, the barest hint of tension now laced the sorcerer's moves. He arced his hand, sending a whip of mist at Starkad the way he had at Afzal. Starkad jumped over it, flipped on the air, and swung with both swords at once. The Niflung parried one and took a deep gash to the face with the other.

Afzal was struggling to rise.

Starkad whipped his swords around in lightning-fast arcs the Niflung barely parried. In a few moves, the sorcerer had gashes on his arms, legs. Starkad was a storm of death. Hervor had never seen aught like it.

Thump thump.

Tyrfing. It wasn't enough for someone else to kill her foe. She had to do it, or the runeblade would not be satisfied. Even now, it tugged on her arm, tried to drag her to Afzal. Hervor grabbed her wrist and pulled back.

"No. No. *No.*" Rather than risk being forced to kill the boy, she hurled herself back at the sorcerer.

Starkad had earned wounds as well. He was bleeding from his temple and from one shoulder. It slowed his left sword ever so slightly, though he had driven the sorcerer back to the river.

Hervor dove into the fray, desperate to stop the pounding in her head. She swung at the sorcerer, whose face now shone with desperation. The Niflung ducked, swept his hand along the water.

Bits of the river froze in spikes that launched themselves at Starkad like a barrage of arrows.

The warrior fell back, dropped one sword as a spike hit him, though he cut aside many others. Hervor lunged forward with her full weight. The Niflung parried. She scraped her sword along his blade, then lurched forward. Tyrfing's point sliced a thin line along the man's chest.

He froze, looking down at the wound with more concern than he'd shown the half dozen Starkad had given him.

He knew.

He understood what the sword would do to him. The wound would not heal, would not close. That scratch would prove direr than had another blade gouged him deeply.

Hervor backed away. The pounding had stopped. Tyrfing had tasted blood. It knew death belonged to it now and that must have been enough. The sorcerer's look of astonishment turned to a glare filled with more hatred than Hervor had known a man's face could show.

He advanced on her, ice coiling around his arm.

Starkad leapt forward and hewed off one of the Niflung's legs at the knee. Even as the sorcerer fell, Starkad spun on and lopped his head off.

At that, Starkad turned to stare first at her, then at Tyrfing, still glowing in her hand.

"Hel will still feast on your souls," the sorcerer's head said. "There is no escape from here."

Both she and Starkad froze, turned slowly to face it.

Blood poured from the decapitated head, its eyes had begun to glaze over. "Anguish ... without end."

It said no more.

Hervor tried to scream but couldn't get it past the lump in her throat.

∮

IN THE MOONS she spent with Red-Eye's Boys, Hervor had seen murder, rape, and all manner of human cruelty. She had since witnessed the burning, tormenting ghost of her own father. Somehow none of that quite compared to being cursed by the severed head of a sorcerer.

Such things were not possible.

They did not happen, save in fanciful skald's tales.

The others had climbed down the slope and were arguing about what had happened. Hervor dropped to her knees by the river's edge and splashed her face. The freezing water seemed to loosen the tightness that had settled around her chest.

She sucked down a long shuddering breath. She knew little of sorcery, save it was the domain of mad men and those more wicked than even bandits. But since claiming

Tyrfing, two of these Niflungar—whoever they were—had come for her. They seemed able to meld with the mist and moreover, he had commanded it like a weapon.

Blessings of the dark goddess Hel?

Someone grabbed her by the shoulders and jerked her to her feet, spun her around. Starkad flung her away from the river and into the midst of the crew.

"You brought them here!"

Hervor grimaced and rose. She was damned sick of him. Instinct drove her to draw Tyrfing once again. But after what she'd just seen, that would prove suicidal.

Any doubt she'd had about Starkad's prowess was gone.

Maybe he truly had received instruction from the war god himself. "I did not know these mist wielders still pursued me."

Behind him, Orvar returned, leaning on the Axe's shoulder. The sorcerer's attack must have allowed him to escape his captors. But how would ...

Starkad raised a finger, working his jaw as if so angry he could not form words. He shut his eyes a moment before he spoke. "You have drawn the ire of the Niflungar upon us. And you did not even think to warn us!"

Warn him? She wouldn't trust Starkad to wash her damned clothes. "You seemed to handle the sorcerer well enough."

"I was *lucky*. And if we are *very* lucky, that was the only member of their kingdom to pursue us to Thule." He looked around at the rest of the crew. "Because I do not relish the idea of facing more of them, especially not if they come in numbers. Would you care to fight three or five or ten such men?"

Hervor snapped her mouth shut, her retort dying on her

tongue. Starkad called them a kingdom. She had not even considered they might come in numbers.

The fisherman's wife, the widow of the man she killed, had cursed her to Hel.

And since then, these Niflungar had come after her. Was it merely for Tyrfing, or did they want to punish her for violating their domain on Samsey?

"So you're telling me beetle-cocking sorcerers are here?" Ivar asked. "Men using ... magic?" He looked at Afzal for some reason, as if the young man ought to be some expert.

Afzal raised an eyebrow at him. "The Art is a real thing, but I know naught of it."

Orvar shrugged off from the Axe. "These mist sorcerers may or may not still be here. Someone else attacked me, and I barely got away. Vaettir, I think. They were taking me deeper into the island."

Starkad glowered. "Perhaps these are nixies. Such vaettir are known to take men captive from time to time."

"What are nixies?" Afzal asked.

Bragi pointed to the waters. "River mer."

"Why would cocking vaettir want to—"

"I don't know, Loud!" Starkad snapped. "Who knows what drives vaettir to do aught?" He spun back on Hervor. "We'll deal with the vaettir soon. First though ..." He stalked closer, blood-stained blade still in hand. "Someone in our midst has proved more liability than ally."

"I might be dead, if not for her," Afzal said.

"Peace, Starkad," Orvar said, fixing Hervor with a long look that could have meant aught. "We have enough enemies."

Starkad glared at Hervor a moment longer, then spat. "Fine. I say we go after these vaettir, follow the river as we can, and search for sign of them."

Hervor ground her teeth. Now they were to risk their lives hunting river mer?

Odin was fucking with her; she knew he was.

But she still needed to kill Orvar. Moreover, Starkad seemed half ready to cut her down where she stood. Some woman must have so riled him against all female kind and done Hervor no favors. She could not afford to antagonize Starkad in the least now. He was her best chance for fulfilling her oath—both their best tracker and their best warrior. To say naught of her desire to make it off Thule alive.

"You would have us take a great chance against these vaettir," Tiny said. "This is not why we came here."

"I agree with Starkad," Hervor said. Everyone looked at her like she was the talking severed head. She needed him on her side, though, at least for now. "We have to follow our own honor."

"You have honor now?" Starkad asked.

Hervor flinched, then tried to cover it. Best ignore that. Arrow's Point would soon see her honor, born on the end of her runeblade. Except ... how was she to even consider striking at him *now*? "These creatures have attacked us at least once, and most like, were the threat on the shores when we first arrived."

Starkad folded his arms. "Afzal?"

"I go with you, either way, Master. My vow is to serve you until I have repaid my debt."

Starkad rolled his eyes, then looked to Bragi.

The skald shrugged. "We all die sooner or later. May as well make it a tale worthy of Valhalla."

"No troll-shit, beetle-cocked vaettir are scaring me off," Ivar said.

Tiny raised his hands in submission. "It sounds decided enough, then. Do we wait for daylight?"

Orvar shook his head. "It would be too long in coming and too short to catch them when it arrived. We have to press on through the night. If we are to do this, we must do it now."

Hervor blew out a low breath. Of course they did.

21

DAYS GONE

One Year Ago

*T*he winter had frozen the lake, allowing Hervor to walk to Bolmso—the island of her father and paternal grandfather, a place that should have rung with the noise of civilization. Instead, the only sounds she heard were the howling wind and a raven's caw.

She wrapped her bear fur cloak tighter about her as she trod onto the island. Snow crunched under her heels, making each step laborious. She should have waited for the storm to break. She should have brought snowshoes or crampons. Then again, she always hated people telling her what she *should* do.

Actually, the lake held hundreds of islands, and she'd had to search a long time to find the right one. This *had* to be it.

A thick copse of trees decorated the shoreline. Evergreens, though fresh snows had weighed down their branches. The raven she'd heard must be somewhere in those boughs, watching her. Like a sentinel in this otherwise forgotten place.

She pushed onward. The trees cut down on the wind's bite, at least a little. She sniffed. Her face still burned with the cold, but she'd live. More snow crunched behind her.

At once, she spun, fumbling with the cloak to free her sword hilt. No one there. Frozen in place, she looked from tree to tree. She had heard *something*. She jerked her sword free. "Whoever you are ..."

The moment she spoke, a reindeer broke between the trees, covering great swathes of land in each leaping stride. Hervor blew out a breath. The isolation was getting to her. She hadn't seen a person in days, not since some fisherman pointed her in this direction. Only a few of the islands even had people living on them.

She sheathed the blade and pressed onward.

On the far shore, a wooden hall rose up. What was left of it, anyway. A large section of the roof had caved in, exposing the east side of the hall. The doors stood ajar, so she slipped inside. This had to be it. Mist clogged the interior.

The hall's heart had been the fire pit, of course. And it had gone long cold now, naught but cinders. Ash.

No one had lived here in a long time.

Hervor moved to the walls. Tapestries still hung there, one depicted great battles with a bear at the heart of them. A berserk. Her grandfather, perhaps.

Traveling around the countryside had eventually turned up skalds happy to weave tales of those otherwise forgotten days. Of the perilous berserk Arngrim, feared by all. So pleased was the king with his champion thegn, he granted him not only the title of jarl but use of a runeblade. An heirloom forged by dvergar long ago.

And somehow she had allowed herself to hope her

grandfather would be here, would tell those stories himself. But there was no one here. This place was dead and forgotten, much as all her kin.

There were not even any treasures left for her to claim. No inheritance. No wealth to hire men to join her quest. The tapestries had value, but they were too large for her to carry back across the lake.

Whatever had lain here was plundered long ago.

An intake of breath from the doorway drew her eye. As she turned, a figure dashed out, running.

"Wait!"

Whoever it was did not stop.

Hervor grimaced and dashed after the figure. The trespasser was short, slim, and very quick. He darted between the trees and leapt over a pile of rocks.

Hervor's feet slid on ice, and she near slammed into the rock pile. Damn it. She scrambled over the rocks, then skidded down a slope.

The boy glanced over his shoulder. Only it wasn't a boy. A girl, maybe twelve winters.

"Stop!" Hervor shouted.

The girl did not stop, dashing behind a tree and vanishing from view.

Hervor panted as she reached the spot. "Girl. I mean you no harm. Come out now." She turned about. The girl's footprints in the snow stopped at this tree. She looked up.

Crouched over a branch, the girl stared down at her.

Hervor folded her arms over her chest. "Come down from there."

"Not fucking likely."

She almost wanted to smile at that. "I'm not going to hurt you. Who are you?"

"I'm the queen of this island, so you best get away before I call my guards."

The queen. Now Hervor couldn't quite stop the smile from reaching her lips. "Call them, then." The girl glanced away to the north, and Hervor followed her gaze. "Is that where your parents are?"

"My father is Odin himself. So you better flee before he arrives."

"Why? I'd be eager to meet the King of the Gods. I have many questions for him."

The girl stuck out her lip and looked around. Probably trying to think up another retort.

Hervor didn't have time to play this game all day. "Come down now, queen. Take me to your people, whoever they are. If you cooperate, I won't harm you. But if you make me climb that damned tree and get you ..."

Indecision warred on the girl's face before she finally groaned. Then she leapt from the tree and landed in the snow in a crouch. As she started to rise, Hervor snatched up a handful of the girl's cloak. No sense giving her the chance to run off again.

"Come on, queen. Lead the way."

With a sullen glance, the girl did so, guiding her to a small house a short distance from the fallen hall. As they approached, an aging couple rose from the shore and walked to meet them. The man had an axe in his hand, albeit one better suited for chopping wood than battle.

"What do you want?" the man demanded.

"This your daughter?"

He nodded.

With a gentle shove, Hervor sent the girl scurrying off toward her parents. "Who are you? What are you doing on this island?"

"It's our home."

"This is *my* island. I claim it as the last heir of Arngrim. And I ask you again, who are you?"

The couple exchanged glances, then the man spoke, lowering the axe. "Come inside. It'll be dark soon."

Hervor nodded.

❧

THE WOMAN OFFERED her water and hot fish, both of which Hervor took gratefully. Even more so, the warmth of their fire. When she had eaten, the man spoke.

"We were slaves of Jarl Arngrim, a long time ago. You though, you're too young to be his daughter."

"Granddaughter. My father was Angantyr."

The former slave nodded, obvious wariness in his eyes.

Hervor licked fish juice from her fingers before settling her gaze first on the woman, then the man. "I have no mind to disrupt your lives. But I will have my birthright, and I would like to know what happened here."

The man clucked his tongue and looked to his wife before speaking. "Not much birthright left here. A long time ago now—we were young then ... what, maybe eighteen winters back, word came the lord and lady's sons were killed in battle. Not just one or two, all twelve of them. Nobody believed it. They'd never lost a battle; they were invincible. Everyone said so."

"But they never came home," the woman said. "Never came back. Winter passed, and in summer, Jarl Arngrim set out himself. We heard later he cast himself into the sea, so we supposed it was all true." She took Hervor's cup and refilled it, then began to clear away the plates. "After that, everyone urged Lady Eyfura to go back to the lands of her father in Holmgard. She wouldn't listen, though, just kept waiting here, like she thought the men would return still."

Hervor cleared her throat when the woman fell silent. "And?"

"And they didn't, of course," the man said. "The princess wasted away. What was left of the population here fled. We ..."

"You thought you may as well claim it as your own."

The man scowled. "I never dared claim it, my lady."

She waved the thought away. "As long as you respect my claim, I welcome your presence here."

"Will you rebuild the great hall, lady?" the woman asked.

Hervor shook her head. "I cannot rebuild my family's home while they remain unavenged. The kings of Upsal and their champion destroyed our entire line." She spit in the fire. "Now I learn they are to blame for the death of my grandparents, as well. No." She ran her tongue over her teeth. No, it was too much. A weight, a burden that only served to reinforce her oath. "Await my return and if anyone should chance upon this island, tell them the last descendant of Arngrim claims all that should be hers."

She would need wealth to challenge the Yngling dynasty.

Hervor knew one sure way to earn wealth. Red-Eye had taught her that.

22

STARKAD

*T*he river ran swiftly, cutting a canyon through the island. Following such a canyon, with ice-crusted walls rising to either side, did not seem over wise to Starkad. Archers could tear them to pieces. But scaling those walls would have taken too much time, even if these water vaettir had chosen to travel above. Besides, vaettir rarely had archers.

Still, this island was wild, well beyond the bounds of civilization. It was possible jotunnar or other dangers lurked here.

The dvergar no longer dwelt in Nordri. Not in any of their great cities outside Nidavellir, though he did not know why.

Nor did it matter.

Wherever dvergar went, they dug up, forged, or otherwise crafted treasures worthy of the ages. The runeblades not withstanding. And Hervor bore a runeblade. The Niflungar would like come for it again. Starkad could take it from her—might even save her life in doing so. Probably

148

not. Probably the Niflungar would still hunt her and then kill her once they realized she no longer bore that blade.

Besides, saving her life was not his problem.

She had wrought her own urd.

He pushed the others hard. They were exhausted, of course, had walked for hours, until day had at last broken. Light was their only ally and a fleeting one. They *had* to push forward. Vaettir liked to lair in old, abandoned places. And what better ruins than a dverg city?

He did not know exactly where, but according to Yngvi, Odin had claimed it lay at the heart of Thule. In this direction. Odin could shove that mystical spear of his up his own arse for all Starkad cared. But his information was like as not true.

With the sun up, the island was warmer. Which was to say, wrapped in a fur cloak he didn't feel his stones were about to freeze off. But then winter had only just settled in here, and it would grow colder still. And unless he missed his guess, their daylight would fade very soon. Already several hours of it had passed.

The ever-present mist had thinned in daylight, especially with that Hel-cursed sorcerer dead ...

Ahead, someone was sitting on the ice by the river. Three men and a woman, all naked. They were camped before a tunnel in the cavern wall.

Starkad held up a hand to stall those behind him. They slowed, now creeping forward. They would have seen the vaettir as well. Orvar moved close behind Starkad, then unshouldered his bow.

"Cold doesn't bother those cocking spirits," Ivar said.

Starkad glared at him and jerked his hand for silence. Leaving the others behind, he began to edge forward in a crouch. The sun dipped below the mountains. Darkness would return in mere moments. And if the nixies leapt into the waters, he'd never catch them.

They needed to get ahead of their foes, cut them off. He glanced back at Afzal, then motioned for him to flank the vaettir. Long winters together had taught the boy well. Hervor broke off and went with him. Starkad frowned. At least she seemed to know how to move without making noise.

The problem was, the rocks provided very little cover. He was going to have to wound one from a distance. Scowling, he motioned to Orvar.

The vaettir had begun to stir with the setting sun. They seemed to take their respite in daylight—the only reason he'd caught them at all, most like. And they were about to leave again. Orvar stood swiftly, drew a bead, and loosed. The twang of the bow drew their eyes but not fast enough. The man's arrow struck one of the males in the shoulder, spun him around and dropped him.

The vaettr screamed in pain like any man might.

The moment Orvar loosed, Starkad raced for the vaettir. As he did so, Afzal charged, shamshir in hand, followed by Hervor who had drawn that shining runeblade. The female vaettir ran to the fallen male while the other two rose to meet the charging warriors.

The sun winked out.

The vaettir Afzal was rushing dropped to all fours and arched his back. A primal snarl echoed off the canyon walls.

Starkad faltered. Oh fuck. He had missed his guess.

The vaettr's neck elongated, popping and shifting, as did his snout.

Teeth jutted from the creature's mouth, growing pointed and sharp, even as his legs melded together. His flesh grew dark, slick. The creature barked loudly.

A wereseal—finfolk. A thrust of its tail sent it skittering over the ice toward Afzal. The boy panicked, stumbling backward.

Hervor leapt in there and cleaved her runeblade into the seal's face. It barked again, this time in sharp pain.

Starkad's own feet skidded on ice as he ran. The Axe and Tiny had engaged another seal, while Ivar and Tiny chased after the female who had headed for the river.

The only light came from Hervor's sword, shining like a tiny sun.

An arrow sprouted from a seal's meaty flesh, but Orvar's aim was off. The darkness must have interfered.

Starkad stumbled as he slid to a stop before the finfolk Orvar had shot. Hervor seemed to have the other one in hand. The seal barked, angling for the water. Starkad interposed himself.

"Resume your human form!"

The seal barked at him, glanced at the cavern. The first arrow had popped out of his shoulder when he'd shifted his form, but he was trailing blood.

The Axe screamed in agony. Starkad spun. The seal they fought had sunk its teeth into the Axe's knees and all but ripped his leg off. The man had fallen, still clutching his axe, while Tiny hacked at the beast with his sword.

In Starkad's moment of distraction, the wounded seal surged past him and dove into the river.

Hervor bellowed and hewed off her seal's head.

They weren't going to get a single prisoner unless Tiny stopped. And given the rage with which he'd set upon the one who'd hurt the Axe, that didn't seem likely.

A horrid sound rang out from the cavern, something between a moan and a growl. Not a sound shifters made.

Not a sound aught human made either.

No, but Starkad knew that sound.

In the darkness, pinpoints of red light opened. Eyes lit with hatred of all life.

Maybe the blood had woken it. Maybe the screams. Maybe the light from Hervor's cursed sword. Whatever the cause, Starkad knew what was coming.

"Fall back!" he bellowed.

The creature that emerged from the cavern moved like a warrior in pain. Bits of sallow flesh clung to exposed bone, reaching out from beneath armor that had survived the test of time better than the draug itself. It bore sword and shield and no doubt knew how to use them.

Hervor spun on the dead warrior, sword readied before her.

Starkad rushed to her side. "Leave this creature to me. Fall back with the others."

"Starkad!" she said. She was pointing at the cavern.

More pairs of glowing red eyes were advancing. At least a dozen pairs.

"Master!" Afzal shouted.

He glanced at the boy. The ice behind them had split. Skeletal hands erupted from that ice, as more of the draugar began to claw their way free.

"We have stumbled upon the gates of Hel," Tiny said. The big man was dragging the Axe away.

His assessment was hard to argue with. Starkad had fought draugar on rare occasions. He had never faced an army of them.

Orvar had scrambled down the slope and was joining the others as they retreated.

The nearest draug lunged at Starkad. He parried on one sword and attacked with the other. The draug blocked on its shield with practiced ease. They fell into the dance as more and more of the creatures advanced. Their war cries sounded more like hisses of things that hated life and light.

Starkad cut the draug's leg out from under it. It fell to the ice, then began to claw its way toward him. He leapt backward. "Retreat! Fall back!"

Ivar was hacking at one that had emerged from the ice. "Retreat where? The cocks are blocking us in!"

Hervor roared, shearing a draug's shield, armor, and body with her runeblade. The creature dropped to the ice and did not move. At least something could kill these monsters.

"Go!" he shouted at her. "Go, forward." He pointed off along the river's path with his sword. "Find a way out of the canyon!"

"We will never make it! You think to outrun the dead?" Another of the creatures flung itself at her, swinging a massive axe.

Starkad's blade caught it in mid-air, stalling it just enough it did not reach her. Hervor hacked off the top of its skull. Its blood didn't flow.

Ivar cried out in pain. A draug's blade had torn through his armor above his gut. Bragi fell back, pressed hard by two of the dead warriors. They would all die. Die and rise as draugar themselves. To suffer in eternal torment.

A black arrow sprouted from a draug on Bragi, and the creature faltered, then crumpled into the ice. And how many magic arrows did Orvar have left?

Starkad shoved Hervor away, then moved to fight off four of the draugar. The dead worked together, a fighting unit. They tried to flank him.

Starkad was faster, able to parry them all, but not attack. They fought without fear, without caring about wounds or pain. And even when he struck them, they barely slowed.

"Get everyone out of here!" he shouted at her again. "I'll buy you time."

"Release me!" the Axe bellowed. "Starkad, go! You're the only one who can protect them. I'm dead from this wound anyway."

Starkad ducked an axe blow, clipped the draug on the face, and rolled away. They were on him again in an instant, but he saw the Axe had worked free of Tiny's grasp and was standing, his own axe and shield in his hand. He could not walk, but he was trying to hold the ground.

And he cast a look of pleading Starkad's way in that instant.

He wanted his death to mean something. He wanted to see Valhalla.

Starkad parried a sword blow and kicked the draug into its fellows. Then he turned and ran for the canyon. Hervor had done as he had bid, ushering Afzal and the others forward. They were running, skidding over ice, her sword lighting the way.

Starkad cast one last look at the Axe. A dozen draugar blocked his view already, swarming over the old veteran.

Starkad ran after the others.

They had reached a dip in the canyon, where icy rocks rose in a pile.

"Up, up, up!" Hervor shouted, pointing.

Tiny was already scaling those rocks, and he yanked Bragi up after him.

Starkad sheathed his swords and scrambled up the rocks as well. The Axe's death would buy them a few breaths at most. The draugar would follow them up the cliff. "Run! When you reach the top, just fucking run!"

Orvar unshouldered his bow once again. Standing with legs wide on a rock halfway up the cliff, the man nocked another black arrow. The draugar were closing in. Orvar loosed. The draug it struck shuddered and collapsed in a heap.

The others had already climbed up past him.

Arrows rained down from above, impacting the draugar but barely slowing them. Starkad glanced up. Hervor and Ivar were both shooting from above.

Starkad leapt up to the next highest rock. His feet slipped, skidded, and he had to steady himself on the cliff. No time. No chance to breathe.

He pulled himself up another rock and another.

The moment he crested the top, he shoved Hervor back. "Those arrows are not doing troll shit to them. Run!"

Ivar loosed again. And again.

Orvar had always tried to save his magic arrows, recover them whenever he could, Starkad knew. But that hardly mattered if they all died here. Now, the man launched another black arrow, grimacing as he did so.

"Die you cock-stomping troll cocks!" Ivar bellowed.

Starkad ripped the skin of oil from his belt and popped the cork. He poured it over the rocks they had just climbed. He'd used so much to trap that Niflung. Had to hope this was enough. "Hold them off a moment!" He struck flint to steel, but it took agonizing breaths to light a damn torch. When it finally caught he flung it down onto the rocks.

Draugar had already surged over them, climbing on each other in a mad rush to add the three of them to their numbers. The flames erupted around them, engulfing several of the creatures and turning them into blazing effigies lit by unholy light.

Starkad grabbed Ivar by the back of his mail and sent him running off after the others.

And Starkad fled, Orvar beside him.

HIS LUNGS BURNED, his legs ached. The others were barely standing, and still he pushed them on. Hervor stumbled, and he grabbed her by the back of the neck and forced her to rise, to keep running. The dead would not stop, not until dawn. Which was long, long hours away.

Afzal was clutching his ribs, gasping. Starkad was failing them all. They would all die, and he could do naught to save them.

The ground here held less ice and had grown rocky. Cracked red earth spread out as far as he could see before them, broken up by numerous shallow craters.

Ahead, steam erupted through the mist like a waterspout. Everyone fell short, Afzal actually dropping to his knees.

It had grown warm. Another geyser erupted farther into the rock fields. This whole area stank like rotten eggs. Sulfur?

"Out of Niflheim ... and into ... Muspelheim," Ivar said between pants.

Muspelheim. The World of Fire. Where the fire spirits Afzal's people bound came from. They used fire spirits to drive away the mist and *its* dangers. Like draugar.

"Get over by the geysers," Starkad said.

"We're like to get burned there," Tiny complained.

Starkad shook his head. Better a little burned than frozen and cleaved by draugar. "Make camp as close to the geysers as you safely can."

Ivar trembled, clutching his abdomen, so Starkad helped him toward the camp he'd selected.

"My gut feels like a beetle cock."

"I don't even know what that means, Loud. But I don't smell shit, so maybe your bowels aren't punctured."

Ivar grunted at that. They both knew if the blade had pierced his intestines, he was in for a long, painful dying. From the look of him, that might still be his urd.

Everyone collapsed, none bothering with tents or bedrolls. Nor did they have wood for fire.

Orvar stumbled from one man to the next, checking injuries of his crew. Their leader was swearing under his breath. The man was losing it, wasn't he? They'd known dangers would lurk here, but Yngvi had known or said naught of an army of the dead.

Tiny sat with his hands over his knees, staring at one of the geysers. The vent blew out small trails of steam every so often, but the big man barely reacted to it.

"Are you injured?" Orvar asked the big man.

Tiny snorted. "Here and there. Naught serious." He scratched his head. "Axe took that beast right in front. It was fast as aught I ever saw."

Orvar nodded. "Shifters always are."

Starkad grimaced. "I should've known, should've ..."

"It's not your fault, Eightarms," Bragi said. "We've all heard tales of finfolk snatching up men and women. I just always thought it mere tales, wild fancies of the far reaches of the North Realms."

Maybe. But Starkad had seen varulfur and berserkir, so why shouldn't other shifters be real as well?

"He was a good man," Tiny said. "Died well."

Starkad grunted at that. The Axe had bought them their escape. Without him, they'd have not made those rocks at all. "He fought for the Ynglings from way back. Never forgave himself for Alrik and Eirik, always somehow thought he should have protected them. You can't save men from themselves."

"No, Eightarms," Bragi said. "You can't save a man from himself."

He had no interest in whatever lesson the skald thought he was trying to impart. Instead, Starkad rose and made his way over to where Afzal had fallen. The young man lay on his side, eyes closed. Asleep?

"Are we safe here?" Afzal asked. "There is fire beneath the ground."

Starkad blew out a breath and looked around. "I think these were lava fields, maybe. The steam from the geysers burns away the mist. Draugar don't like fire, so they may not come here. I hope. Either way, we can't run forever."

Afzal offered a half chuckle that turned into a cough. "I cannot run another step."

Starkad patted him on the shoulder. "Then rest."

"I may sleep, Master. I doubt there is rest to be had in this place. The island is tainted."

Could an entire island be cursed? In Starkad's experience, vile things lived in places where Mankind did not walk. Actually, so-called civilized Realms were not much better. Men could be nigh to as vile as vaettir and without the excuse of coming from some alien world. Starkad should know. "You want to leave?"

Afzal groaned. "I thought that would go without saying. Only Ivar feels the need to state such obviousness."

Now Starkad chuckled.

"Master, could we get back to the ship?"

"I don't know. The draugar block the way we came." He did not mention the other problem. The one that had niggled him since the Niflung had first attacked.

The sorcerer might well have killed the men they set to

guard the ship. Even had he not, the finfolk might have attacked. Five of the original crew were dead for certain.

They could sail the ship with but a few men but could not row it with a small crew. If they were becalmed, they'd be well and truly fucked. Starkad had seen that happen and it ... he'd not ever wish to repeat it. Then again, winter storms could well kill them or throw them so far off course they'd never reach the known world again.

They had no easy escape from Thule.

But the men did not need to hear that. Faced with dangers beyond mortal ken, they had already drawn nigh to their breaking point. Starkad needed to drive them forward, keep them from dwelling on their losses or the dangers. Because if they realized how far beyond hope they had traveled, they might well turn on each other.

The others, like Afzal, had probably begun to doubt the mission to winter here and prepare for a colony. And that meant they needed a fresh purpose.

That, at least, Starkad could give them.

23

HERVOR

*D*eep sleep held her and, even knowing she dreamt, Hervor could not force herself to wake. She lay in darkness, the only light streaming from Tyrfing in her hand, the only sound the pounding of her heart. The blade craved blood and, unsated, it was willing to settle for hers.

In the darkness, shadows moved. With the clarity of dream, she knew them for the ghosts of her kin. The twelve sons of Arngrim, whom she had promised vengeance. She had sworn an oath upon the sword in her hand, and now, those ghosts watched her. Growing inpatient, unable to escape their torment while her vow remained unfulfilled.

They did not speak and yet, Hervor knew—they understood her promise.

If she failed, if she died without revenging them, their urd would become hers. A wandering shade haunted by her failure and unable to ever fully cut ties with Midgard.

She woke with a start, sitting up before she had time to realize how much her body protested. The pains sleep had dulled slammed back into her. Her wounded back, her swollen ribs, and now numerous cuts from draugar blades. Her throat was raw, parched. Funny though, this place no longer seemed to reek of sulfur. She supposed she had just gotten used to it.

"You wake," Starkad said.

She turned to find him sitting, watching her.

"Ugh." She stretched. "What do you want?"

"I ..." He shook his head. "You brought some of this down on us."

She snorted. "I did not force any man to come here, nor seed this island with shifters and draugar. You're simply an arse who's scared of women."

"I fear *naught*, shieldmaiden."

Then he was a fool, too. Plenty on Thule seemed worthy of fear.

With a grunt, Starkad rose and cracked his neck. "I will speak to everyone. Come. Get up."

Wonderful. Standing hurt even more than sitting, but she followed Starkad to where the others had gathered. Bragi and Ivar sat, the latter half curled over the wound in his gut. She could slump down again and join them. Her aching legs begged her to do it.

But then, she couldn't trust herself to be able to rise again after that.

She did not think she'd ever been so tired in her life.

Orvar, their supposed leader, was now looking to Starkad as if he might have the answers.

Starkad paced around, pausing to pat Afzal on the shoulder. Finally, he turned to look at everyone. "This is a place of fire. And it seems the draugar will not pursue us here. I don't know whether we are safe from the finfolk— perhaps so. Maybe they don't even know where we are. It does not matter." He turned, sweeping his arm out to indicate the cracked, barren landscape. "It matters naught, because we have no food. No water. There is naught here to sustain us, even if we wanted to remain. Nor can we go back the way we came. The draugar likely lie in wait there. And the dead have no end of patience."

"We can travel up, through the mountains," Tiny said. He stood with his arms folded over his massive chest. "Avoid the canyons and they might not find us."

Starkad nodded. "Perhaps. Maybe we could make it back to the ship."

Ivar coughed. "Assuming those cock-thumping finfolk aren't waiting for us there."

"What do they even want of us?" Tiny asked. "Do they eat men?"

Bragi clucked his tongue. "Tales say the finfolk take men to be husbands to their women, and women as wives." At that he grinned at Hervor.

She scowled at him. There was not a damned thing amusing here, least of all shifters abducting men or women for forced marriages.

"Wait ..." Ivar said. "You think they wanted Orvar to ... fuck a seal?"

Well. Maybe there was something *slightly* amusing.

Orvar spat and glared at Ivar. "Keep it up, Loud. Maybe you can fuck one of my arrows."

Starkad cast a glance at Orvar. "I think we must discuss this land."

Orvar groaned, then nodded. "Look here all ... I ... have an idea where the draugar came from. In the days of the Old Kingdoms, maybe even before that, the dvergar had four great cities in the four corners of the World. This island, Thule, was home to the northernmost city, Nordri. And those draugar must have been their human warriors or else

warriors sent against them by one of the Old Kingdoms."
Orvar pointed toward the heart of the island. "Either way,
their city was lost, abandoned. And filled with a dverg
hoard. Gold, silver, gems—more wealth than we could
carry."

Hervor worked her tongue over her teeth.

Dverg gold for the taking ...

No wonder Yngvi and Gylfi had partnered on this expedition. If Orvar spoke the truth, this Nordri could make
everyone here wealthy enough to claim a jarldom. At the
least. And dvergar crafted things too, objects imbued with
power. Tyrfing was forged by the great smith Dvalin.

What other wonders might his brethren have made and
left behind here?

Of course, with such wealth, the Ynglings would become
that much more difficult foes to destroy. Well, first thing
came first. She still had to deal with Arrow's Point. Even
were she willing to break her vow, she did not relish the
thought of spending eternity as a restless ghost in punishment for the transgression.

"Dverg gold ..." Ivar said. "It tends to cost more than it
buys. Steal from them and they may curse you."

Starkad shook his head. "No dvergar live here now.
Thule is dead, long dead and nigh to lost to the ages."

That Niflung had called this place vile and had warned
they would all be dragged down to Hel. He had known
about the draugar. How many more of the creatures might
dwell here?

"We come back with that gold, and men will be telling
our tales for a hundred years or more," Bragi said.

"I like taking stuff," Ivar said.

"We don't know what might lurk in this Nordri either,"
Hervor said. "Maybe the finfolk have gone there ... maybe

more draugar live there." Still, if they went to the city, it might offer the chance to fulfill her vow. And if they managed to plunder some gold on the way back, she'd make certain to get her share. She could worry about stopping the Ynglings from getting theirs later. It was a long way back to Upsal.

Afzal sighed and rubbed his eyes. "You really think the seven of us can face down an unknown number of vaettir? Forgive me, Master, but our last fight with these finfolk cost the Axe. And that was against four of them, not expecting us."

Ivar spat. "We weren't exactly expecting naked people to turn into seals and try to bite our faces off."

"Look," Starkad said. "We don't know where the finfolk are. I do have a general idea where to find the city. We can continue north, out of these lava fields, and search for the city. Either way, we have to press on."

Ivar groaned as he rose. "Then what are we waiting for?"

Hervor shook her head. More walking, more searching. More wandering in the night.

24

DAYS GONE

Three Moons Ago

A few moons of raiding and piracy had earned her a small share of booty and a loyal enough crew. Sure, she'd had to kill their former captain for the position. But few men wanted to follow a leader with no head, so she'd given them an easy choice.

They had stopped at a town on Sjaelland to resupply before setting out for Samsey. As the largest island of the Morimarusa, Sjaelland was home to numerous seaside towns, each within the domain of one jarl or another, all paying homage to Hrothgar. The island was fertile and thus immensely valuable. Legend claimed the Vanr Gefjon had dug up the whole island and sown it, though the Vanir were all gone now.

Those prosperous towns had provided a large sum of plunder, though of course not from the domain she visited now.

"I don't like it," Viggo said. "Men say the island is haunted. No one goes there."

On raids, all men were equal or so the thought went. In practice, the crew was hers, and Viggo was the most respected of the rest. He'd earned a reputation for once cleaving a man from skull to sternum—exaggerated, perhaps, though he was a big man. They walked together through the town while the rest of the crew was out trading for ale, bread, and the like. Or looking for slave girls to bend over when their masters were not around.

"It will be a short stop," Hervor promised. She shifted the sack she carried over her shoulder. Its contents had soaked through the canvas and began dripping blood on the ground. More than one townsman gave her a wary look.

"And a wasted one."

Hervor ran her tongue over her teeth. She couldn't exactly refuse to tell the crew where they were meant to sail. On the other hand, Viggo's reluctance to go to Samsey was problematic. They passed by a smithy, and the warrior paused to examine an axe most men would have needed two hands to wield. Sacrificing a shield would never be worth it, but a man Viggo's size could do more, manage more. He had his uses.

"How does an island become haunted?" she asked.

He pricked his thumb on the tip of the axe. "Too many men die without any proper sending, no pyre. No völva."

"Which means?"

Viggo offered a bronze arm ring to the smith, who nodded. The warrior slung the axe over his shoulder—it was too large to sit on his hip, even had he not two other axes there already. "Means ... they come back as ghosts, draugar, whatever."

He had his uses but was not the smartest man on her crew. It didn't matter. She didn't recruit for brains. "It means people lived there once. People lived there and left behind all they had when they died. Ruins means treasures, and stories of hauntings mean not many men go after that treasure. Silver, maybe even gold."

Viggo grunted now, eyes lit with the glimmer of interest. And she did hope to find plunder there, though most importantly her father's sword. Anyone who wielded a runeblade would find him or herself the subjects of a skald's tales. Those were the ones who did great and terrible deeds, who shaped history and found lasting fame. And with such a sword, she could begin to avenge her father.

The trouble was, she didn't even know for certain where on the island to look. And if Viggo was any indication of the rest of the crew, they wouldn't want to spend long there.

Fortunately, this town was famed for its völva. Word said she heard the voices of the gods, dreamed the past and future. Such a woman held promise for Hervor's errand. The sack was not heavy, but it felt awkward, especially trying not to let it stain her clothes.

"Go back to the ship. Make sure everyone is ready to leave at dawn."

Viggo shrugged and trotted off.

Hervor wandered the town, asking for directions until she found the völva's house. Animal skulls adorned the fence around that house. A deer, a wolf. The big one must belong to a cave lion. Other skulls she couldn't even be certain about. A rabbit, maybe. She swung open the gate and approached the house. The door stood open, so she ducked inside.

The place stank of burning weeds and strange herbs. The witch had no furniture, just benches built into the walls, half of which were laden with mushrooms, animal skins, or pots filled with Odin alone knew what. The fire in the pit had burned low, casting the room in such deep shadow it took a moment to spot the old woman.

She sat on one of those benches, gnawing on a branch. Only a few teeth remained in her mouth, and those were oddly pointed, like a wolf's. Her eyes were glazed over, milky white. She spat a piece of bark out as Hervor approached.

"Seer."

The woman slurped, sucking down black goop that had dribbled over her lip.

Hervor knelt before the woman. "Men say you know many things."

"Men say many things. Rarely are all true."

"Can you help me?"

"No one can help one intent to destroy herself."

Hervor frowned. "I'm trying to restore the legacy of my blood."

"A legacy of blood, yes." The witch didn't look at her, so much as at the space behind her. She giggled a little, then continued to gnaw on the stick.

"Tell me about Samsey."

The seer snorted, coughed, and spat. The thick phlegm landed less than a foot from where Hervor knelt.

Hervor frowned, then opened the sack and drew the heart out of it. She tossed the cold, bloody thing at the völva's feet. "I hear you collect hearts."

"Ehh." She sniffed, then snatched the thing up. Squeezed it. "Ehh. Not beating."

"Of course it's not fucking beating!"

The völva licked the heart. "Mmm. Stag, a strong one."

"Did you expect a human heart?"

She licked her lips. "Ehh. That's the best, of course. Deep lives, deep souls, lots of light. So much darkness." She giggled.

Hervor leaned forward barely able to stop herself from clutching the old witch by the shoulders and shaking her. "Where does my father lie?"

"In burning torment, in freezing lament. In cold ground as was the wont of fallen lands, wakeful and grim."

Cold ground. "He was buried?"

"But not forgotten. Left behind, yet lingering. Layers upon layers of warped agony."

Buried in a grave, perhaps. But she had said something about fallen lands. Maybe she meant the Old Kingdoms. They entombed their dead in barrows. "Where on the island do I find these barrows?"

"So many questions you ask, and none the right ones." She giggled again. "If you ask the right questions, you won't even need the answers."

Hervor threw up her hands. "Fine. What is the right question?"

"At last! You inquire after wisdom. Good, good." She sniffed the heart again, before setting it down in her lap. "Won't save you, though. Too stubborn to listen to wisdom when freely given ... and you'd think to bargain for it? Hehehe. The gods are watching, little girl. They watch while you fumble around in the dark."

"The gods can keep their riddles. I only ask upon which shore I should make land. I gave you the filthy heart, now tell me, witch!"

The völva shook her head, uttering a chittering sound like a rabid squirrel. Then she licked her lips. "Like a child you stumble, until the children you will anger. They too are wakeful, now. Wakeful, mindful, wrathful. Go then, shield-maiden, make land upon the southern shores. And if you so dare, wake the dead and embrace the urd laid before you."

The south. A place to start at last and worth the effort of

hunting down the deer. If perhaps not quite worth the irritation of dealing with this crone.

"One last question, I will answer. If a good one you ask."

Hervor stood. "I have no more questions for you, witch."

"More's the pity then. The answer might have offered you solace when the night grows long."

Hervor sneered and turned away but looked back before she exited. "The answer would have been one more riddle trying to warn me about something that would only make sense once it had become too late. Such solace does good for no one. I will have my vengeance, and I will make my own urd."

The völva favored her with a wide, toothy grin. And then she laughed. That laughter continued to ring out of the house as Hervor fled back to the street.

It followed her all the way back to her ship.

25

HERVOR

*T*he crashing of water heralded their approach to the great gorge long before it came into sight. They came upon it from a frozen plateau, her crampons digging into the icy shelf as the sound drew nigh.

Across the gorge, steep, icy cliffs dropped down to a series of shelves, each pouring more and more waters into a gorge that split the island in half, running farther than Hervor could see in the mist. Vapors wafted out of that gorge like the forging of the World between fire and ice at the beginning of time. Maybe it was here, where the World began, caught between Niflheim and Muspelheim.

Everything but the falls themselves had frozen, and even amid them, ice crusted over rocks in great mounds that looked to have been built over winter after icy winter.

The others looked as bemused as her, staring into the abyss. Starkad, who had somehow become their leader, stood motionless, as if transfixed by the Otherworldly beauty and horror of the vista. Hervor could not blame him. Bragi mumbled lines in verse, as if trying to find words to capture the experience. Afzal had cupped his hands in what she could only assume was prayer. Tiny was supporting Ivar, who had turned sallow, probably burning with fever.

Orvar stood at the gorge's edge, staring down into the abyss. One good shove ...

"I'm going to build my palace up here," Ivar said, though his words sounded half garbled. "Live like ... an Ás. Claim the whole damned island. Ivarsland. That's what I'm going to call it."

"I think this place is already claimed," Tiny said. "By Hel."

"Hel can suck my—"

"Weapons," Starkad said.

"Weapons?" Ivar said. "I don't usually call it—"

Starkad drew his blades and pointed one in the direction they had come from, over the plateau.

Hervor stared into the mist, seeing naught.

At first.

Then the shapes emerged, clambering over rocks, advancing toward them. The dead came from the mist, a few at first. Then more and more—more than she could easily count.

"Dead cocks trying to steal my palace," Ivar said while unshouldering his bow.

"How many of those magic arrows you have left?" Starkad asked Orvar.

"Uh, one."

"Then shoot the first one," Starkad said. "After that, those with bows try to put arrows in their eyes. Maybe we can blind them."

Ivar chuckled. "He thinks I'm Arrow's Point to make a shot like that."

Hervor's fingers brushed over Tyrfing's golden hilt. It was humming, calling her.

Eyes lit with hellish gleams appeared, drawing nearer.

"Can we run?" she asked.

"Dawn is long off," Starkad answered. "We'll not make it. Not all of us."

Tiny slapped her on the back. "Let's see the runeblade one more time, eh?"

Yes. Tonight, Tyrfing would feast not on the living but on the dead. She jerked it free of its sheath. It had grown warm, angry. Like her.

Orvar, Ivar, and Bragi launched several rounds of arrows at the advancing draugar. The first, hit by that magic arrow, crumpled in a heap and did not rise. The others barely slowed. Shafts stuck out of their chests, shields, even skulls. And still they came on.

"I hate dead people," Ivar said. Their bowmen switched to melee weapons.

And the draugar surged among them. Hervor lost track of the others as she hewed, ducked, blocked on her shield. A draug with an axe leapt at her. She jutted her shield out, smacking it in the face and sending it crashing onto the ice. Another advanced with a sword. Tyrfing sheared its weapon arm off at the elbow.

Both the fallen creature and the one-armed one continued to come after her, forcing her back. The one-armed one grabbed the rim of her shield and pulled. Felt like it would rip *her* arm off. Hervor let her arm slip free of the straps and the draug fell over backward from its own effort. She spun, swiping Tyrfing at the other draug, which had risen to its feet. The runeblade cut through its skull. This time it did not rise.

The one with her shield did, though, and ran at her swinging it like a weapon. Hervor dodged backward and swung Tyrfing. It cracked the shield, wood splintering under her blow. Shame. That had been a good shield, well made.

The draug tossed aside the useless boards and lunged at her like it meant to strangle her with its single, rotting hand. She couldn't get Tyrfing back into position fast enough, so she dove to the side, rolling.

Another draug jumped on her. Its weight knocked her on her back. The stench of decaying flesh hit her in a wave.

The draug atop her chopped down with an axe. Hervor ducked her head to one side, let go of Tyrfing, then caught its arm with both hands. It continued to drive the axe toward her face with unearthly strength. Those glowing eyes were boring into her, as if it would consume her body and soul alike. It opened its mouth, revealing canines unusually sharp, dripping with blackish saliva. That mouth lowered toward her face even as its axe pressed down.

Hervor cried out, straining to keep the rusted axe blade from biting into her forehead.

The draug's head flew free from its shoulders, and all the strength went out of its limbs. She thrust it aside, snatched up Tyrfing. Starkad stood nearby, already engaging more draugar. Odin's spear, he was fighting five ... no *six* of them. And had still diverted himself to save her.

Panting, she scrambled back to her feet even as two more of the dead warriors charged her. When not chasing prey, they ambled like men in agony. But on the battlefield, they were every bit as fast as the living and twice as strong. At least.

But she was no novice. She had trained her whole life with a blade. She was the daughter of Angantyr, famed berserk and champion of Bolmso. Hervor bellowed a war cry and flew into the nearest draug. It parried, dodged, fought like a man.

With both hands, she grasped Tyrfing and chopped straight down at the creature. It parried. Or tried. Its blade snapped in half, and Tyrfing bit into its skull. She jerked the blade free just in time to dodge the attack of the other draug.

The impact numbed her arms. She gave more ground. Another of the creatures broke off from Starkad and charged her. They must have realized Tyrfing was the greatest threat. And they'd come to take it from her, to try to steal her family's legacy.

Over her dead fucking body.

She bellowed again, defying them. Exhaustion had slowed her, but she had left that behind.

Father ...

She would do him proud.

One of the draugar bore spear and shield. It thrust at her. She leapt back, knocking the point aside with her sword.

The other rushed her with a two-handed axe. It swung the weapon in a great overhand cleave. She barely twisted out of the way. The axe split the ice by her feet and bit a full foot down into it. The draug jerked on its weapon like it had stuck.

Hervor swept Tyrfing across its neck and spun, turning to face the spearman again. Not fast enough. The spearpoint caught her left arm, scraped along her mail, and tore a chunk out of the iron and her flesh both. The blow spun her around, screaming. She was stumbling to her knees, but she continued to turn, swinging Tyrfing. The runeblade lopped off the draug's leg and sent it crashing to the ground the same time as her.

Screaming she clambered atop it and ran it through. Blood streamed down her arm.

She looked up.

Tiny was hacking away with his broadsword. Starkad had gone to help Afzal who was hard-pressed, unable to hold the dead back with his curved blade.

And three of the draugar surrounded Ivar. One had caught him in a bear hug. Even over the raging battle, Hervor could have sworn she heard bone breaking in that embrace. Ivar buried his axe in the draug's skull. Another of the creatures latched onto his arm and bit down on his shoulder.

Hervor stumbled to her feet, ran toward him.

The third draug drove a sword straight through his back. Ivar shuddered. His head went limp.

Hervor slashed across his killer's chest before it could free the blade. The draug dropped. The one that had bit Ivar released him and flung itself at Orvar.

The pair of them stumbled toward the waterfall's edge. They struggled, caught in an embrace, the draug crushing the life out of Orvar.

Hervor glanced around. Mist blanketed everything, and no ally in sight ...

This was it.

This was her chance.

She stalked closer. Finally, she could avenge her family. And none of the others would know. They'd think the draugar responsible. She launched herself at the pair, swinging Tyrfing. Her blow sheared through the draug and sent Orvar pitching over backward.

Falling into the gorge.

Vanishing into mist.

She'd done it ...

A heavy impact drove her backward, and she fell to the ground beneath another draug, skittering close to the edge of the plateau she had just shoved Arrow's Point off. The draug had no weapon but rained blows upon her with its hands. Even through her armor, those blows felt like getting hit with a mace. Blood stung her eyes.

She flailed, trying to dislodge the creature.

It bit her shoulder as it had done to Ivar. Its maw was at once burning and freezing, sending pulses of agony through her. She shrieked in agony, twisted. Somehow she managed to roll atop it. It tore great gouges out of her shoulder. She wanted to weep from the pain. Instead, she somehow managed to rise halfway. It shoved her again, and she fell onto her back. It leapt for her. She jerked her knee up to her face and kicked out. Her crampons drove through the draug's eyes and skull. The creature's arms flailed at her.

She pushed away with her leg, lifting it off the ground. "Hurts, doesn't it!"

With her left hand, she patted around until she closed on Tyrfing's hilt. Awkward, but if Starkad could fight with either hand ... she rammed the blade upward, impaling the draug. It struggled a moment more before going limp. Finally, she dropped her leg and rolled. It took both hands pushing against the corpse to free her foot from its skull.

A chilling hand grabbed her injured shoulder and hefted her aloft, heedless of her screams. She tried to grab up Tyrfing. The draug that held her kicked the blade. It skittered along the ice and pitched over the plateau, falling into the rising mist of the gorge and vanishing into the night.

"No!" she shrieked. "No!" Father's sword. Her legacy, her inheritance! Her honor, her oath, her *life*.

She slapped the draug's skull with her left hand. She might as well have punched a wall. It raised her to its face, lifting her off the ground with one hand. Those glaring, crimson pinpoints of light. Reaching into her. Hating her with a fire beyond imagination. Its loathing of her so eclipsed her hatred of Arrow's Point and the Ynglings, she felt like a child having a tantrum.

This was the enmity of Hel, a cold hatred of all living things. Of her.

Tears welled at the corners of her eyes. Pain, fear, or some other primal emotion she could not name.

With a gasp, she tore free her eating knife from its sheath around her neck. This she buried in one of those hateful eyes. The draug flailed, spun. Shrieked in defiance of her petty attack. It shoved her free. She stumbled backward, skidding on ice.

Her foot slipped.

And she pitched backward, tumbling into the mist.

PART III

Fourth Moon
Year 27, Age of the Aesir

26

STARKAD

*T*he last of the draugar fell into a heap. Spewing spittle, panting, Tiny hewed into the still crawling corpse, then stomped on the skull. At last it shuddered and gave out.

Starkad wiped his swords in the snow. Gore and grime coated them, more than fresh blood. Vikar's sword had chipped on a damn draug's helm. Starkad stared at the blade's edge in disgust. If he kept using it, his brother's blade might actually break. It needed more tending than he could do here—a proper forge.

"Master?" Afzal asked. The young man bore a gouge above his left eye and was favoring one arm.

Starkad nodded at him, then looked to Bragi. "Stitch up Afzal's cut before he loses too much blood."

"Hervor went over the gorge," Afzal said. "We can't find Orvar-Oddr at all."

"I saw her fall," Starkad said. And Orvar must have gone over as well, if his body was not here.

"Is she ..."

"Dead?" Starkad shrugged and turned to peer into the

mist rising up beneath the falls. Yes, she was almost certainly dead. But they were all looking to him, wanting him to tell them they had a chance of escaping this island.

Tiny knelt by Ivar's corpse, mumbling about Odin and Valhalla.

Bragi had moved to sit before Afzal, inspecting the wound but casting glances Starkad's way. So it was like that. Four of them left, and they didn't want to believe Hervor or Orvar dead.

He glanced back at those falls. Could either have survived that? He couldn't even judge how far down it was, but if they had fallen into water then ... maybe? If so, neither would live long in the frigid cold.

He blew out a long breath, then looked to the others. "Tiny. Burn the corpses, especially Ivar. We don't want aught getting back up. Bragi, make sure everyone is fit to move when I get back."

"What are you going to do?" Tiny asked.

In answer, Starkad strode toward the cliff and began to lower himself down, feet first. The rocks were slick with mist and ice. Trying to climb down to the bottom would most likely end in a broken neck.

Damn Hervor.

Bitch didn't even have the good sense to die where they could be sure of it. Now he had to go looking for her useless arse and rescue her like some maid in a skald's tale. Except this whole endeavor was turning out more like a ghost story around a campfire than any tale he wanted a part of.

His crampons scraped on ice.

"Hervor!" he shouted down in the abyss. "Orvar!"

No answer save the raging torrent of water across the gorge. Deeper and deeper he climbed. His arms ached after swinging those swords, after too long without sleep, without rest. Without sunlight, save a few hours. The far north held a perilous appeal, a place where a man could test himself to the limits.

Starkad had not yet found his limits, but it was beginning to look like he soon might.

Ice crumbled away under his fingers. Starkad clutched tighter, pulling against the gorge wall. Under all that ice, numerous rocks jutted from the cliff's side. In summer—as if there were summer here—he might have climbed this with more ease. But then, the challenge was why he had come.

Still, it had come with a higher price than he'd expected. A lot of dead men. Rolf, the Axe, Ivar, and the others. Probably Orvar. And *now* a dead woman too. Another dead woman weighing him down, his fault. His mistake. And hers, Hel damn her. She had tricked her way onto this trek, and it had cost her. That knowledge ought to have absolved him of failing her.

Somehow still his stomach felt inflamed, his cheeks burning.

Hervor wasn't Ogn. Bragi had said that. And still, she was dead. Had he been faster, maybe he could have saved her. The fastest man was the only one who counted. He thought he was the fastest. This night, he hadn't been fast enough.

Some hundred feet down, he came to a tiny ice shelf just above the water level. The falls crashed upon rocks, running out in a raging torrent of rapids. Those rapids would crush anyone caught in them, smash either of them like a broken toy and drag them under never to see daylight again.

"Orvar!" Starkad edged closer. "Hervor!"

Just the echoing cacophony of the waters, the rapids.

"Can anyone hear me?"

The shelf didn't run far, but Starkad skirted the edge of it, back and forth. She had fallen here. Her broken body didn't lay on the ice and that meant the rapids. He slammed the side of his fist against the ice of the gorge wall. She had no chance. Even had she survived the fall, she'd have drowned. And he'd never find her.

"You stupid, stupid girl." He paced the shelf again. "Damn you!"

Hervor was not Ogn.

But Starkad should have protected her.

He had failed her, and he was failing the entire party.

༒

PANTING WITH EXHAUSTION, Starkad at last threw one arm over the top of the rise and yanked himself up on the ledge. The others sat there now, staring at him. Two pyres burned out over the ice field. They had heaped the draugar corpses together and set them alit. The smaller pyre—Ivar's.

Ivar the Loud.

The man had escaped servitude in Nidavellir thanks to Orvar. He was a brute, a murderer. A mad man even, who enjoyed fighting even more than a man ought to. And now his daughter would never see her father again.

Afzal scrambled to his feet and offered Starkad an arm, which he accepted. The Serklander helped him up. "You didn't find them."

"No. There's naught down there but rocks and rapids. They're both gone."

"We're all going to die." Afzal said it without emotion. Coming from him, it sounded almost prophetic.

But Starkad didn't believe in prophecy.

No ... No. Fuck Odin and his riddling dreams.

Starkad clapped Afzal on the shoulder. "If we die, we will die well. But plan to live, and I think you will."

The Serklander looked back to the south.

"You want to flee, try to make it back to the ship."

Afzal nodded. "The draugar are dead so ..."

He trailed off at Starkad's shaking head. "The one's we burned are gone, yes. We don't know how many more are left out there. Yes, we might make it back to the coast, reach the ship."

"Is that not what we ought to do then?" Tiny asked.

Starkad scowled, cracked his neck, and looked to Bragi. Even the old skald seemed ready to give up. The man was running his thumb over the shaft of one of Orvar's black arrows, recovered from a corpse. Like that sole missile might somehow protect him. Bragi's age had caught up to him, no doubt.

All the men wanted was for Starkad to tell them they could go home. But how could he do that? Turn away in defeat after all of this? No. Never. "I came here to find Nordri, and I damn well mean to do so. I will plunder the dverg city of its riches and so enrich our friends and allies. To do less would be to allow Orvar and all the others to have died in vain. And I will not allow that."

"They say lust for dverg gold has blinded many a man," Bragi said.

"Turn back if you wish. Go hide on the ship and await my return. If you're lucky, I will bring a trinket for you. I for one intend to find what we fucking came for."

Afzal sighed. "I go where you go, Master."

"You do not owe me aught. Do as you wish, boy."

"I go where you go, Master."

Starkad spat in the snow. If the Serklander thought he

could shame Starkad into giving up, he was sadly mistaken. "So be it. And you two?"

Tiny shrugged. "If I go away laden with gold, at least something useful will have come from this trek. I don't relish returning to Dalar like a whipped dog, tail between my legs. I just want to make certain we *do* return."

Bragi waved his hand to encompass the three of them. "Fools, every last one of you. But, yes, I will come with you, if only to ensure future generations learn of your foolishness. I expect to name the tale, 'Starkad's Folly.'"

"Skald," Starkad said. "I find you less amusing once the mead has run dry."

"Then perhaps we should be hunting mead instead of gold."

Starkad snorted. He looked to the sky. Hard to orient himself in this place, but he thought north would be that way, beyond more mountains. "Let's move."

27

HERVOR

*H*ervor's throat hurt. She must have sucked down a great deal of water. Groaning, she opened her eyes. Her whole body was sore, but it was not the well of misery it ought to have proved. Instead, her injuries had faded to dull aches. Even the wounds on her arm and her shoulder had scabbed over, though they stank of seaweed. She lay on her back under an outcropping of ice. In the gorge?

Nearby, a half dozen people sat in a huddle, each swathed in great bundles of fur, including lined hoods. They spoke in soft tones, their tongue strange, unrelated to Northern at all.

Her armor was gone, and she had lost all her weapons in the fight with the draugar. Not a good situation to wage battle in.

She sat, trying not to grunt with the effort. Still, one of them looked at her. A woman, maybe her own age. The shifter had hair black as onyx and eyes near the same. Stranger still, her skin was dark, even deeper in tone than that of the Serklander. Triangular tattoos marked her forehead.

For a long time, the woman stared at Hervor. It was impossible to read those dark eyes, but her mouth was very stern.

These finfolk had saved her from the river, treated her wounds. Why?

"What do you want from me?"

They all looked to her now. One spoke in their strange tongue and received an answer from the nearest man. They argued—or it sounded like argument. The second man had Tyrfing in his lap.

Hervor rose, glaring at him. "Return my sword."

The man stood too, looked at her, then followed her gaze to the blade he held by its scabbard. He held it up, shook his head roughly, and then slipped the strap over his shoulder.

Hervor stormed toward him. "Listen you trollfucking son of a—"

The woman leapt up and closed the distance between them in an instant. With one hand, she grabbed Hervor's hair; with the other, she raised a bone knife to her throat. "No." Her accent sounded thick, confused.

"You speak Northern?"

"No," the woman said with a glower. "No. Blade. No."

Hervor grabbed the woman's wrist and twisted. Tried to. The shifter jerked on her hair so hard Hervor fell over backward and banged her arse on the ice.

"No blade. No troll. No."

The man with her sword said something in their own language, then the woman released Hervor's hair. She sheathed the knife, then leaned close to Hervor's face. She offered a hand.

Hervor stared at the outstretched arm. This shifter didn't seem intent on eating her or killing her, though she was a far cry from friendly. Still, it was better than being gnawed on by seal teeth. Hervor took the woman's hand, then the shifter yanked her to her feet with such force it hurt her shoulder.

"No troll. Troll. Troll rock. Walk."

Hervor jerked her arm away from the finfolk woman. "Yes, I can walk. I have no fucking idea what the rest of what you said means. But know this—that sword is *mine*. My legacy, my family heirloom. That oaf can't keep it."

The woman's eyes narrowed in apparent confusion, and she shook her head. Hervor had probably spoken too fast for her. Which was fine. She didn't really care if the finfolk understood her. After a moment, the shifter grunted, grabbed her shoulder, and pushed her forward out of the overhang.

They walked a long time, long enough to be certain they'd already carried her out of the gorge. The finfolk carried no torches, didn't seem to fear the mist, or breathing it in.

"Fire."

"No. Fire. No."

So they didn't care if it drove her Mist-mad. Maybe they didn't even realize the danger. Hervor waved her hands through the vapor. "This is poison to me." One of the other males was carrying her travel sack. It would have a torch. She pointed at it.

The woman spoke in her own language, and the male trotted over, handed her the bag.

Hervor pointed again. "Fire." She made a show of breathing deeply. "Fire." She shook her head. "No mist."

The woman banged her teeth together in a gesture that could have meant aught at all. Then she fished through the bag and tossed Hervor a torch.

Hervor stared at it, then at the woman. "Flint and steel?" She pantomimed striking the two together.

The finfolk woman rolled her eyes, then dug through the bag some more. Eventually, she grunted and just shoved the whole bag at Hervor. They waited long enough for her to light a torch. At least she would not go mad now. A small comfort.

They passed over hills until the sea came into view. On the ice by the shore rested two long, narrow boats. More like pointed, hollowed-out tree trunks than a rowboat. Animal skins were stretched over the hulls. Maybe even sealskin, to keep out leaks.

"Cousin of yours?"

The woman looked back and forth between the boat and Hervor as if trying to sort out her meaning. "Insult?"

Hervor snorted. Yes, that about covered it.

The shifter smacked her on the side of the head. The blow came so fast Hervor hadn't even braced for it. It dropped her flat, left her world spinning, eyes out of focus.

"Insult. No." The shifter might have been shaking her head. Hard to tell with everything spinning.

Hervor groaned, staring up at those strange lights in the sky. So the finfolk did not care to be insulted. No verbal sparring with them, then. She rubbed the side of her head, and her hand came away smeared in warm blood. Bitch was strong. Not as strong as a draug but stronger than a man.

"In boat. Get in."

Right. Hervor rose, swayed, steadied herself. The finfolk male with her sword boarded one of the other boats, along with two other males. In that boat lay a body: Orvar-Oddr, the Arrow's Point.

His chest rose and fell in slow breaths.

Son of a troll! Hervor took a step toward that boat before

the shifter woman grabbed her and pointed to the other one again.

There wasn't much point in fighting them. Not now. She had no weapons, not even her damned knife. And they were each stronger than her. With a sigh, she sat on one of the planks that served as seats, glare locked on Orvar's body. "Where are you taking me?"

"You. Kiviuq." The woman sat across from her while other finfolk took up the oars and shoved the boat into the sea.

"I'm Hervor. I don't know what Kiviuq means."

The woman pointed to the other boat.

Hervor shrugged and rubbed her head.

None of this made sense.

Only one thing she could say for certain. A man on that other boat needed killing.

28

STARKAD

*T*hey had walked a long time, the others following Starkad, resting on occasion, especially when the sun came up. Those few hours seemed very far between, and only then did they find solace. As the sun set, the night crept in, and with it, whispers and the unshakable feeling of being watched. Vaettir must have inhabited every rock, lake, and mountain on this island. Long away from the influence of man, Thule had grown wild.

But the dvergar had once tamed it and then abandoned it. Their wealth was the stuff of legends. As would be anyone who possessed such treasure. Yes, of course, men already told tales of Starkad Eightarms across half the North Realms. But one could always become more famous, more known. Look at Odin. A man who had made himself a god —in the eyes of so many now, he had always been a god. For they could not imagine a mortal rising so high.

Their group had taken to following an icy river back toward its source. Ever, Starkad scanned the banks for the bodies of Orvar or Hervor and ever he saw naught. Nor did he expect to.

The river ran from somewhere up in the mountains ahead, cutting a swatch through valleys. Perhaps it eventually emptied into the sea. That was where corpses would have been washed away, if not taken by the finfolk. Either the others had not considered they walked in the wrong direction to search for their companions, or they too realized the futility of it.

His gut wrenched at the thought of leaving them behind, in the mist. But. Be it his curse or his own damned nature, Starkad could not make his feet steer away from Nordri. He *had* to see it.

Mountains such as these appealed to the dvergar. Perhaps they reminded them of their own world. Though, if the dvergar were homesick, why did they come to Midgard at all? Why not leave the Mortal Realm in peace? Perhaps the motives of all vaettir were unfathomable. Following the river into the mountains was more like to lead to Nordri. It was hard to be certain either way, of course.

The old skald coughed. "When we get back to Sviarland, I'm going to be a whole moon resting by the fire. I'll have some pretty maid bring me the drinking horn all night long, never let it fall empty."

"Huh," Tiny said. "You let the maid serve you. I'll serve her. You know? With my big—"

"Yes, Tiny," Bragi said. "We get it. Are you certain there's not some other reason everyone calls you Tiny?"

"Just because I'm the smallest of my clan. No other reason at all. Troll arse."

Starkad held up a hand to silence them, then pointed to the mountains. In the valley ahead, the river disappeared underground. That meant a cave. And alongside an underground river seemed a good place for a dverg city. Even they must need fresh water to drink. At least Starkad assumed they did. Ivar and Orvar both probably knew more of the creatures, but they were gone now.

Ashes.

Starkad pushed forward, the others following behind, silent now. The river did indeed run into a cave—one carved out of ice. A shelf of rock ran alongside it, covered in snow at the outside, then mere rock farther in. His torchlight refracted off the frozen ceiling, casting light far down the tunnel.

Deep. Very deep. And very quiet.

Starkad looked at the others. Thus far, it had only been an idea. A man had to pick a direction and start walking. Now though, it became real. "This location seems right for Nordri. A tunnel like this one—maybe this very tunnel—must lead to the city. If we push on, maybe we'll reach it today."

"But?" Afzal asked.

"But we didn't find Hervor or Orvar's bodies," Bragi answered for Starkad. "Could be a chance they yet live. If we go underground, they'd never find us."

"Then what are we doing here?" Afzal demanded. "Should we not be searching the waterways?"

Starkad grimaced. Probably they should be. But it wasn't that simple, not really. He *had* looked for the pair, and no sign of either. And there might never be one.

Either way, it had to be the crew's choice and a real choice. Starkad pointed down into the ice cave. "Bragi's right. We should have found the bodies of our people. But we didn't. We don't know if they live at all, though it seems unlikely. If they do, we don't know where they are. We lost the finfolk trail a long time ago and who knows if we could ever find it again. So. We have to decide whether to leave the treasure we think we found behind to go hunting the full island for those who may be corpses."

"You cannot weigh a man's life with gold," Afzal said.

Bragi sighed. "Boy, all men's lives are weighed in gold and silver. A warrior wins glory and riches by raiding, fighting, and killing. Kings claim and hold power by the slaughter of their enemies, by sending their own people to die. And men go gladly into battle if they think it might make them rich. Wealth is the only defense we have against the World and its ravages."

Afzal shook his head. "You try to justify your greed with fancy words."

"I don't need to justify a desire for wealth. Life does that on its own."

Tiny stepped around Starkad, inspecting the ice walls. "Stunning. The dvergar made these caves?"

Starkad shrugged. "Maybe they're natural, maybe they're made. Does that matter?"

"No." The big man shrugged, then pointed down the tunnel. "Orvar-Oddr came here, led his own damned mission to find this place. So Ivar and everyone else who's gone to Valhalla or down to Hel, they did so to find this fucking city. And now you want to turn around and go looking for him? I don't think so. For all we know, Orvar already made it back to the ship. If not, he's probably dead. Hervor too. Either way, let us get what we fucking came for!"

His voice echoed down the long tunnel, ringing out again and again, far louder than Starkad would have liked. He waved him to silence with an angry jerk of his hand. Hel alone knew what might lurk down there. The last thing any of them needed was to announce their presence.

"So. I think we know Tiny's vote. And Bragi?"

"I'm forced to agree. Find Nordri, claim what we can,

and get off this cursed island. Too many of us are dead already. Going after Orvar only invites more losses."

"Afzal?"

The Serklander worked his jaw, then scratched his head. "I go where you go, Master." The words seemed laced with acid. The young man didn't want to go to Nordri nor leave Orvar-Oddr and Hervor. Maybe that made him more of a hero than the rest of them.

Either way, Tiny and Bragi's arguments made a great deal of sense. Starkad could not and should not overrule them. They had come to Thule for Nordri. It was more than that, though. He *had* to see this city where men had not walked in long ages. He had to know and witness it for himself.

Maybe that was part of his curse.

And maybe that curse extended to all those around him.

29

HERVOR

They paddled until the sun rose, then drove the boats onto the bank. They had followed the coast all the way, and Hervor could not be certain, but they seemed to be in a fjord. Based on the sun, probably on the northern side of this island. Odin alone knew how far away from where they had first landed.

Hervor couldn't even guess how much time had passed since she'd fallen into the gorge. She'd been unconscious for a while. Long enough for them to treat her injuries. Even those on her back. Which, now that she thought of it, meant they must have removed her shirt.

A warrior couldn't afford too much modesty. Still, it made her wonder what else the animal men might have done with her while she lay senseless. She scowled at the thought.

The woman directed her to follow, while the men pulled the boats away from the fjord. Hervor did so, until the woman indicated a spot by some rocks. Then she lay down against those rocks.

Daylight must have meant time for a nap. And if what

she knew of shifters was true, it also meant they could not shapeshift. The sun locked them in human form. Which probably meant this was her best chance.

As she sat, watching the shifters, the men led Orvar to where Hervor sat and threw him down beside her. He collided with the rock, a satisfying *oomph* escaping him as he hit. Slowly, the man sat, shook himself, and looked at Hervor.

"You're here too," he said. No hint of ire, no indication he realized she had been the one to shove him over the falls.

Hervor bit back her response. If he didn't know she planned to kill him, she might more easily gain another chance. She glanced at the shifters as they settled down to rest. Soon, they might sleep, and she could escape. Until then, perhaps the best way was to put Orvar at ease as well.

She turned back to him, feigning a hint of warmth. "A draug sent me tumbling over the falls."

"Me as well."

Hervor grunted. "So ... are not you the one they call Arrow's Point?"

Orvar groaned. "I have not used that name in many years. Not since I gave over pirating and the like ... but I was. A long time ago, yes."

"And how does the legendary Arrow's Point find himself overcome by *seals*?"

Now the man grimaced and looked to her, then the sky. "Hard to sleep when it's so blasted bright above, yes? You'd think now would be the best time to move."

"Not for shifters."

"No, more's the pity."

Hervor too sat up against the rock. The man had already grown comfortable with her. So let him talk. Let him damn himself one step more. Soon, he'd reach the gates of Hel. "Bragi said your father gave you magic arrows."

"Black arrows, true, forged by dvergar in the depths of Nidavellir, I think. Vile, toxic things, apt to kill any they pierce. Many a dverg-wrought craft works like that. Twisted bastards revel in death."

Dverg-crafts, Hervor knew only too well. Not so very far away, a finfolk man held Tyrfing, her legacy. If she could claim that, she could strike down Orvar and the finfolk both. "There were nine arrows?"

"No, six. I always managed to reclaim them before ... before this place. My grandfather stole them from a king in Kvenland, long ago. My father gave them to me, then, when I left my homeland. I went raiding and pillaging and adventuring across all the North Realms. So many adventures. So many lost friends. And those arrows fastened that name on me, Arrow's Point. None withstood them."

"Was that how you killed the sons of Arngrim in that ... famed battle?"

He blew out a long breath. "Not a tale I like to dwell on, girl. But I suppose we all have ghosts behind us. After all those years of murder and plunder, I came upon a great champion in Sviarland. And so, of course, wanting to know who was the stronger of us, I challenged him to a holmgang ..."

30

ORVAR

A great many men and shieldmaidens had gathered to watch the holmgang, a veritable army on both sides on the island. Some, I had brought with me from my crew in Nidavellir. Many more though had come to watch Yngvi's champion Hjalmar fight.

I remember, pacing around the man, panting and exhausted. It felt we'd been battling for days. Who could say? I had lost any track of time. Nor did my foe look any more steady on his own feet. Neither of us had given ground despite the countless blows we each had struck.

I spit out a mouthful of blood. By Frey's flaming sword, I wasn't even certain what blow earned me that coppery taste. Staring down Hjalmar, I tossed aside my battered shield. Another blow would have shattered it anyway, as had been the past two.

Hjalmar grinned and flung his own shield aside. "Maybe we ought to have tested wits instead of brawn."

"I would find it hard to match insults with a troll's wife."

Hjalmar flexed his arms. Probably as sore as my own. "You mean to say you do not speak to your own woman?"

Several of the onlookers laughed at that.

I tried not to smile. "I most often whisper my tales in the ears of your lady while we lay in tangled furs."

"Alas, champion of Nidavellir, I am not married. Perhaps a man from dverg lands has mistaken my goat for a woman?"

"More likely I mistook your mother for a goat and sent a slave to draw her milk."

Hjalmar chuckled and wiped blood from his brow. He looked to the sun, which now that I checked, had already settled low on the horizon. Maybe too late to leave this island and reach the mainland before nightfall. After meeting my gaze, Hjalmar drove his sword point first into the ground. "Champion."

I did the same, grateful for any chance to let go of the weight. My arm felt apt to fall from my shoulder. I nodded at my foe, slowly working my sword arm. "You wish to yield?"

Hjalmar laughed. "Odin's spear, man! I would acknowledge you as an equal. Come, why should we meet death at each other's hands?"

I rubbed my face. Hel, perhaps this Sviarlander was right. And it seemed these people had accepted the Aesir as gods. I had heard rumors of such people, stories they had overthrown the Vanir even. Hard to credit such tales, at least back then. Now I know, of course.

"Come, Arrow's Point," Hjalmar said. "Feast with us."

I looked to my men. Several of them nodded. Well enough. "Come then."

We returned to our camps.

None among us wanted to cross even a short stretch of the sea at night. Not given the choice. So the two crews joined together and built great bonfires to hold back the mist. My gut growled in anticipation of the roasting fish.

Hjalmar stalked over to his fire, hair dripping wet, and sunk down beside me. "I suppose I ought to be honored my fame has reached so far north."

I shrugged. "A king's housecarl who had fought a draug and won, protecting his new king. Yes, men speak of that even in far Nidavellir."

Hjalmar blew out a breath. "Not a story I tell sober."

"It's fortunate my men have brought ale then." I motioned to his people, who dragged a cask of it over to the fire, then brought mugs to each of them. I scooped a mugful for Hjalmar and offered it to the Sviarlander.

The man downed it all in one swig, belched, and wiped his mouth on his sleeve. Then he cracked his neck and stared at me. "You want to know so badly?"

I spread my hands. Few men fought draugar and walked away. The wakeful dead could not easily be sent back to their graves. I had slain one, once, at the cost of the lives of three of my men.

Hjalmar cleared his throat. "Last summer, around the solstice. King Alrik and his brother Eirik set out riding. No man knows what they quarreled over, but they killed each other. And they lay in the snows, unburied and unburnt."

And I knew what that meant. "The mist ..."

Hjalmar dipped his mug in for more mead. "Yes. The mist raised them. I don't know what happened to the king, but his brother Eirik was taken by a fell rage, and he came after the sons of Alrik. Our champion Starkad was away, searching for the king." He shook his head, then drained his mug again, before blowing out a long breath. "It came in the night. Got through the walls—I don't know how. The main fire pit dwindled to cinders."

I almost choked on my mead. No one let the main fires

of a house go out. And that a creature of the mist like a draug could exert such influence ...

Hjalmar nodded at me as I coughed. "Yes. Hard to believe, is it not? But it did. Alrik has two sons, Yngvi and Alf. By chance, it came for Yngvi, who I had called upon that very night. The new king is already a man grown, and together we drove the creature into the hearth. I'd swear its shrieks came from the mouth of Hel herself." The man unlaced his tunic to reveal a series of long scars running at an angle along his chest. Five of them. "Eirik did that with his fingers."

"You took a wound to save your king. I would call your fame well-earned." I clapped the Sviarlander on the shoulder. "And if it pleases you, I would say we should leave this island not as foes but as brothers. For it seems I have finally met my match."

Hjalmar stared at me a time. Then he drew a knife and sliced open his palm. I took the blade and repeated the gesture. Then we clasped hands.

"Brothers," Hjalmar said.

"Brothers."

31

HERVOR

*O*rvar's voice trailed off, clearly pained. And he mumbled something under his breath. Then he rolled onto his side. "We best also get some sleep. No sense in opening old wounds."

Hervor nodded affably until he closed his eyes. Old wounds? Those wounds had never closed. And now she must open all new wounds, as vengeance demanded.

And before she could do that, she needed to escape and reclaim Tyrfing.

She waited until Orvar too seemed settled, crept past the sleeping finfolk. The moment she put some distance between them, Hervor ran. Dashed out over the ice field, ducked behind the nearest rock pile, and then scrambled from that to another.

Why could there not be a damn forest when she truly needed one? These shores seemed naught but tundra, though rocks and hills at least gave her some spots to hide. Naught as suitable as trees though. Trees she knew.

Glancing over her shoulder, she made for the nearest hill. Not over it, she would stand out too much, but around it, into the valley it created with another hill. She had to keep moving. Her people were south, and if she could somehow reach them—find them again—she'd be safe.

She almost laughed. Her people. Odin's spear!

That party worked for the Ynglings, her enemies. Starkad might have saved her life—twice—but he'd also beaten her bloody. She owed him for the latter, but maybe she'd call it even. Still, he'd probably protect her from these Hel-cursed finfolk. Maybe even help her escape Thule.

The island did not suit Mankind.

Something whooshed behind her, and she turned.

Before she had finished moving, cords flew through the air, caught around her legs, and sent her toppling over. Large bone weights slammed against her shins.

The finfolk woman was running toward her. Hervor rolled over and tugged at the cords. They were some kind of sinew strands, tough and wrapped around her legs so many times she'd spend far too long unwinding them.

She yanked, pulled, tried to free her leg.

The finfolk woman grabbed her tunic. Hervor beat at her with her fists. That earned her a blow to the side of the head. She reeled and pitched over into the snow. The finfolk woman yanked her head up and punched her across the jaw. The blow left Hervor dazed, unable to even surrender.

She wanted to surrender. It was enough. Enough.

The other woman hit her again.

Hervor lay back in the snow and groaned, then the finfolk woman slumped back on her arse.

After a moment, she cuffed Hervor on the side of the head, this time not hard enough to do real harm, though it stung. "You. Trouble."

Hervor chuckled, choked on her own blood, and spit it out. "My mother would agree." She chortled. Gods, the woman had called her an evil, spiteful child. She supposed she was. Maybe not so much had changed.

"No man. *Woman.*"

"Wait, what?" Hervor mulled it over a moment. "You're irked because I'm not a man?"

The finfolk woman thumped her own chest with one finger. "Naliajuk. Naliajuk take you. Husband." She roughly grabbed Hervor's groin and shook it. Not a sensation Hervor enjoyed. "No husband."

"Nope. No husband down there."

"All human men. Get you."

"Hervor."

The finfolk woman glared at her. "Hervor. Now give. Kiviuq."

One of the males. Starkad had said finfolk abducted men and women for spouses. So this Naliajuk had fished her from the river, thinking to claim a husband. And when she had removed her armor to treat the wounds, she'd gotten an unpleasant surprise. And so decided to give her prisoner to this Kiviuq.

"So you don't want me, huh?" Hervor laughed again. Just as bad as Starkad—no love for women. Not that Hervor intended to marry a fucking seal of any gender.

"No man."

"Right. So you'll give me to Kiviuq. Why, what do you care? Who is he to you?"

"Mmmm." Naliajuk looked around and gnawed on her lip, then cupped both hands around her womb.

"Your ... lover?"

The finfolk woman cuffed her again. "Mmmm. Kiviuq. Naliajuk." She pointed to her womb.

"Your son."

Now she rolled her eyes. Again she pointed to her womb. "One. Woman. One."

"One woman? Same woman? Born of the same woman? Your brother?"

"Br-brother." Naliajuk nodded now.

Possible she meant they were twins, but it didn't really matter. For whatever reason, Naliajuk had not handed Hervor over to her brother just yet. Maybe there was some ritual for it since she had been the one to capture Hervor.

Hervor rubbed the blood from her face with the back of her hand. Several painful bruises had already started to form. Naliajuk had given her quite the beating. "Why don't you just leave us alone? I don't want to be *anyone's* wife."

Least of all a man who seemed more animal than human.

"Mmmm. Human. Fresh human."

"Yes. I'm human. But why don't you marry your own kind?"

Naliajuk gnawed her lip again, then shook her head. "Human. Best. Take human, win ... respect."

Respect. She probably meant having a human bride would bring her brother honor. Hervor shook her head. She wished she could explain to the woman there was no honor in abducting a wife. Then again, even mortals had been known to do so.

Men were willing to do a great many things for lust or profit. And she was no innocent to think her wishes should mean much to this animal.

Naliajuk yanked Hervor up by her arms and roughly dragged her back to the camp, not bothering to untangle her feet. The motion sent fresh jolts of agony through Hervor's wounds, but the finfolk woman ignored any of Hervor's grunts of pain. Finally, Naliajuk deposited Hervor back in the same spot. This time, she wound a cord around Hervor's hands, binding them together.

A man did the same with Orvar, who fixed Hervor with a level stare through the whole process.

"What the fuck were you thinking?" he asked when the finfolk pulled away again. "Did it not cross your mind to coordinate an escape attempt?"

If he only knew what she planned to do to him when she escaped. Hervor worked her swollen jaw. "You were too busy resting. I saw a chance to go for ... help. And I took it."

Orvar sneered. "From now on, girl, you listen to me and follow my lead."

"Why? What good have you wrought on this island, Arrow's Point?"

Now he sat up straighter. "You will heed my words because King Yngvi funded this expedition, and the king appointed me to lead it."

"Just how long have you had your mouth around his cock, anyway?"

Now Orvar's sneer turned into an outright glare. "Watch your Hel-cursed mouth, shieldmaiden. The pain you endured in that beating is naught compared to what lies before us if we fail to work together."

Perhaps he might have a point at that. Hervor could avenge no one while bound by finfolk, nor was she keen to marry this Kiviuq and bear his ... pups.

So.

Once again her temper had endangered her goals. She bit her tongue, as if that might help suppress the boiling rage in her gut. "So ...you're right. I was ... rash. We bide our time, then."

"Yes."

Now his guard was up with her. His own anger inflamed.

And her chance at both escape and revenge dwindled while that blaze lingered.

"Fine then. Tell me about this Hjalmar."

"What?"

"If we are to pass hours like this, at least let us not be bored."

Orvar worked his jaw as if weighing that, then shrugged. "You are a strange one, Hervor."

"I have been called worse."

"As have we all, I suppose. Hjalmar ... Hjalmar was a housecarl to king Yngvi, as I said. So when we proclaimed ourselves brothers, he brought me to Upsal and presented me at court. Yngvi embraced me and bade me join them all for a feast, while his brother, Alf, watched, reserved. I did not ... much know what to make of either.

"Yngvi and Alf shared their kingship, determined not to turn on one another as their father and uncle had done. I thought it a strange choice, one fated to invite bickering amongst them. And yet nigh to two decades have passed since, and they remain loyal to one another thus far."

"And Hjalmar?"

"Oh ... that feast marked the dawn of good times, when I would become something other than the Arrow's Point. Good times, of course, never last."

32

ORVAR

*T*he kings sat me at their own table, availing me of their hospitality. I knew, even then, they hoped to enlist me in their raids and wars. Nor was I opposed to some mercenary work, here and there.

"So," Yngvi said between bites of mutton, "Arrow's Point. You've led a great many raids in your time. I have a mind to do so as well. I would like it if you would join me."

I glanced at my new blood brother, but Hjalmar was staring at the young princess. What was her name? Yngvi had mentioned it, but I had taken little note. There were a great many women there, shieldmaidens too, each more into the fullness of womanhood.

I cleared my throat. "Where do you think to raid? West to Kvenland?"

Alf snorted. "My brother is convinced Odin wants him to claim islands in the Morimarusa for our people."

"Odin?" I looked now to the other king. "This Ás usurper?"

Alf opened his mouth, but Yngvi answered. "The Aesir are the new gods. They have taken Vanaheim and named it

Asgard. Our neighbor, King Gylfi of Dalar, spoke with Odin, King of Asgard."

Well, that was new. "These Aesir visit men?" Stories told that the Vanir had not walked upon Midgard in uncounted generations. A man could send prayers to Njord or Frey or Ullr, and maybe they would answer. But the Vanir did not show themselves. And now a new race of gods had supplanted them. Some might call it just, I supposed. If gods were not above justice. And if I believed it all.

"So Gylfi claims," Alf said. "Father thought him a liar, intent to promote his own importance."

Hjalmar was whispering something to the princess now, and she was smiling. Neither seemed to be paying attention to the conversation. At the time, I thought it well for him. Would that I had known what would come of those whispers.

I did not. I cared more for the words of the kings.

Yngvi motioned to a slave for more ale. "Gylfi rode through here, two moons past. Told of his encounter with the High One, the one he said could only have been Odin. Rumor claims Gylfi learned some of the Art from a wandering wizard."

"Which is all the more reason to doubt him," Alf said.

"I agree it is unmanly," Yngvi admitted. "But still. If anyone could recognize a god when he saw one, would that not be a sorcerer?"

Time would tell. I had made no judgments about gods, nor did I see this as the time. I slapped a hand on the table, and Hjalmar started, looking at me. "I have indeed raided into Reidgotaland before. If you would go there, King Yngvi, then I will come with you and my blood brother. Most of the kings there are not strong."

Alf rolled his eyes. "Starkad has warned against this. He says sorcerers dwell there and Odin sends us to our deaths."

"Starkad is young," Hjalmar said. "What does he know of the World?"

"Young yes," Alf said. "But well travelled and the finest swordsman I have ever seen."

I had met Starkad some few winters back, in the court of Harald of Agder, back in Nidavellir. Fierce warrior, but as Hjalmar said, still young at the time.

Yngvi shrugged. "If you do not wish to go, then stay here and run the kingdom, brother. And Starkad—if he returns, if he ever finds our father's ... well, if he returns, he can ensure you remain safe here."

Alf scowled at the insult. Yes. Shared kingship did not seem over wise to me.

The feast ran fell into the night, and even after, King Yngvi and others sat long at the drinking table. Alf excused himself, as did Hjalmar.

I followed my blood brother. The man stumbled a little, half drunk, perhaps. He wandered outside to piss, and I gave him a moment, warming myself by a brazier.

Hjalmar returned, blinking against the firelight. "Is the room not to your liking, brother?"

"It is quite comfortable. I was more concerned with things here not being to your liking."

Hjalmar groaned. "I've had a bit to drink. Perhaps we could save the verbal bouts for tomorrow."

I rubbed my hands together. The mist had grown very thick this night, seeming to encircle the brazier but never quite encroaching into the fire's warmth. Like it was hungry for our souls. "I'm not having sport with you. I do see the way you look at that princess, though. And she is what, thirteen, fourteen winters?"

My brother warmed his own hands over the fire, eyes wistful. "Ingibjorg. She's Yngvi's daughter, yes fourteen winters now. Well past marrying age, but her father holds out. He wants a better match for her than a simple housecarl."

"Even one who saved his life?"

"Even so."

Hard to say whether that made Yngvi a bad king or a great one. Politics were everything. And true, a princess was far above a housecarl, nor could Hjalmar likely afford sufficient bride price. The latter problem, though, might be solved with these raids.

"Yngvi plans to sail to the Reidgotaland islands soon. You want to win the princess's hand? Impress him. Win glory, win spoils, and show him how much he has to gain."

"You think the king would agree then?" Hjalmar murmured something unintelligible before looking at me again. "She would marry me if he'd allow it. She's said as much."

I was never going home again. Never could I look upon the lands of my birth, for fear of a fool prophecy. This place though, it felt right. And Hjalmar was a good man, my blood brother. I sniffed. "Brother, I swear to you. Fight with glory, with valor. I will help you win the hand of Ingibjorg, no matter how long it takes."

Hjalmar clasped my arm, then embraced me.

Those were the good days, however brief.

33

STARKAD

*T*he ice caves delved deeper and deeper, through glaciers and into the mountains. Ice gave way to rock, natural at first, and then clearly worked stone. They wandered long before coming to stairs carved from the rock. These stairs descended for over an hour, until Bragi had begun to complain about his old, aching legs.

"Be silent," Starkad said. One wall had dropped away, leaving a fall into unknown depths. On the other wall though, dvergar had carved a long, sprawling mural depicting Hel knew what. He held the torch closer, just out to his side, until the skald decided to come have a look as well.

Starkad kept glancing at the carvings as he descended. They showed two great armies of mighty beings, gods perhaps, as they seemed to have mastered various winged beasts, serpents, even varulfur. And between them stood the twisted and misshapen dvergar, forging weapons, even wading into battle. The deeper they went, the more the dvergar fell in battle, their broken corpses decorating fields, until, at the end, they seemed to cower before a shining sun.

A massive crack split the sun down the middle, as though someone had intentionally defaced it.

"What does this mean?" Starkad asked.

"Oh now I can talk?" Bragi asked. The skald snorted. "Legend says the sun is anathema to dvergar, turns them to stone even."

"And the rest of it?" Afzal asked.

Bragi shrugged. "Maybe they were fighting the Vanir or the alfar or some other divine beings from ancient times. I can't imagine it depicts aught human."

Starkad stifled the urge to correct the skald. The Vanir had once been human, after all. Even the glorious alfar, when they walked on Midgard, did so by possessing mortal hosts.

Either way, the mural depicted something akin to Men, even if they had left part of their humanity behind. His time among the Aesir had taught him such things. But the Sviarlanders didn't need to know it and, of greater import, they certainly did not need to know *how* he knew such things. He had walked away from those self-appointed gods and never looked back. Bad enough men seemed to have figured out he studied swordplay under Tyr.

No, his companions didn't need to know the truth.

Tiny spit over the edge of the stairs then chuckled as his phlegm vanished into the darkness.

Starkad cuffed him on the back of the head. "If you're not interested in dverg history, fair enough. But do not draw attention to us. The dvergar have gone from here, yes. That does not mean naught might lurk here. We have already seen vaettir aplenty on this island."

The big man glared at him, sneered, then began to descend the stairs again. Starkad looked to Bragi and Afzal, who now both stared at him. He cocked his head after Tiny, then started back down the stairs.

Later, the mural depicted mist billowing out of an island. On and on it went, until it seemed to engulf all Midgard. Was that island Thule? Did the dvergar mean to imply *this* place was where the mists first escaped Niflheim and entered the Mortal Realm? Starkad ran his fingers over the mural. The island in the mural seemed different than he thought of Thule, but who could say. It wasn't like they'd carved an actual map.

"The beginning of the Fimbulvinter," Bragi said.

Starkad grunted.

"It's true then," Afzal said. "There really was a time before the mists."

Such things were an obsession for Odin. Small surprise he had sent men to this island, though why he had not come himself, Starkad could only guess. Contending with the Niflungar, perhaps. The would-be god had his fingers stirring a great many pots.

Starkad swept his torch away from the mural and descended after Tiny. All this history tasted bitter, just served as a reminder of the slowly suffocating world. He would not be drawn into Odin's wars or quests. He'd left such things far behind.

All Starkad wanted now was to see this world, every hidden depth of it.

The stairs ended in the middle of a great landing that spread out farther than the torchlight in both directions. The dvergar had worked the floor smooth, though they left numerous stalagmites in place. Decorations, maybe.

Afzal reached the bottom and paced around a bit. "Which way, Master?"

Starkad turned about, torch high over his head for

maximum effect. No clear indication but better to pick a way than seem indecisive before the men.

Without a word, he started walking in one direction. This landing was wide as any great hall. Wider, like a yard perhaps. But underground, something must bound the sides of it. He altered his course at an angle of his original one, until at last a rock wall came into view. All he had to do was follow the walls, and he'd find an exit from this chamber.

He continued along that way rather long before coming to an opening, the depths of which retreated away from his torchlight. Starkad stepped into it. Light reflected off a solid surface several dozen feet away. An alcove? It stank of rot, mold, and dust.

And then dust shifted. It wafted up from the floor as though a wind swept through the underground chamber, impossible as that sounded. Firelight glinted off metal. Starkad leapt backward, away from the alcove as pinpoints of red glare opened. He collided with Tiny, shoved the big man back, and flung his torch at the rising draug.

It shrieked at the flames, a sound of torment, of damnation. Flames leapt over the creature, engulfing its rotting clothes as it stumbled forward.

Starkad drew his blades, and the others did the same. The draug swung a giant, rusting axe. Starkad leapt to the side and rammed Vikar's sword into the draug's face while lopping off one of its arms with his own blade.

The fiend fell backward but did not lose its grip on the axe. Blinded, it swung the weapon wildly with one hand. The axe collided with the wall, casting out a shower of sparks. Tiny roared and hewed into it with his broadsword. Once, twice, and it toppled to the ground.

A moan echoed through the great chamber. Followed by another. And another. On and on, the tormented, hellish cries rang out. Draugar waking, stumbling back to life—or at least into motion.

Starkad sheathed Vikar's sword and snatched up his torch from where it had fallen. "I think we know what happened to the city of Nordri."

34

HERVOR

*J*ust off the shore, an arching rock rose from a shelf of ice, looking like some bent-over jotunn. Or giant troll. Naliajuk had said Troll Rock. This then was where they'd planned to take Hervor. They banked their boats right up against the ice shelf, then leapt out on it. The males dragged those boats up onto the ice, while Naliajuk grabbed Hervor by the elbow and pulled her toward the shore.

A village neared, though not one with houses exactly. It seemed the finfolk lived in domes of ice a short walk from the sea. Little huts, really, though Hervor couldn't guess how they built them. Maybe the ice here never melted. Even summer could not break the grip of this freeze.

The breath of Hel had blown over Thule, and the finfolk had either welcomed it or made the best of it.

The finfolk woman led her past several of the ice houses, toward the center of the village. An arch of bones rose there —whale ribs by the size of them. What the fuck?

Naliajuk yanked her away from the bone arch, pulling

her along until they reached one of the ice huts, while her brother pulled Orvar away.

That finfolk man Kiviuq, the very animal they wanted her to marry, had now claimed Tyrfing. The shifter probably had no idea of the value, power, and dire nature of that blade. He had not yet drawn it, but if he did ... well. There would be murder in this village tonight. It was a twisted justice, one fit for a thief who had claimed her legacy. That still did not answer how to go from that justice upon the finfolk, to her revenge against Arrow's Point.

Hervor had to stoop to enter the hut Naliajuk shoved her toward. The interior was lined with fur from a snow bear. Quite the hunter, whoever had brought one of those down. She couldn't stand upright, but the fur was soft, so that didn't matter. The interior was surprisingly warm, comfortable even, at least compared to the frigid wind outside.

The finfolk woman crawled over to where she sat, then continued to move around her, like a wolf circling prey. She looked innocent, young. But seals were predators and dangerous ones at that. A hunter who forgot that wound up like the Axe.

Inside the hut lay several figures carved from walrus ivory. Had Naliajuk made these? Hervor reached to pick one up.

Without warning, Naliajuk grabbed Hervor's hips, patted them. Checking her bones?

Hervor dropped the carving and clenched her fists. She *might* be able to overpower Naliajuk if she caught the finfolk woman off guard. But running through the village she was not like to make it far. Better to tolerate the strange inspection. She'd get her chance later.

Then the finfolk woman grabbed her breasts, squeezed. Hervor stiffened. Yes, that was too much. She shoved Naliajuk off her. "Listen you fish-brained beast. No one touches me like that without my permission."

Naliajuk gnawed her lip a moment. "You. Baby."

"So I'm a baby because I don't want to be groped? By another woman, no less?"

Naliajuk patted her own womb. "You. Baby?"

"Do I have babies? No." She shook her head. "Gods, no." Imagine her a mother. Not a pleasant thought for her *or* the unfortunate babe.

Now the finfolk woman frowned. "No baby."

"No."

"Broken?"

Hervor sneered. "No. I'm not fucking *broken*. I just don't want a Hel-cursed baby!"

Naliajuk jerked back, raising her hands in signs of defense, almost like claws. She arched her back like she was about to shift into a seal. "No Hel. No speak. No."

Well, that was interesting. The shifter didn't like anyone invoking the name of Hel. Of course, völvur and old men said the same, but she didn't know many warriors who didn't curse in Hel's name. The queen of Niflheim was the fear, the real power behind the mist. She was death—the worst kind of death.

Hervor raised her own hands in surrender. "I understand. Don't say her name."

Naliajuk nodded.

"You want to know if I *can* have a baby?"

Again, that simple nod.

If she said no, would they release her? More likely, finding her a poor wife, they'd eat her. "I assume so. If I wanted to. And I don't. No baby. No husband. Give me back my sword and that other man. Let us go. We don't want to marry you. We don't want to fight you."

Words she'd never said to anyone in her life. She always loved a good fight. But the shifters were not men, and facing them in combat was a foolish risk. Besides, they outnumbered the remaining crew.

Naliajuk crawled for the door, then looked over her shoulder and pointed at the furs Hervor sat on. "You. Stay. No leave." With that, the finfolk woman left her alone in the ice house.

When she was certain the woman had left, Hervor crawled to the edge to peer outside. No guard, though plenty of the fur-wrapped finfolk wandered around in the village. Naliajuk was there too, talking to Kiviuq, and others.

They had bound Orvar to the bone arch with strands of sinew and torn his shirt away from him. He stood there, shivering, as finfolk pelted him with stones of ice. Hit him in the chest, back, face.

Oh. That was delicious. Here, at the end of the World—the slayer of her kin. Bound, broken. His cheeks pale with impending frostbite, maybe even deathchill. The mighty Arrow's Point rendered limp and impotent and well primed for her blade. If she *had* her damned runeblade. Tyrfing's absence was a raw, gnawing hollow in her gut.

There was nowhere to run. Not now. She needed a plan. And she needed the rest.

She crawled back into the center of the hut, wrapped the fur over her, and curled up to sleep.

SOMEONE GRABBED her by the shoulder. Hervor jerked awake, twisted around, and snatched the man's wrists. Kiviuq. He broke her grip with ease, then grabbed her arms.

She stared daggers at him. Right. She would marry this animal when the fields of Hel melted.

The finfolk man gnashed his teeth at her.

She tried to pull back, but he was too strong.

After an overlong pause, he shoved her toward the doorway.

Outside, several of the other finfolk stood around the whalebone arch. Orvar knelt nearby, arms wrapped around himself, his skin tinged blue. Had he given in and agreed to wed one of these creatures?

Kiviuq followed behind her, seized her by the shoulders, and shoved her over to his sister. Naliajuk caught her arms and leaned close to her face.

"Now you. Marry?"

"Go fuck a troll."

"Troll. No troll. Marry human. Give baby."

"Go. To. Hel!"

Naliajuk flinched, looked around. Some of the others made signs of warding. Naliajuk flung her to the ground.

The impact stunned her. Only for an instant, but then two finfolk were on her, each yanking her up by one arm. They pulled her arms apart until her shoulders felt ready to pop out. Like that they lifted her off her feet and carried her —kicking and flailing and spitting at the trollfuckers—to the bone arch. Each tied one of those sinew bands around her wrist, then released her.

Hervor stared up at the woman. "Why do this to us?"

Naliajuk pointed at Orvar. "Man. No wife. Say no. No."

Huh. "So he has to *agree* to marry the finfolk woman?"

"Marry. No hit. Husband, no hit."

Huh.

One finfolk pulled a bone knife.

Hervor spit in his face. "Do your worst. I've been cut before, fish rat."

The finfolk glared, then snatched her tunic and began to saw at the laces.

"What the fuck do you think you're doing?" she demanded. She strained against the sinews binding her. "Get off of me!"

The fabric didn't give way near as easily under the knife as the laces had. Blade was probably better suited for piercing. But her shirt did cut. He ripped it off her, leaving her shivering in her linen undershirt. This he pinched between two fingers, inspecting it as if surprised to see another layer down there. Shifters probably never wore undergarments. Just more clothing to remove when they wanted to shift.

Finally, the finfolk began to saw through the linen as well.

"I will *kill* you one day for this." Hervor glared at him. She'd skin this fucking animal for his pelt.

When the male had finished his work, he leaned in an examined her exposed breasts, though only for a moment. He nodded in apparent approval—wasn't that wonderful—and backed away.

She stood there, shivering and unable to cover herself for either warmth or modesty.

Neither of which mattered as soon as the first ice ball hit. It struck between her shoulder blades and stung like she'd been hit with a weapon. It knocked the air from her lungs and for a moment, she couldn't breathe. Couldn't scream in pain. Before she could even catch her breath, another ball hit. This one striking her ribs. The villagers were each gathering up stones of ice, mashing snow around them with both hands. One by one, they hurled ball after ball at her.

Except for Naliajuk and Kiviuq. The brother and sister

both stood side by side, arms folded in near identical poses. Watching their people torture her but not taking part.

"Why not?" she spat at them. Why shouldn't they join in? Was there some rule against beating your intended wife? Wouldn't that be the quaintest law—you could have your wife beaten. Just couldn't do it yourself.

The beating continued for some time.

She tried to look up, watch those iridescent lights in the sky. But after each blow, she found herself instinctively trying to curl into a ball. To protect her face. None of the ice stones struck her there. Maybe they knew they might crack her skull like that.

And then the pelting stopped.

Hervor coughed, moaned, looked up. She had long since fallen to her knees, supported as much by the sinews pulling at her arms as aught.

One of the villagers approached her with a bowl, carved from bone and lined with animal skin. Water in the bowl. They didn't want her to die of thirst, at least. She raised her head more as he neared, trying to sip from it. The finfolk held the bowl just out of reach.

Hervor groaned. She'd have to arrange some special revenge for this one. He was fucking taunting her. Her!

The man suddenly heaved his arms forward. Ice cold water splashed over her. The shock of it left her gasping.

"I will ... die ... like this." Could barely speak through her chattering teeth.

The finfolk man tossed the bowl aside. Then he punched her in the face. Her head jerked back under the force, only the sinews keeping her from falling over. Pain blinded her. That and he'd hit her over one eye. She tried to blink it away, but that eye wasn't working. A sharp slap on the other cheek jerked her back to alertness. The male slapped her again and again and again. Until her cheek felt on fire.

At last he backed away, looked to Naliajuk. The woman approached and knelt in the snow beside Hervor. With one hand, she lifted Hervor's chin, forcing her to meet her gaze.

"You. Marry. Kiviuq. Give babe."

Hervor stared at Naliajuk. Did the other woman feel aught for her suffering? No. Why should she? This was normal to her. Had Hervor felt aught when Red-Eye's Boys had raped or tortured those they'd come across? Maybe. You learned to block it out, to stop thinking of the other person as a person.

It didn't take long.

By the second or third time, it became habit.

How much easier then, for these creatures that were not even human?

And they would beat her down, eventually. Sooner or later, everyone broke. She was strong, defiant. But no one lasted forever. She should just give in, agree. Would wedding the bastard really be any worse than this? She'd slept with men she didn't like before. Sometimes opportunity, need, or sheer lust mattered more than love or desire.

Everyone broke sooner or later. But Hervor had always figured herself to be one who'd go later. Much fucking later.

"Why don't *you* marry him?" she said. "Give your brother a few pups. Make us all happy."

Naliajuk shook her head and released Hervor's chin. She backed away.

And then the ice stones began again.

Hervor groaned in agony. She wanted to weep at the pain, at the frustration, at the utter hopelessness of this place. But she would not. She would not break in front of these animals. Not now, not for as long as she could manage.

THE COLD WIND had scourged Hervor more effectively than any lash. By the time they released her from the sinew bands, she could not walk, could barely move her arms enough to cover herself. Deathchill was taking her. The thought seemed idle, far away.

To embrace the end seemed the easiest way forward. The only remaining option.

Naliajuk carried her to a bonfire in the midst of the village and there dropped her on the ground.

Hervor lay unmoving, unable to even stir. Or care. She had failed in her quest for vengeance and would now sink into the Realm of spirits, trapped forever. It ought to have horrified her, but she could not bring herself to form an emotion, any emotion.

Her flesh stung as the fire began to infuse its warmth back into her. With surprising gentleness, Naliajuk bound her hands to a post carved from another whalebone. As if she could rise. As if she could run.

There was no escape from Hel. And her breath had blanketed Thule.

THE FINFOLK WOULD NOT LET her die. The fire eased just enough warmth into Hervor's limbs to keep her alive.

"You're awake."

Not by choice. Hervor groaned. Someone had wrapped one of those fur coats around her while she slept. Naliajuk, probably. Misplaced concern or simple refusal to let her prisoner escape, even into death?

She cracked open her eyes. Orvar-Oddr was bound to

another whalebone post nearby, leaning with his back against it. A fur coat on him too. Did her face look half so bruised and beaten as his? By the feel of it, it must.

Hervor shivered, forcing herself not to whimper with the pain of it. She would not let this man see her weakness. She had no fucking weakness, damn it!

"I should not have come to this place ..."

No shit. No one belonged on this island. Not in a long, long time.

"I guess I was running from my past ... I felt like I failed the Ynglings in letting Hjalmar die for letting Yngvi's daughter ... what nonsense. Hjalmar brought it all on himself, in a way. He knew what he was about. And still, I let Yngvi call me back, call in old loyalties. As if it might make up for what they'd lost."

Gods above, the man was rambling like deathchill was setting in. Ironic, that the cold would ultimately deny Hervor her vengeance.

So keep him talking, keep him coherent. Wait for her moment. Every single fucking one of the Ynglings needed to pay, yes, but if she brought down Arrow's Point, maybe it would grant Father some measure of peace.

"What do you mean, Hjalmar brought it on himself?"

"He ... we did as Yngvi had wished and raided into Reid-gotaland. Moons of blood and slaughter. And after, things turned against us. They always do."

35

ORVAR

*T*hat summer had been kind, at least to me. We had made three raids into Reidgotaland, even established a settlement on one island. The last, in particular, had pleased Yngvi who planned to inspect it now that summer was returning again. We'd heard little from the settlement over the winter, small surprise. No one wanted to sail the Morimarusa with the risk of storms. To do such and test the patience of Rán was to invite the sea to cast her net over you.

Leading those raids had won me renown and booty both, enough so I'd even taken a wife among Yngvi's people, Eira, the daughter of one of his jarls. She was young and like to give me many children, I had thought.

With the breaking of winter, I'd returned to Yngvi and Alf's halls by the River Fyris. Already, those halls were thick with the kings' gathered people, all eager to know when they could next raid.

Hjalmar sat among those men, casting frequent glances over at Ingibjorg who sat beside her father. She seemed to be offering discreet smiles to the housecarl whenever her father was occupied in conversation or drink—which was often. The couple had clearly not yet received Yngvi's blessings.

Shame that. Had Yngvi relented sooner ... well. He did not.

And I strode over to my friend Hjalmar and clapped him on the shoulder. "So glum, brother? The winter moons have passed! You ought to leave your mood with them."

Hjalmar grunted in acknowledgment, then beckoned me sit. I did, and slaves brought mead out for me, followed by a steaming hunk of mammoth flesh. The hunts had been kind to some, it seemed. Mammoths are dangerous prey, but they do well to feed a large host.

The thegns were debating where they ought to strike next, as if the choice were theirs and not up to Yngvi and Alf.

"We ought to have taken Samsey already," Sveinn said. "It's central, decent-sized, inhabited only by a few fishing villages. Would have made a better spot for the colony."

Another scoffed. "You ever seen Starkad Eightarms fight, man? If he says a place isn't for men, I'd take his word at it."

I had been one to argue for taking Samsey as well. It looked prime for it, with a small population. Yngvi, however, still trusted the word of his father's champion Starkad, who claimed sorcerers laired on that island. Men best left undisturbed.

And if true ... well, a wise man wants naught to do with sorcerers. Mad men, every one of them, and their hearts blacker than a troll's.

A slave approached and whispered something in Hjalmar's ear. My blood brother rose and accompanied the man away.

"It's a big enough island," Sveinn said. The thegn was young, but I had seen him fight. A brave one. "You really think a few sorcerers lay claim to all of it? Arrow's Point! You've raided all over the North Realms—you ever see a sorcerer? Ever had one rise up to stop a single raid?"

I shook my head. "Völvur here and there, but they don't get involved. They don't work their seid on raiders, we don't cut off their fucking heads. It works out for everyone."

The thegns laughed. No, I didn't know much of true sorcerers. But magic was real. I had no doubt. My arrows told me that much. Those arrows had real power. I wanted no fight with anyone who wielded such Otherworldly ability. It was possible for a man to be too brave.

Oh. Yes, and I *had* challenged Starkad to a duel, to first blood.

Gods. I'd wanted to see who was truly the best. Starkad had bested me before men had even finished placing their bets. The man fought like a god of war, one to make Frey himself envious. Or Tyr, this new Ás war god. Some claimed the god had but one hand and could still best any foe, mortal or otherwise. Starkad had two hands, but was so fast he'd *earned* the name Eightarms.

I've never seen aught like it, before or since.

Hjalmar returned to the center of the hall a moment later, guests behind him. "My king, may I announce the twelve sons of Arngrim, Jarl of Bolmso." He spoke with a loud voice that rang through the feast hall. He did not quite hide the look of disdain on his face.

And like that, our high times ended.

"Who is this Arngrim?" I asked Sveinn.

"A jarl in Ostergotland. Rumor has it he's a berserk and so are his sons."

I scowled. A berserk as a jarl. That was new.

"There's more, though. Some say he killed Gylfi's son-in-law out in Holmgard, took the man's daughter as a wife by force."

"Gylfi's granddaughter?"

"No, different mother, from before."

Still, bold to strike against one tied to Gylfi.

King Yngvi rose to greet the newcomers. King Alf remained in his seat.

There were twelve of the men, each clad in a bearskin, each bearing arms that looked well worn. Blood splatters still caked furs of more than one of those berserkir.

Hjalmar stepped aside but did not return to his seat beside me. The housecarl seemed to mistrust these brothers even more than Sveinn did. I had to stifle the urge to touch my sword hilt. Aught that so discomfited Hjalmar sent my blood racing with ease.

Starkad was there too, sitting on the far side of the table, his two blades on his back. If trouble started, the young man would be ready, I knew, and I pitied the man who drew a blade on him.

When Yngvi had retaken his seat, one of the sons of Arngrim strode forward from the others. "Thank you for your welcome, King Yngvi. I have travelled far to reach your table. I am Hjorvard of Bolmso."

"On what errand?" Alf asked.

"Because word of your daughter's beauty has spread through every kingdom in Sviarland. And thus, I made my vow before the sight of the new gods that I should make Princess Ingibjorg my wife. I will marry her and no other."

Yngvi looked to his daughter first, then to his brother. Alf whispered something in his ear.

"Would he consent to this?" I asked Sveinn.

"The brothers are well known for their prowess. I doubt the king wants them as enemies."

Hjorvard cleared his throat while Yngvi listened to whatever Alf advised. "Come now, my king. Tell me swiftly the result of my errand."

I glanced to Hjalmar, who by now was gnashing his jaw. My blood brother looked to me, and I nodded back. My friend had to speak now, before it was too late.

With a return nod, Hjalmar strode forward again. "Lord king!" Yngvi turned to him. "Since I came to you, I have won great battles in your honor. I alone stood beside you against the draug. I have served well and brought you riches on many raids. Please, my king. Grant my request, and honor me with your daughter. You know my heart has always been set on her." Hjalmar pointed at the berserkir. "These men are famed, yes. But famed for their wickedness. They plunder the weak, rape everywhere they go, even in your own Realm. You cannot give Ingibjorg to a man such as this!"

At his words, the berserk brothers hurled back several angry shouts. Some reached for swords, axes. Yngvi and Alf's warriors responded in kind, rising from the table.

Yngvi sat a long time, staring first at Hjalmar, then at Hjorvard, and at last at his brother. He turned back to the center where the brothers and Hjalmar stood. "You are both great men. Hjalmar is correct—he has done me honor and served my family well. Hjorvard's fame and noble lineage have also reached us and I ... I could not refuse either alliance."

"My king?" Hjalmar asked.

Yngvi held up his hand. "No. In such a case, it is only fair to let Ingibjorg herself choose."

The princess's eyes widened, and her mouth worked wordlessly. Poor girl had probably never been asked to speak before such an assembly before. Women rarely were.

I guess you'd know.

Finally, Ingibjorg rose from her seat. Looking at Hjalmar. A very good sign. "You are very fair, Father. And I would rather have the man I know to be good than one of whom I know only tales ... many evil. I choose Hjalmar as my husband."

The gathered sons of Arngrim looked at one another. I could have sworn I felt their outrage, and several more put hands upon weapons.

Before any drew, Starkad stepped between the brothers and the kings.

Hjorvard looked to the champion, then to Hjalmar. The berserk spat. "I do not accept this man as my equal. I challenge you to face me in combat, Hjalmar. Face me in holmgang or be cursed by all you meet as an outcast. If you dare marry before meeting my challenge, you will be despised by all, and my father shall consider it an act of treachery against Bolmso."

Hjalmar stormed forward. "Naught will hold me back, berserk. But as the challenged party, I will name the time of our holmgang. Nine days from now, at *dawn*."

Good. He would not allow the berserk to fight in moonlight.

Hjorvard glowered. "Then I will name the place. The island of Samsey, where your people fear to tread. Do not think we have not heard how you sail around it, avoiding it as cowards. Come there, meet us if you have the souls of men."

Starkad opened his mouth, looking like he might object.

"I will be waiting for you," Hjalmar said. "Ready to cleave your head from your shoulders."

Hjorvard spat again, a gesture repeated by each of his eleven brothers in turn. With that, the sons of Arngrim stormed out of the hall. Evening was already upon them, but berserkir do not fear the mists as other men do.

Perhaps they were already Mist-mad.

When the doors had slammed shut, Starkad spun on Hjalmar. "Fool! Samsey falls under the domain of the Niflungar! Why do you think I counseled avoiding the place? Now you will go and risk their wrath, and for what?"

"For Ingibjorg!"

"You could have fought for her hand on any island."

I rose now, joining the others in the center. "I find it hard to trust these berserkir, and their choice of a dueling island worries me."

Yngvi shook his head. "Perhaps so, but the time and place is set. Hjalmar cannot back down now."

"Then I will take a crew with me," I said. "And we will make certain this is no trap and that these brothers intend to fight with honor."

"I will have no more part of this," Starkad snapped. He pushed past me, muttering about what men did for women. The man seemed young to be so jaded.

I did not yet know him as well as I do now.

I watched the champion go, thinking him a fool, then strode over to my blood brother. "Come. Let us eat and make plans. First for your battle, then for your wedding."

36

HERVOR

*A*nd so the duel had been set.

Except it wasn't a duel, for twelve men had died instead of one.

Hervor might have asked more, but Kiviuq came and dragged Orvar back to the whalebone arch, and finfolk beat and cut and mocked him.

Hervor watched, flinching at the worst of the blows. The man rarely cried out, and she had to give him credit for courage. And almost, she could understand him following his blood brother to Samsey.

Had it not ended with the death of her family.

Blood demanded blood.

And Tyrfing must have ... vengeance.

Eventually, the finfolk returned Orvar to her side and flung him down.

He struggled to rise until they bound him to a stake once again.

Hervor shook her head. "Odin's spear, man. Why didn't you just marry the damned seal already? Close your eyes, stick your cock in, and pretend it's a woman."

Orvar coughed, spat blood, and cast a weary glare her way. "And why haven't you, girl? As if you can't get on your hands and knees and take it. Or maybe for the same damn reason. You don't want to be forced into a marriage, much less agree to spend the rest of your life here. Give the marriage vow and that's an oath, yes?" He scoffed, then shook his head. "And it *would* be a woman, anyway."

"Oh?"

"Of course it would. Shifters are people possessed by Moon spirits."

Some few lived among men, true. But Hervor found such an idea hard to credit—that shifters might themselves be a kind of victim. Forced to live under the thrall of some vaettr. "Maybe you're just worried that, if you gave it to her good enough, she'd start barking like a seal."

He grumbled something under his breath. "You have a lot of anger in you, shieldmaiden."

"I think we've both got plenty enough to be angry about." She tugged on the sinews. They stretched but did not come close to breaking.

"Indeed. But slinging your petty insults won't get us out of this situation."

"No? And what would? Do you have a fucking army hidden away in your arsehole? Maybe you're owed a favor from Odin himself? At this point, I would settle for a damned knife. But you've got naught but troll shit. If you did, you'd have freed yourself already."

Orvar shifted against the post, groaning in plain discomfort. "I have *you*."

Not likely.

"I was thinking while they beat me. If we work together, we might be able to slip away, steal one of those boats."

What a lovely thought. "How?"

"We'd have to put them off their guard. Here, in the middle of the village, everything is against us. But if we agreed to wed them—"

"Like Hel."

"Hear me out. We agree to wed them. One of the ones who understood some Northern told me they have a sacred place, like a temple, where the weddings are held. Maybe we'd have more chance to break free from there than from here."

She spat. "Or maybe we'd find ourselves being fucked by wereseals. You may be that desperate for some release, but I'm not."

"I'd say you could use some."

Now she spat *at* him.

The phlegm landed well short, and Arrow's Point scowled at her. "You're naught but a spoiled child. This may be our only chance, and I find your anger toward me sadly misdirected."

If he only knew. The words bubbled on her tongue, as ready to explode as if from one of those geysers.

Arrow's Point: murderer, slayer of all the sons of Arngrim.

The very man who had destroyed her house, her legacy. And there he sat, watching her, oblivious to his own guilt. Not knowing he faced down the very woman who would crush him and send his soul screaming down to Hel.

She clenched her jaw. He ought to know. But if she told him, he would be more on his guard. More prepared for her. She would still find her moment to strike. She had to.

"Tell me," she said, unable to bite back the words, "did you betray the sons of Arngrim?"

He scoffed. "Because you think I'd betray you, girl? For Odin's sake, no! I betrayed no one. We ... we came to Samsey.

The longship anchored only a few dozen feet offshore, but the mist around Samsey obscured the whole of the island. So much so, I almost found myself wondering if we had really arrived at land at all. Frey alone knew what kind of creature or vaettr lived in such a Hel-cursed place. But the berserkir had insisted on the place so, we went there."

"Sometimes honor demands we act against our better judgment."

"Right you are. And I did."

37

ORVAR

*M*utters spread among the crew, words like troll or draugar bandied about. Even jotunn. I thought the latter unlikely. Such monstrosities were said to lay in Utgard, beyond the protection of the Midgard Wall, and very few came past the wall. That, at least, I felt confident about. The men though had begun to whisper prayers to the Vanir or the Aesir, depending on their wont.

Torch in hand, Hjalmar moved up beside me. "Shall we?"

Jotunnar aside, the place suited me little. "Perhaps it's best if we scout this place ourselves, leave the others to ensure our ship remains secure. Even if the brothers have laid no traps, Samsey has an ill-repute and a worse feeling to it." Aught that frightened Starkad ought to leave other men fleeing as fast as they could.

But my blood brother could not well back down from the challenge now. No, we were committed.

"As you wish." Hjalmar leapt over the gunwale and landed in the sea up to his waist.

I followed. The waters were freezing, colder than any lake, even in summer. I could not quite stifle my gasp.

"That'll wake you up," Hjalmar said.

I snorted, best I could with my stones freezing off. We waded over to the beach.

Gods, the mist was so thick I could barely see five feet out. I pulled another torch from my belt, then lit it off Hjalmar's. Best we both carried one in a place like this.

"I doubt that Hjorvard's ever been here."

I grunted in agreement. Not even a berserk would have chosen this place, had he known. At least I would think not. Berserkir were half vaettr themselves, but still. This place looked like some vision of Niflheim.

Hjalmar set out, waving the torch in front of him. I followed a few steps behind, constantly checking our flanks. I could not well use my bow while holding a torch. If we came upon aught out here, we'd need swords, and we'd have very little warning. It was tempting to draw immediately, but we might have been there hours, and even that slight deadening of my arm from fatigue could slow me, cost me my life.

"I do not care for this place," I said.

"Look," Hjalmar pointed at hills barely visible through the mist. "Is that ice? Has it not melted?"

No it hadn't, not even in summer. Indeed, an unnatural chill had settled over this island, like winter had loosened its grip but refused to depart entirely, even for a few moons.

We walked a long time, the ground beginning to slope upward. As it did so, the ice grew more prevalent and our steps became more difficult, slower. I hadn't packed crampons or aught else for climbing on ice. Hadn't thought to need it in summer.

"Eightarms said this place is claimed by sorcerers," Hjalmar said.

Yes. And some of the other warriors had disdained him for it. Men like Sveinn, brave enough, but now remaining on the ship. Leaving Hjalmar and I to explore this place.

We turned aside from the icy slopes.

If the berserk brothers had laid any trap, it would not be up in the hills or frozen mountains. And any dangers lurking there were best left alone, unwoken.

In truth, though, it was not the dangers of the island that undid us, but those of the berserkir.

For we did not betray them.

They betrayed us.

A thick forest covered the lower shores of Samsey, and we searched it several hours without sign of life save for a few ravens here and there. If there were ravens, there must be food for them, but I saw no game.

Dawn had drawn nigh as we returned from the forest back toward the ship.

"Are you prepared?" I asked. "You had no sleep in the night."

Hjalmar snorted. "Could you sleep the night before you were to duel a berserk?"

Not a chance—not even a duel against a man. A man's blood boiled too hot on such nights, and there was no cooling it for sleep.

A great howling rang over the island as the sun began to rise. Many voices raised in a battle cry that seemed more bestial than human. I exchanged a glance with Hjalmar, then we both knelt in the forest. That sound had come from the ship.

We crept forward until we could see the edge of the shore. Screaming men leapt over the gunwale and waded ashore, many of them. All had swords and axes drawn, visible because one of them shone like a ray of sunlight. That one illuminated the face of the eldest of the berserk brothers, Angantyr.

No one moved on Hjalmar's ship. The brothers had slaughtered every last warrior and sailor, then come ashore, laughing, panting, and coated in blood.

All our men, our friends, allies.

All dead.

And us, alone against the twelve berserkir hunting us.

38

STARKAD

*T*he tunnel opened into a great cavern where the roof vanished into shadow and countless pits dropped into chasms far below. There, nestled between stalagmites and crevices, rose blocky stone buildings, each probably home to a family of dvergar.

Starkad crouched at the threshold, looking for a way in.

Battlements crested not only the houses, but towers spread through the city. Arching bridges connected these rooftops and towers, creating a lattice-way of paths from which archers could rain death down on would-be attackers.

A river encircled half the city, one sent into tumultuous rapids by numerous rocks spread around it. This left few approaches to the dvergar save for the tunnel he'd just come from.

None of those defenses seemed to have saved Nordri.

No dvergar walked the streets. No, but neither were those shadowed paths empty. Numerous pairs of glowing red eyes lurked in darkness, patrolled ancient byways, or stood watch atop those towers.

Starkad knelt at the tunnel's exit, not quite certain where to go.

At the city's heart rose a circular palace, each tier slightly smaller than the one below, creating the appearance of steps. Atop that palace stood a statue of a dverg. If he could see it from here, it must have stood thirty feet tall or more.

The palace would hold the great dverg vaults, for certain, yes. But how to reach it? If they brought torches into the city, the watchful draugar would spot them with ease. The mist had not seeped this deep underground, so they could breathe without fire's blessing. They could not, however, see in the dark. Not like a draug or dverg could.

"Ideas?" he whispered to Bragi.

The skald rubbed his beard. "Make an offering to Odin, and pray for aid."

"Useful ideas?"

The rubbing continued. "Keep just one torch, low to the ground, and stay hunched over it. If we stick to the lower paths, maybe they won't be able to spot the light."

Tiny extinguished his torch and drew his sword. "We do that, we walk among the thickest of them."

"We can't fight them all," Starkad said. "And we've come too far to go home empty handed." Moreover, on Nordri's very threshold, he would not be denied. He would look on the fallen wonder of the once-great kingdom. "Afzal, keep your torch as Bragi has said. Bluefoot, you stick close to him and help shield the light. Tiny and I will go first, blades ready. Don't fall too far behind, and don't get too close either."

Starkad drew his own blades, then traded glances with Tiny. The big man nodded grimly. They might not all walk out of here, and they both knew it. But anyone who did make it ... dverg gold would change his life forever.

In a crouch, he crept forward, a few feet ahead of Tiny. He trusted his own stealth more than that of the giant back there. Tiny was useful once they were *already* discovered. And useful if he wanted to be discovered. Otherwise, less than ideal. For that matter, they were lucky Ivar the Loud wasn't with them. The man would have no doubt announced their whole party to the draugar.

Starkad grimaced. No. They weren't lucky he was dead. He'd been a nasty arse with a foul mouth, but no worse than the rest of them for all that.

He pushed into an alley and crept along until it connected with a main street.

Scuffling footsteps sounded from that main byway. Blades hovering a hair off the ground, Starkad slipped forward more. Just another step. A draug shambled by, dragging a maul behind it—a hammer big enough to crush a troll's skull. Or to turn a man into a bloody puddle.

Starkad waited for the draug to pass, then rose, dead silent. He fell into step behind the draug, timing his footsteps to its shuffle to disguise their sound. When he drew close enough, he slashed with both swords. The draug's head flew clean off. It twisted, writhing. The hammer flew into the air, kicking up dust as the creature spun with it. Starkad dropped to his knees and let maul soar over his head. The draug's clumsy attack had spun it around so he was behind it again.

Starkad thrust both swords up, each punching through a lung—or where a lung would have been if they had not rotted away.

The draug wiggled soundlessly on the blades, unable to shriek out fury or warning without a head.

Tiny stepped up and lopped off each of its arms, then

Starkad flung it down, off his blades. It landed on the hard stone and flopped around there.

"How do we kill it?" Tiny asked.

The severed hands had begun to crawl toward them, using fingers like climbing picks. Ever closer, as though it would strangle them itself. Afzal jerked a hand to his mouth, muttering in his Serklander language.

"Only fire would do it for sure," Starkad said. "And we cannot afford to get their attention with that. Move, steer wide of it."

They pushed on through the city, pausing several times to let groups of one, two, once even three draugar pass. The creatures seemed wakeful, tireless, though not overly alert. They must not yet know Men tread among them. If they learned of it, their numbers would let them box in Starkad and his party. One misstep, one premature turn, and they would face an army of the dead keen for their blood. The thought of it sent his pulse racing. These moments were what he lived for.

Darting from one alley to the next, they came to face the grand spire palace. The heart of Nordri, the former home of a dverg prince. Like all vaettir, the dvergar were invaders, corrupting Midgard. No doubt Mankind would have fared better had all vaettir left them in peace. But they had come here, so he might as well claim what he could of their spoils.

A pair of draugar stood on either side of the massive archway leading inside the spire. The doorway was so tall a man three times his height could have walked through without stooping, and each side of the arch was worked into an intricate design, like a dragon coiling around the whole entrance. No doors, just the two guards. And a wide-open space of two dozen feet between the alley and the draugar.

Starkad was fast on his feet. Very fast. But probably not

so fast he could close the distance to the two draugar and kill them both before either one raised the alarm. And then he'd have draugar climbing over one another trying to reach him and his people.

They were so close.

Afzal tapped him on the shoulder, then pointed up at the spire palace. Each tier above the first had a balcony where the inhabitant could walk the walls. A balcony meant an entrance. The problem was the lowest balcony was probably twenty feet up, and those dvergar-worked walls would be smooth as silk. No climbing them.

He looked back at Afzal, who now pantomimed pushing up with his palms. Lift someone to the ledge. Huh.

Starkad beckoned the party back down the alley, and around, so they could approach the palace from the rear. With no sign of approaching patrols, they ran for the palace wall.

"Tiny's the biggest," Afzal whispered. "He can lift you."

"What's the boy on about?"

Starkad glanced around. If they were doing this, they needed to do it fast. "Brace yourself against the wall, then lift me onto your shoulders. Then I'll lift Afzal until he can reach the ledge. Afzal, you scramble up there and lower a rope down."

"Did you eat troll shit for the day meal? You think I'm lifting the both of you?"

"Now!" Starkad spat through gritted teeth. "Before they see us all."

Grumbling, Tiny did brace, then set his hands, fingers locked together. Starkad sheathed his swords and used the step to climb atop Tiny's broad shoulders. The man grunted and growled as Starkad set his feet and turned.

"Hurry up, you troll lover," Tiny said to Afzal.

The Serklander next stepped into Tiny's laced fingers. Tiny vaulted him up to where he could step into Starkad's. Tiny gasped, grunting at the weight as Afzal climbed onto Starkad's shoulders. From there, the boy leaned back just a little. Starkad grabbed his ankles, trying to steady him.

"I've got it," the Serklander said. "Help me."

Starkad pushed up on his ankles, and suddenly the weight lessened. He glanced up. Afzal had himself supported under his arms. An instant later, he rolled over the lip of the balcony.

"How about you get off of me, you oaf," Tiny said.

Starkad did jump down, even as Afzal threw a rope over the edge. He looked up. "Are you braced against the side?"

"Yes." The boy's whisper came out in a hiss that might have been fatigue or fear. Probably both.

Starkad grabbed the rope and began to climb up, hand over hand. It took longer than he'd have liked. He was tired, he supposed. He reached the lip and rolled over. Then he took the rope from Afzal. "Tiny, get up here. Bragi, take cover in the shadows."

"No way," the skald snapped. "I'm getting my share."

"Fine. Tiny comes up first."

Tiny began to climb. Even with his feet braced against the balcony's edge, the weight of it threatened to rip the rope from Starkad's hands. Behind him, Afzal grabbed the end to lend support, slightly easing the burden.

Once Tiny was up, pulling up Bragi proved an easy enough task.

"We still have to watch ourselves," Starkad said. "Find the riches, take what you can, and get out. And keep your voices down."

With that, he pushed forward, following the wall until it led to an opening. The outer balcony was mirrored by an inner balcony looking down on a landing in the first floor. A winding staircase led up to this balcony and onto the floor above.

A mortal king would have hidden his greatest riches in the tower. But the dvergar were creatures of earth, stone. Maybe they would go down. Starkad peered over the side. In the center of the room sat a pair of low thrones on a raised dais. This was a great hall. A single draug reclined against the back of one of those thrones. Guarding something?

Starkad pointed the creature out, then stalked over to the stairs. The others followed close behind. He crept down, moving a few steps at a time, then checking to see no draugar had moved. Not those guarding the front door nearby, nor the one behind the thrones. He motioned for the others to remain on the stairs, then continued down.

He descended a few steps, then paused. Checked.

His racing heart sent his pulse pounding in his ears. Starkad had not felt this alive in a long time. Perhaps Thule was cursed, perhaps the mists had come from here. Either way, it proved the most extreme reaches of Midgard. And that meant only the greatest men in history could survive it.

He wanted to be one of those men.

He would be one.

He edged forward. Ever forward.

The draug lived—so to speak. Starkad had seen the gleam of its eyes from up on the balcony. So it was at least wakeful, watching. Perhaps watching either side of the dais for sign of an enemy approach. The sides, yes. But above?

Starkad slipped onto the front of the dais, then—careful to make no sound—onto the stone chair of the fallen dvergar king. He climbed onto the back of that chair and peered down at the draug. It didn't move. Watching for foes from the wrong direction. Starkad would almost have felt sorry for it … were it not an abomination of the natural order of life.

Sword in hand, he leapt off the throne and plunged his blade straight down into the draug as he fell. The clang of metal on metal rang out as his weapon scored armor. Starkad jerked his sword free, tearing out ribs and flesh in the process. Then he cleaved into the draug's skull to be certain it lay still. As with the others, it continued to writhe. Dead already, it could not die, save in flame. But headless and impaled, it posed a bit less of a threat.

Starkad looked to the main entrance. No draugar came rushing for him. They hadn't heard his little scuffle. He supposed he was due a little luck, after all.

He motioned to the others to join him, then knelt before the area the draug had guarded.

He ran his fingers along the stone. The seam was so fine you couldn't even see it, but he felt it. A block that did not quite belong with the mold of the rest of the floor. He pushed on the slab. It didn't move.

There had to be some way to open this.

"Check the thrones," he whispered when Afzal neared.

The boy did so, running his hand over one throne while Bragi examined the other.

"What is it?" Tiny asked.

"The vault, I think."

"You think? After what we just went through—"

"It's my first lost dverg city. Now stop whining and help."

Tiny grunted, then began pushing and prying on the floor. "Gold so close I can taste it. And here this big fucking rock is in the way."

"Try tasting the rock," Bragi offered.

"Is this …?" Afzal began. A slight click came from the throne he inspected.

Without further warning, stone began to grate on stone. Tiny scrambled off the slab as it began to slide into a hidden alcove beneath the floor. This opened up a pit with a short staircase leading to the base of it. The roof here was smaller than a man's height. Even Afzal would have to stoop to walk here.

Starkad leapt down into the pit. His feet skidded on something. "Afzal. Torch."

The boy tossed the flame into the pit. Immediately, the whole tunnel began to glitter. Gold and silver coins ran the length of the space. In their midst sat gem-encrusted goblets, dverg-wrought blades, gilded chain fit for a king. There were emeralds and rubies and lapis lazuli and opals. Enough gems to buy a kingdom.

"Thor's thundering cock," Tiny said when he looked down.

"We have reached the Otherworld," Afzal said.

Bragi snorted and jumped down into the now crowded tunnel. "Nope, boy. Just the best of this one."

Starkad pressed on, back into the tunnel, to examine the gilded mail. From what he knew of dverg work, they made naught without practical use, so he had to assume—appearances aside—the armor would turn a blow. Maybe as well as Orvar's famed magic shirt. He lifted the chain to inspect it, admiring the way the light glittered off it. Not the most practical for stealth, perhaps. But certainly elegant.

Coins and gemstones clattered as he tugged the mail free of them. As they did, they exposed a hand. Taut flesh failed to fully cover the skeletal fingers beneath it. That hand flexed.

Another draug here, in the vault.

"Back!" Starkad barked.

The others grumbled, then saw what he saw and ceased filling their satchels with plunder.

Starkad had taken a few steps back. The tunnel was too tight to properly wield his blades. They needed to face this creature out in the open. "Up the ladder! Out of the pit, now!"

A sword burst free from the treasure hoard, scattering priceless wealth as it rose. A series of runes ran the length of the blade, each radiating a faint iridescent light. A pit opened in Starkad's stomach.

This was not just a blade.

It was one of the nine runeblades. And that meant its owner was no ordinary draug.

Afzal had already scrambled back up the ladder with the torch. Starkad shoved Bragi toward it, then began pulling himself straight up the wall. It wasn't so tall, after all. Seeing his reaction, Tiny did the same. They crested the ground level just before the draug finished freeing itself from its hoard.

The creature's eyes glowed red, like any draug. And yet, a bluish flame seemed to waft off its head and spread from its mouth. It bore a crown around its helm, one set with a gleaming ruby reflecting the same unholy light as its eyes.

Starkad jerked both swords free.

"Go! Take out the ones guarding the entrance and find a way out of here."

Tiny stood shoulder to shoulder with him, broadsword in hand. "We can take one more."

As it stepped from the pit, the draug rose to its full height, at least as tall as Tiny. It looked to each of the party. And it continued to grow. Its mass rippled outward, its armor inexplicably growing with it. Those indigo flames only intensified as the draug grew.

Starkad fell back a step. And another.

In the back of his mind, he knew Afzal and Bragi had broken, run for the entrance as he'd told them. The fiend had now grown to twice Tiny's size. It was not a mere draug. It was a dark god of the dead, fit to challenge a jotunn. They had awoken some ancient power that ought to have been left sleeping. Perhaps the very reason the Niflungar had not come here to try and claim this runeblade for themselves.

Starkad had wanted a challenge. He'd wanted to know who was the best.

But if he fought this fiend now, fought and lost, his people would die. Without him to protect them, their deaths were nigh to assured. He swallowed. "Tiny, go. Help them!"

The big man made no further objection, turning and running for the exit.

The draug plodded toward Starkad with great lunging strides.

The runeblade—it had grown too, hadn't it—hefted above its head. A shield big as Starkad was protected the monster. At the last moment, Starkad dove forward, rolling between the draug's legs. The runeblade sheared into the floor and gouged a great swathe of stone.

Starkad rose and swung at the draug's legs. His sword clanked off a chain greave. He dared not remain, instead immediately leaping away again. Even as he did so, the draug spun on him, slamming the edge of its shield into the floor where Starkad had stood a breath before.

Without looking back, Starkad scrambled to his feet and made a break for the entrance. Tiny and Bragi had already felled the two draugar there and were waiting for him, beckoning him forward. And that entrance was so tall even the giant draug could pass through. Wonderful.

Great crashing footfalls rang out behind him. It would

overtake him in a few strides. Now he did look back, just in time to see the runeblade sweeping down on him. Starkad skidded to a stop and fell over backward, sliding just under the blade's arc.

He scrambled forward, helped up by Tiny's swift grab. The big man shoved him out of the palace, and they all dashed for an alley.

A bellow erupted from behind them, a sound like all the damned of Niflheim shrieking in agony. It went on and on. Starkad passed into the alley, then guided his men around it and around another. Running blind, just to keep that thing from spotting them, from tracking them.

A draug voice answered the hellish scream with a mind-rending shriek of its own. Another and another draugar joined that profane chorus, until the whole city echoed with it. Hundreds of them, no doubt.

All screaming for the blood of men.

All hailing the wakening of their king.

39

HERVOR

*A*fter another round of beatings, the finfolk threw Hervor into an ice hut beside Orvar.

She groaned, then rolled over to look at him where he sat.

Everything hurt.

Her eyes burned. Her muscles ached. Breathing was agony.

Her godsdamned *hair* hurt.

"Listen, girl. I've been thinking … we need to agree to this. We have to say we'll marry them without actually giving an oath." He paused a moment, clearly in pain himself. "And we need to get them to bring us both at once."

Hervor groaned again, not bothering to sit up. "Why would they do that?"

He shrugged. "Tell them you won't marry unless it's a joint wedding."

"Because that's not fucking suspicious."

"So tell them I'm your father, and you won't be wed until you see me wed first."

"My fa—" She snapped her jaw closed. Her father? Her

father! This monstrous, murderous, trollfucking bastard who had helped *kill* her father. And he wanted her to claim him as such! She could barely form the words through her clenched teeth. "It would dishonor my actual father to claim another as such."

Orvar grunted in acknowledgment, then sighed. "Perhaps. But a reasonable man will understand the extreme circumstances. Sometimes a lie is the only chance."

She stifled a bitter laugh at that. Of all the tales she'd heard of Angantyr, all the ways her father was described, reasonable had never made the list. And this man had left him to burn in agony, writhing in torment until the end of time, had Hervor not come and claimed Tyrfing. Her father's ghost might no longer burn, but still it writhed. Maybe watching her, even now, waiting upon the fulfillment of her oath. That was his only hope, no doubt his sole solace.

And if one more lie—no matter how vile—was her only chance at fulfilling her oath, then she would lie. She had done worse. Would yet do far worse, if it meant avenging her family.

She sighed. "Very well. I will agree to the wedding on your conditions. What's your plan?"

He grimaced. "We do not know aught about the temple or their ceremonies. I don't have a plan, save to look for an opportunity and seize it."

Not elegant. But then, such was most often Hervor's plan as well. After all, she was still seeking the opportunity to cut Arrow's Point down.

And soon, she would find it. And she *would* seize it.

THE FINFOLK FERRIED them over the sea in those long, narrow boats of theirs. Behind Troll Rock rose a temple carved from ice, looking much like a hollowed-out iceberg with a peak carved into a spiral.

Hervor had never seen aught like it. Glorious and ominous, jutting from the sea.

The moon had risen. A full moon. For these shifters, that was probably an auspicious time. Many seals lounged about on the iceberg's surface, some even within the temple. A few stood in human form in there, wrapped in those heavy fur coats.

Orvar had a hand inside his coat. The man had worked off a piece of whalebone and turned it into a shiv and had assured Hervor this would work.

Problem was, shifters didn't die easy. Naught possessed by a vaettr did, but shifters were especially resilient. On the other hand, maybe she didn't need them to die. Just to fall into chaos. That might let her reclaim Tyrfing and maybe even strike down Orvar in the process.

The boats bumped the iceberg, and one of the finfolk grabbed her by the shoulders and yanked her onto the ice surface. Another did the same to Orvar, and he stumbled, no doubt still weak from the beatings and cold.

He looked to her. She feigned a slight smile. Bastard.

They had to duck to pass through the entrance of the temple, though the interior rose ten feet above her head. Inside, Kiviuq smiled at her like he was pleased—like she ought to welcome the forced union. Hervor inclined her head to the finfolk, forcing the hint of a smile as well.

Who could say where the beast ended and the man began? Orvar claimed they were people. If so, it meant forcing a marriage was all the more despicable.

Norns wove a crooked and cruel urd for men and

women. They alone had such a right. For anyone else, stealing freedom of choice made you no better than any other thief. Worse, maybe, since choice counted for more than worldly goods.

Hervor chuckled under her breath. Then again, she'd stolen plenty and taken more lives than she could count.

None of the finfolk had brought weapons to the temple. Perhaps it would have profaned this ritual. They worshipped the moon, clearly.

A hole in the iceberg's peak allowed moonlight to pass inside, reflecting off the ice. Beside Kiviuq and Orvar's woman stood another man. A priest perhaps. The priest raised his arms into the moonlight, staring up at it and chanting in their strange language.

"Aningan," he said, and all the gathered finfolk repeated the word several times. The name of the moon?

The man who had brought them began to guide them toward their would-be spouses.

Orvar offered Hervor the slightest incline of his head. Then the man jerked free the shiv and jabbed it between the ribs of their guide.

The finfolk doubled over in pain. Hervor reacted instantly, grabbing the man by his hood and flinging him in the midst of the temple. Shouts of chaos went up at once, but Hervor was already running, ducking her head back out of the temple.

The seals outside stared at them, clearly not certain what had just happened. Hervor jumped in the boat an instant before Orvar leapt into the other one.

"Go!" she shouted, shoving her boat away from the iceberg with one oar.

And he set to paddling away from the rock, down south.

Hervor, however, began to paddle back toward the village.

There was something she needed even more than freedom.

"What in Hel's name are you doing?" Orvar shouted at her.

"I'm not leaving without my father's sword!"

"Odin's spear, girl! Your father will understand!"

Hervor ignored the murderous bastard. Oh, she'd have something for him, soon enough.

"Hervor!"

"Go to Hel!"

She continued toward the village, only a very short distance from Troll Rock, sparing a glance behind her. The seals had already begun to dive into the sea. The human form finfolk were shedding their clothes, preparing to do the same. Orvar too started after her.

Even better.

She rammed her boat right up on the shore, leapt out, and started running into the heart of the village.

Orvar's boat would hit the ice in a moment. Hervor dashed toward Kiviuq's hut. All the finfolk had gone to the ceremony, leaving the village in eerie emptiness. The angry barks of seals drawing closer meant it would not stay that way long.

She ducked inside the hut, easily spotting the sword leaning against one wall, then crawled over and grabbed it. As she came back out, naked and screaming finfolk rushed toward them.

Hervor jerked her blade free from its sheath, and it gleamed like a ray of sunlight. She sliced through the attacking finfolk with a single mighty blow that opened him up from his neck to hip. He fell. A small army more was closing in, though.

"Run!" Orvar shouted and raced out of the village.

Oh. Damn it.

Hervor chased after him, not sheathing Tyrfing.

Orvar cast a glance back at her, at the sword. His eyes widened like he'd finally realized. Finally.

"Your father's sword?" he shouted back at her.

Hervor screamed in fury like a woman possessed and lunged forward, swinging at him.

Orvar skidded on ice, dropped to one knee, and rolled under the blow.

Hervor spun, swinging again. "For my father!"

Orvar rolled away, unable to claim his feet. "Stop. We have no time!"

She paid him no heed, slashing and thrusting while Orvar fell back. He clearly knew a single touch would end him.

"Daughter of Angantyr!" he shouted at her. "I did not kill your father."

Now she panted, advancing with a steadier pace. An executioner moving toward the condemned. This bastard would die. "You killed my uncles. You damned them all to eternal torment. I owe you twelve deaths, though I can dole out only one."

By now, the finfolk had caught up to them and moved to surround them. Hervor glanced at them but continued to advance on Orvar. Naught else mattered more.

"You cost us everything!" Orvar said.

Hervor cocked her head toward Kiviuq. The finfolk man's glare ought to have melted all the ice on Thule. She didn't care.

"You were right," Hervor said. "I *can* let a wereseal fuck me—if it means getting my revenge."

"You're Mist-mad, girl."

The female finfolk, Naliajuk, stepped forward, forestalling Kiviuq. "No. No blade. No fight."

Hervor pointed Tyrfing at the woman. "Stay out of this or you'll be next, bitch. Arrow's Point dies this night."

Glowering, Naliajuk raised one of those corded weapons above her head and began to twirl it. Other finfolk did the same.

Oh damn it. Not now. Not this close.

She roared and charged Orvar. He dove to the side, amidst the finfolk.

And then Naliajuk flung the weapon. The cords wrapped around Hervor's legs and sent her stumbling down to the ice. Tyrfing slipped from her grasp and skidded along the ground for several feet.

"Bastard!" Hervor shouted at Orvar.

The man tried to rise, but Kiviuq grabbed him by his coat, yanking him off the ground. The wereseal held him eye to eye for a brief instant. And then he cuffed him on the side of the head.

Hervor wanted to relish it, until Naliajuk began raining such blows upon her as well.

A barrage of them that went on and on until darkness finally enveloped her.

40

STARKAD

*T*he shuffling gait of draugar boots filled nigh to every street in Nordri, the sound occasionally overshadowed by the thundering footsteps of the giant draug king. Starkad and the others crouched in an alley at the city's edge, watching a patrol of five draugar amble by. They might have been able to ambush the patrol, take them down. More like than not, though, the noise of battle would draw others. And far too many draugar clogged these unholy streets for Starkad's small party to overcome, saying naught of the king himself.

No, they could not fight. And the draugar knew they must have come from the main entrance, and so they now patrolled the thickest around it. Starkad had scouted that alone, searching for any way through. None presented itself, no matter how long he looked.

And so they had skirted the edge of Nordri, hunting for any other way out. It was hard to be certain in the darkness, but it looked like other tunnels did run out of the main cavern. Unfortunately, those all lay on the far side of a freezing river.

Maybe the dvergar had once used boats to cross, but if so, none remained now.

When the patrol had turned a corner, Starkad scampered forward, keeping low to the ground until he reached the next alley. The last such refuge before the open rocks in front of the river. The others dashed after him, Afzal creeping closest behind.

"Master?"

Starkad stared at the river. Numerous rocks jutting out of the water turned the river into icy rapids so swift even a draug would face destruction, smashed to pieces under that force.

"Planning to fly?" Bragi asked.

Starkad scowled at him, then shook his head. Desperation made even good men arseholes. "Those rocks look just close enough together a man might jump from one to the next."

Bragi's mouth dropped open, and he sputtered a few times before he spoke. "You got troll shit between your ears? Ice and water coat every one of those rocks. You'll break your ankle on the first one and find yourself swimming for just long enough to die of deathchill."

The skald had a point. It would prove difficult, especially for an old man like him. But Starkad had no alternative to offer. "The choice is yours, Bluefoot. All of you. Take your chances against an army of draugar—out in the open where they can surround you—or balance on the rocks and find another way out of Nordri." He rubbed his face. He was chilled, starving, his eyes wanting to close on their own. The others probably fared even worse. "We can't stay here. If we fight, maybe valkyries will carry our souls to Valhalla." Starkad had his doubts such a place even existed. He preferred fights with a chance of victory. "Or try the river and at least a hope of life."

"I'm for trying the rocks," Tiny said. "Let the dead alone to rot."

Afzal nodded at the big man's words.

It was decided then. And they all looked to him. Hardly a surprise. Starkad glanced up at the nearby buildings and the bridges that connected them. No patrols. Now or never then.

He scrambled to the river's edge and leapt out to the nearest rock, three feet from shore. As Bragi predicted, his foot slipped on the slick surface, and his knee slammed down onto the ice. That hit jolted him like a bolt of tiny lightning. He managed to throw his arms around the rock's point. His effort kept him from plunging into the river, save for one foot. Stifling a groan, he scrambled properly onto the rock and rubbed his knee. They were looking at him, of course.

He nodded to them in reassurance. "It's easy."

The next rock was a bit closer but angled away from him. And he'd have to make a standing jump. Swinging his arms back and forth, he built some momentum. Then he jumped forward. He landed on the surface, and his feet skidded along it, nigh to tossing him into the river once again. Arms wide he caught himself, flailed, then immediately jumped to the next surface before he could fall. This one was bigger, sticking up like a swollen knuckle. He wrapped his arms around it, turned to the others, and beckoned them on.

Afzal came next, making that first jump with a bit more grace than Starkad had. Of course, he'd seen the danger and could prepare for it. Obviously. Starkad held up a hand to stall him there.

He hadn't been able to stand on the next platform, and neither would Afzal. Which meant Starkad needed to be clear of this one. Unfortunately, Bragi held their torch on the backside of the river. Starkad could barely make out the next rock, much less be certain of his footing. He had convinced them to try this way, though, so he had to see it through.

He leapt once again. This time he landed on a low rock, fell to his knees, and skidded forward. He scrambled to his feet. There, the far side of the river—maybe six feet out. Making a standing jump as far as he was tall didn't seem practical. That meant he'd need to run on this icy platform. Marginally less suicidal than taking on an army of draugar.

Marginally.

Grunts behind him told him Afzal was already making the next jumps.

So.

Time to do this.

Starkad backed up to the edge of the rock. Deep breaths. Always had to keep one eye on where you wanted to land and one on the ground before you. Good. He could do this. He'd made farther jumps than this.

Three running strides forward and he flew through the air, cleared the gap with room to spare. He landed in a roll, banging himself up on solid ice. That would leave a bruise.

But this led to another ice cave. From what he knew of dvergar, they always had another way out of their homes. They'd never let themselves get trapped or pinned. So multiple ice caves must have led down to Nordri.

Afzal made the last jump, falling just short. His feet pitched into the water.

Starkad lunged at him, caught his wrists, and jerked him ashore. "We'll warm ourselves by a fire soon."

The Serklander nodded and clapped Starkad on the arm in thanks.

Tiny was making his way closer, and Bragi too, bearing their light.

A twang sounded, barely audible over the rushing river. Bragi, standing on the first rock, jerked. Then he pitched forward, an arrow jutting from his back. He seemed to fall with agonizing slowness. Starkad's mouth opened to shout in a warning that came far too late or in denial.

The skald fell into the river.

His torch went out, leaving them in darkness.

Absolute darkness, save the pinpoints of red light across the river. Tiny, glowing eyes. More and more of them.

"Thor's thundering cock!" Tiny bellowed, standing on some rock in the middle of the river.

Starkad dropped to his knees, fishing blindly through his satchel for another torch. "Get down, Tiny! Low! They can still see you!"

Where was it? Where was the damn—there! He pulled the torch and then his flint and steel. Clank.

A spark.

No flame.

Spark. Spark.

"Fucking do something!" Tiny shouted.

"Be quiet," Afzal snapped. The Serklander's voice came from low to the ground. Smart man, staying down. Not so smart staying nigh to where Starkad tried to light a torch though.

Spark.

Twang.

The sound of a shaft hitting ice.

"Troll shit!" Tiny shouted. "I have to jump."

Spark.

"Not in the dark, you imbecile!" Starkad shouted at him.

Spark.

Twang.

"Gah!"

A spark caught on the oil-soaked rag around the torch. Flames sprang up.

"Stay down," Starkad said to Afzal, while himself rising and moving away from the Serklander. Standing, he gave Tiny more light. And made himself a better target. Maybe he should have taken the time to wear that gilded dverg chain.

An arrow whooshed by him.

Tiny leapt and leapt again, landing on the shore beside Afzal. Blood was trailing down his arm. The Serklander grabbed him and jerked him up.

Twang.

Starkad jumped back an instant before an arrow struck where he had stood. He raced for the ice tunnel, not bothering to order the others to follow. They would follow. They all wanted out of here. So had Bragi Bluefoot. The man had fastened his name by plunging into frozen waters. And now he had ended the same way.

Poor bastard.

Another shot clattered against ice behind them, but they were out of range. Still, the draugar knew where they had gone. Sooner or later, they'd find a way across. Starkad ran on and on, pushing past exhaustion and fatigue.

He could do naught for Bragi. Just one more friend dead, one more ally he'd failed to protect.

Giant slabs of ice narrowed the cave, forcing them to squeeze through one at a time. No worked ice, this. The dvergar must have simply taken advantage of the terrain they'd found.

Past the ice slabs, Starkad climbed steeply upward until light beckoned ahead.

Real light. Not the flicker of a dying torch refracted off ice facets.

Lungs burning, Starkad pushed onward. A little more. Just a little farther.

The cave opened out not far from the shore. In daylight. The mist had thinned, revealing a glimmer of the sun, and a dusting snowfall. Starkad stumbled several more paces before collapsing in the snow. The others did the same.

He glanced back at the cave. Daylight would buy them time. A little time. But they didn't know how long since the sun had risen, and it would last at most maybe four hours. Probably less.

A thin strip of land led to a mountain rising up out of the sea. Steep, which probably meant treacherous, narrow passes. In narrow passes, numbers amounted to a lot less, and he could hold his ground against a great many foes.

"Get up!" he struggled to follow his own advice. "Get up, make for the mountain."

"Master," Afzal complained. "Please. A little rest."

"We cannot afford it."

The Serklander groaned but did rise, stumbling in the process. "Then let us make for the ship."

Starkad glanced at the shore. Based on the sun, it ran east to west, and their ship lay south. They might follow the coast to the ship, but it could take days. "We wouldn't make it. They'd be all over us long before we got there."

Tiny pushed himself up and started walking toward the mountain.

"What hope is up there?" Afzal said.

At that, Tiny glanced back at him. "Don't you get it, boy? The mountain is the only hope we have left. The hope for a glorious last stand. This is the last time you'll see the sun. Tomorrow, you'll be dining at the table of Hel or else in Valhalla, feasting and fucking valkyries if you're lucky and brave. I am for the latter urd."

Afzal looked to Starkad as if hoping he would contradict the big man. But he couldn't. Tiny had the truth of it. Moreover, Starkad doubted Valhalla existed. Hel, though, everyone knew she was real. And she was sending her vile servants after all of them.

41

HERVOR

*T*he finfolk had dragged them back to the center of the village and once again bound them to the whalebone arch. No one had stripped Hervor this time at least. Instead, they all stood round in a circle, staring at her and Arrow's Point. The murderous bastard sat five feet away from her.

Close enough, she could have strangled him were her hands not bound.

Kiviuq paced around them, hands behind his back. Every so often, he cast a glance her way, eyes lit with something beyond fury. A mix of anger and confusion, perhaps, as if the man could not quite understand why she had betrayed him.

Simple people.

Naliajuk was another story, though. She quivered with visible rage while one of her people spoke softly to her. The female pointedly avoided looking at Hervor. Maybe shamed that the offering she'd brought her brother had acted thus? Well, they had tortured her, so they deserved what they got.

The night wind stung her cheeks, and she had to fight to

271

keep her teeth from chattering. To allow that would make her look weak. She couldn't afford to look weak.

"Your petty foolishness cost us everything," Orvar said to her.

"Had you not murdered my kin, none of this would have happened. Even had you deigned to offer them proper pyres and set their souls at ease, we might not have come to this. So spare me your accusations."

"You have no idea what went on back then." He strained against his bonds like he intended to come closer to her. "Men fight, they kill, they die. I fought for my family, and yours were hardly the innocent victims you seem to imply."

Naliajuk stormed over, cutting off Hervor's reply. "You. Bad."

Hervor couldn't stop herself from chuckling at that. "Yes. I am a bad woman. He is a bad man. And your whole tribe is made up of evil seals."

"You. You kill. Lie. Mmmm." She worked her fingers and gnawed her lip. "Make ... bad. Front of god."

Orvar sighed. "I'm sorry we profaned your ceremony. You left us no choice. We must return to our people."

"No. No go. No free. Now you fish."

Hervor raised an eyebrow. "Our punishment is fishing?"

"No. You fish." She clanked her teeth together.

Oh. Oh, Odin's spear. "You're going to *eat* us like fish?"

Naliajuk knelt beside her and thumped Hervor's forehead with her finger. "Bad. Woman bad. Punish." The finfolk grabbed her ankle and lifted it toward her mouth, then gnashed her teeth in front of it. "Bottom." She again tapped Hervor's forehead. "Top."

Hervor shuddered at the mental image. It sounded like they intended to eat her alive, from the toes up. "You can't be serious. That's horrific. If you want to kill us, do so and be done with it."

Naliajuk shook her head. Her eyes almost—*almost*—seemed to hold pity. "Bad. Front of god. Bad woman. Bad man. Punish."

Hervor jerked forward, pulling against her bonds until her face was a breath away from Naliajuk's. "This man destroyed my family."

"You. Father?"

"No! Odin's spear, no!"

"Lie?"

"Naliajuk, please. Listen to me!"

The wereseal slapped her. The sting of it, the strength of the blow, sent Hervor toppling back down on her arse.

Naliajuk shook her head and rose as Hervor struggled back to her knees. Damn. Not a single moment of this trip had gone as planned. Niflungar, draugar ... and now it would end with her eaten alive by wereseals. She worked her jaw where Naliajuk had hit her.

A new man came running into the village, shouting something in his own nonsensical language. Kiviuq and Naliajuk both turned to him, then strode to where he stood, panting. They traded words. Pointing. Angry shouts. Gestures she assumed were rude. More arguing.

"You should have talked to me," Orvar said.

Hervor ignored him, keeping her focus on Naliajuk, who stood shaking her head as if to deny what this new man was saying.

"This was not the time for your vengeance. Even your father knew to make a proper challenge. I shouldn't be surprised though, I guess. He too cheated in the end."

"Lies!"

"Do you really think anyone agreed to a duel involving

twelve berserkir against two mortals? I wasn't even supposed to be involved—"

"And you should have stayed out of it. If I have to come back as a draug myself, I will have my vengeance."

He snorted. "You won't come back as a draug after they eat your fucking body."

Naliajuk spun on them and stalked back over, her jaw working as if she could not quite believe what the other man had told her. She looked back and forth between Hervor and Orvar, gnawed her lip, and shook her head. "You. Your people. Bad. Wake dead."

"What are you talking about?" Orvar asked.

But Hervor knew. "The draugar."

"Draugar. Draugar bad. Draug prince. Much bad."

Draug prince? That was new. "Are you saying the others woke up some prince? A leader among the draugar?"

"Dead. Going. All island, going. Hunting. You people. Bad."

The finfolk did not care much for the draugar it seemed. Feared them, even. Rightly so, she supposed. "Will you fight them?"

"Fight. No fight." She shook her head. "Maybe leave."

"Leave?" Orvar asked. "You plan to abandon Thule? This prince is so bad you will give up your homes?"

Naliajuk sighed and rubbed her arms, looking far more like a woman than a beast. A frightened woman who knew she was losing everything. Hervor knew that feeling all too well.

Orvar cleared his throat. "What if I kill this draug prince?"

"You?"

"Yes. I have fought many dangers in my life. Release me, and I swear upon my bow and my sword, I'll destroy this draug or die trying. You plan to kill me anyway. You have naught to lose."

For a moment, the wereseal stood there, running her tongue over her teeth. Then she spoke to her brother in their own language. He shouted angrily. Others joined in.

After a few moments of this, Naliajuk grunted and turned back to him. "You. You oath."

"You have my oath as a warrior. I will slay the draug prince."

She nodded and cut him free with a bone knife.

Orvar rubbed his wrists, looked at Hervor, and shook his head.

"Wait," she said. "Wait! You can't leave me here. I'll go too. Naliajuk, I can fight the draugar too. I've already killed many of them."

Orvar scoffed. "You're fucking joking. You just tried to murder me while I was unarmed and helping you escape."

"Naliajuk!"

The wereseal looked back and forth between Orvar and Hervor. Confused.

"Come on now," she said.

Naliajuk looked to Orvar.

No. No, not good. She couldn't let *him* decide her urd. Thor's thundering cock, no. "Orvar?" Hervor said. "Orvar! I swear. I swear on my sword, on Tyrfing! On Tyrfing, I swear to bury our quarrel until we have dealt with this prince."

He folded his arms and looked around the camp. At the finfolk all waiting to eat her alive. He shook his head and sighed.

"An oath on your weapon was enough," Hervor said. "You know an oath on mine is too. Who would dare violate an oath on a runeblade?"

The man sighed again, then looked to Naliajuk. "I will take her. Every sword will help."

The finfolk moved to her side and cut her free. "You. I take. I take you to others. They run."

Starkad and the rest of the party. Hervor nodded.

With a sudden motion, Naliajuk grabbed her by the coat. "You. Fail. Draugar do bad. You. Worse than we."

Worse than being eaten alive? Hervor did not want to imagine any such thing. "We won't fail."

THE FINFOLK SAT Orvar and Hervor in the same boat, Kiviuq paddling them around the shore. Toward a draug prince. Hervor did not wish to dwell on it, and yet now, thanks to another oath, she had to kill the draug before she could finish Orvar.

"You think you know everything," Orvar said without warning. "You think you understand what happened on that island ... most like before you were even born."

"Why should I believe aught you have to say for yourself?"

"I *told* you. I came back to my ship to find my crew, my people, slaughtered by your kin. By that very sword you now carry, cursed vile thing it is. I should have recognized it sooner ... should have looked more closely at such a blade, much as I hated the sight of any dverg-wrought weapon. Angantyr bore that, the worst of the berserkir, looking much like a fiend of the mist himself. Glowing and flaming and drenched in blood."

42

ORVAR

*W*e were desperate, you know, and nigh to mad with grief over the loss of our people. And in that state, we watched the berserkir stalking closer to our hiding place.

"Odin preserve us," Hjalmar mumbled. "What is that sword?"

I spat. "A runeblade. Arngrim is said to wield Tyrfing. The jarl must have gifted it to his son."

Hjalmar groaned. "This was not Angantyr's fight at all. It was to be between myself and Hjorvard."

"And now it is twelve on two, and the twelve are barely human. Come, brother. Let us slip off into the forest. There must be some other way off this island."

My blood brother glanced back at the woods behind us, then at the ship we had arrived on. "My brothers in arms are murdered in the night. Even could I walk away from that, we have never fled from our foes. Let us not start now. We will be Odin's guests in Valhalla tonight."

I blew out a long breath and shook my head. Hjalmar spoke truth, I supposed, little though I liked it. We had fought many battles before and never ran from any foe. If I was to die, I would do so with honor. Not that I intended to die. I rose then, drawing my sword. "I have no wish to meet this Odin. At least not yet. So, our only choice is to kill all twelve of these berserkir."

Hjalmar too rose, drawing his sword. "What do you think? Will you take Angantyr and Tyrfing? Or try your luck with the other eleven?"

I shook my head. A man with a runeblade or over-whelming odds ... but I could see why Hjalmar would split us thus. Angantyr was not only most famed, but that sword would give him a fell strength. Still, I had a shirt woven by alfar. Maybe it could turn even a runeblade. "I'll fight Angantyr. Your armor won't stop Tyrfing."

Hjalmar's eyes were locked on that glowing blade, as if seduced by a woman in firelight. "No, brother. You have never taken precedence over me in any battle. You think to take the glory for yourself today? Angantyr is mine. I will kill the berserk for Ingibjorg and then none may say I did not win her."

I opened my mouth to object, but Hjalmar charged forward, racing for Angantyr with a battle cry.

And I had no choice.

I raced after him, sword and torch high. "They fight alone!" I shouted at the other berserkir. "And let the strongest and bravest among them win."

Hjorvard looked first to Hjalmar, who now parried and danced with Angantyr, then to me. The berserk flashed his teeth, then strode forward.

This was it then. I tossed the torch to the beach and slung my shield off my back. I barely had it in hand when Hjorvard reached me, screaming in a mindless rage. The berserk's sword cracked off my shield. The impact rang through my arm and left my shoulder stinging. Hel, the man was strong!

Already Hjorvard had reeled back for another strike. I stepped aside, dodging again and again.

Rather than try to block those mighty blows, I dodged them, batting them aside with my shield only when necessary. On the third blow, my shield cracked. Trollfucker had inhuman might and stamina. I wasn't going to outlast him. Hjorvard fought with more ferocity than skill though, always on the offense, unrelenting.

Just how good was my alfar-woven shirt, I wondered? It had turned blades before. I dropped my shield low, granting the berserk an opening. As expected, the man leapt, intent to chop me in half. I allowed the blow to connect, swinging with my own attack rather than trying to defend myself. The attack slammed into my abdomen and hurled me from my feet for a bare instant before I struck the beach. My gut felt like it had been kicked by a mule, and I gasped, struggling to turn over.

Finally, I rose to my knees.

Hjorvard had fallen, a great gash along his neck.

I rose, hand to my stomach as the other brothers roared in amazement. Had the man hit me anywhere else, he might have broken ribs. The next brother bellowed at me, slathering and wild as a cave hyena. And still, it seemed they had enough honor to face me one at a time.

This next brother leapt forward, swinging his axe in great swathes that could have cleft a man's skull in one blow. I danced to the side, swept my shield upward, and hewed low at the same instant. My sword bit through the second brother's kneecap. Even a berserk could not stand without those. I leapt on him, slamming the rim of my shield down onto his throat. Bone crunched under the blow.

I had not even risen when the next bellowing brother crashed into me. I raised my shield, and the man collided with it. The force of it shattered the shield and sent me tumbling end over end through the sand. I rolled over on the beach even as the man raced forward, sword raised.

Unable to think, I flung sand in the man's face. The berserk stumbled a moment, giving me time to rise and swing my own sword. I opened the man's gut with one blow, then rolled away. The dying berserk flailed wildly, intent to chop me down even as his intestines spilled out over the beach. The stink of blood mixed with shit hit me as I stumbled away.

Another brother was racing in on me now. As blind and enraged as all the others. I slipped a dagger from my belt with my free hand. As the brother neared, reeling back for a killing blow with his axe, I surged forward under his arms and drove the knife into his belly. The berserk barely slowed. A meaty fist slammed into my face and sent me tumbling away. I lost my grip on both my sword and the knife.

I did not dare stop for them, though. Instead, I rolled through the sand without even looking. Dust flew a heartbeat later as that axe crashed into the spot I'd lain. The dying berserk swung again and again, forcing me to give ground and scramble away.

But the man was slowing. Gasping for breath, I managed to gain my feet, then raced over to snatch up my sword. Even as another brother raced for me ...

43

STARKAD

*A*s Starkad had hoped, they had found a narrow pass on the mountain slopes. There they had felled a tree and built a bonfire. He had considered forbidding it. The flames would announce their location. But then, the draugar would find them sooner or later in any case. Better that he and the others should get warm and face their end with strength.

Darkness had settled in once again, save for the winter lights in the sky. Starkad warmed his hands by the fire. He'd have thought their foes would be upon them already. But still they had not come.

Afzal was smoking the last of his herbs and blowing out great puffs of the strange-smelling stuff. The Serklander had relaxed once he began to sample his foreign poisons. He always did so. And perhaps those herbs truly did open his mind, allowing him uncanny insight. Always so hard to be certain.

"What do you see?" Starkad asked him.

Afzal let out a long breath before answering in a raspy voice. "Shadows stirring, beneath the ground."

Tiny snorted. "I salute your wisdom, boy. A blind babe could have guessed that much. Perhaps next you will tell me we will face snow? And ice, maybe?"

Starkad glared at him, waving him to silence. "What else, Afzal?"

The Serklander rubbed his eyebrow with his index finger. "Men are searching for us, wandering the mists."

"Men? Or draugar?"

"The Arrow's Point ..."

Tiny straightened at that. "Orvar lives? Where is he?"

"He lives ... I think. But not for long. None of us have long left. The mist is closing in, coiling around us like a serpent."

Pleasant image. Starkad pulled Vikar's sword and set at it with the whetstone. A man had to keep his weapons in order. Even in times like these. Especially in times like these. His sword and Vikar's sword—they were all he had of an old life. If he died here on Thule, that life and all they had been would be lost, forgotten.

Still, Afzal claimed none of them had much time left, and Starkad could not argue with such a prophecy. Sooner or later, the draugar would come for them.

That they had not yet done so perhaps meant they too could not cross the river. So they would come from another exit, travel the long way around. But they would come. Starkad had woken that vile king, and he could not imagine such a being would suffer living Men in his domain.

"What do you see of the draug king?" he asked Afzal.

Afzal shut his eyes and breathed deeply. "Old ones ... forgotten. Heirs of fallen glory wake for vengeance."

"The fuck does that mean?" Tiny demanded. "How about something useful?"

Starkad stared into the flames. "I think it means he was a

prince of one of the Old Kingdoms. Each of them bore a runeblade. If so, he's waited here for centuries."

"So ... he bears a runeblade."

"Indeed."

"Such a prize ..." Tiny said. "Such a prize would well please Gylfi."

Starkad scowled now. He had come here for such prizes, even had he not known specifically he sought the blade. But treasures ... "What claim do you have to this, big man?"

"As much claim as any, and I have asked for naught else thus far in Gylfi's name."

Starkad spat. "I lead this party now."

Tiny shrugged. "Because we lost Orvar? Such matters naught. All are equal on a raid, and Gylfi holds as much stake here as Yngvi. They've had oaths on the matter."

Starkad sneered. "It matters naught, in any event. Had we not lost Hervor and her runeblade maybe we ... well, that no longer matters. I suppose like any other draug, the prince will burn. Cut his legs out from under him, chop off his head, and set him alight."

"You going to do all that?"

Starkad shrugged. "You seek to claim the damned blade. I thought you were offering."

"If I have to."

Starkad chuckled. "You're a brave man, Tiny. You know ... I don't think I even know your real name."

The big man spat and shrugged. "Does it matter?"

"Very soon now, we will fight a glorious battle side by side. And then we will die. I ought to at least know what to call my brothers in arms in such a battle."

Tiny grunted. "Well, it's Ecgtheow. But everyone calls me Tiny anyway."

Starkad offered his hand. "I'm honored to fight by your side, Ecgtheow."

The big man clasped his arm. "No, I am honored. Men call you a god of war."

Starkad shrugged. They said the same thing about Tyr, and he did not care to be tied back to that bastard.

"If we can kill this prince ..." Tiny said.

Starkad waved it away. Whatever point the big man made, he was not willing to cede such a prize. Not after all it had cost.

Finally, Tiny cleared his throat. "We have a choice before us. We can stay here and wait for them, allowing our strength to wane from hunger. Or we can skirt the shore as your slave suggests."

"Afzal is not my slave."

"The point remains. You expected them to be upon us long before now. We have gained what rest we can already. Waiting longer means we grow weaker. On the shore, we might find some food—fish, game, something."

Starkad sighed. Tiny was right. He had come up this mountain to die. If they left, they surrendered the most favorable location he'd found to face an army of draugar. If they remained though, they'd still lose. Not so unlike being back by the geysers. They'd gained a measure of safety in exchange for any hope of survival.

But they didn't want to vote on the matter. They wanted him to decide, to save them. Even Afzal was watching him now, eyes clouded with his poison, yet still aware enough. Intent, awaiting the word of his master. And not wanting to die.

Fair enough. Starkad had never been one to stay long in a single place. "We've rested. If Orvar is alive, is looking for us, he'd probably head toward the ship. So will we. We follow the coast and make as good a time as we can while hunting for food. None of us want to die hungry."

"I don't want to die at all," Afzal said.

"Everyone dies, eventually." He clapped the Serklander on the shoulder. "But maybe … maybe we can at least make it off this island."

Afzal sighed and rose. And then he hurled his pipe off the side of the mountain.

"What was that?" Starkad asked.

The boy rubbed his eyebrow again. "You're wrong about one thing, Master. I won't make it off this island. Of that I'm certain."

More prophecy at the end of a pipe. Starkad gripped him by the back of his head and drew Afzal close to his face. "Listen to me. Your urd is in your own hands. Make the most of it."

When the boy nodded, Starkad released him and set off, back down the mountain.

44

HERVOR

*T*he only sound came from the water lapping on the shore and gentle rhythm of Kiviuq paddling. Naliajuk sat beside her brother in the boat, staring at Orvar and Hervor. He had insisted she sit in front of him, where he could keep an eye on her.

She had sworn an oath and on Tyrfing no less.

She would not break it.

According to Orvar's story, Angantyr had been a worse murderer than even Hervor. Did it matter? He was still her father. Besides which, how was she to believe a word the man said? Maybe Orvar would not have embellished the tale before knowing her identity ... but now? How could he not skew the telling to cast himself as a victim?

As innocent.

No one was innocent, after all.

Not Orvar. Not Hervor. And probably not the sons of Arngrim. Maybe they had been raping, pillaging, monsters. So had Red-Eyes' Boys. And they'd been Hervor's people.

She kept twisting around on her seat, wary least he

should plunge a knife in her back. Would his oath bind him, as well, or was he faithless?

"There's not many of us left," she said.

"Us? You think you're one of us now?"

If he told the others she'd attacked him like that, maybe any one of them might kill her for it. Even old Bragi Bluefoot might do her in for such treachery and name it the will of the gods. And Hervor liked Bragi.

She grimaced, not willing to acknowledge Orvar's point. "The Axe fell when we first woke the draugar. And I saw Ivar get stabbed just before I got separated from the party."

"And you murdered Rolf yourself."

She groaned. "That was an accident ... look, Starkad must be leading them now."

"Obviously. There's no finer warrior in the North Realms."

"He hates women."

Orvar shrugged. "I'm starting to see why."

She clamped her mouth shut at that.

An explosion of water ruptured the silence once more, an instant before a massive form breached the surface several dozen feet away from the boat. Sleek black-and-white skin. The orca hung in the air for a breath before crashing back down and disappearing beneath the sea.

Naliajuk had clutched both sides of the boat, eyes wide, jaw trembling. Frozen in terror.

Kiviuq stared at the spot where the orca had vanished, muttering about Aningan.

The finfolk feared the orca. Maybe they hunted them, too. But the part of them that were seals, they felt a primal calling back to their nature. Their instincts, their heritage.

Like Hervor. Driven by primal rage.

So then, had she judged Orvar without knowing the man?

No.

No, whatever twisted words he spoke, it did not change that his hand had nigh to ended her entire line.

"So tell me then," she said. "Tell me how you killed the last of my kin."

"Hervor ... you know how it ended. And I already told you how it began. We did not start this fight ..."

"Yes. Justify yourself. Tell me."

"What good will come of the rest of this story—"

"Say it!"

Naliajuk and Kiviuq looked over at her outburst.

Hervor ignored them. "I want to hear you say how my father died. Leave naught out, Arrow's Point. Tell me the truth—all of it. Tell me how you murdered him."

Orvar let his head slip into his hand. "You ... arrogant, fool child. I have something better for you. I will tell you how Angantyr murdered my brother."

45

ORVAR

I had slain all but one of your uncles, and as the last circled me, I tossed aside the broken hilt of my sword. Rage wafted off the berserk so thick I could have almost seen it. But the man did not charge in. Perhaps the sight of ten of his brothers dead and dying on the beach instilled the barest hint of self-control in him. Though bleeding from a dozen wounds, I must have seemed tempting prey.

I knelt to pick up the axe of one of the dead berserkir.

My lungs felt aflame, every breath agony. I wanted to pitch forward and lay in the sand and sleep, to rest for days. Whatever happened next, skalds would sing of this battle. I had slain ten men in single combat, one by one without a moment of rest. Not just ten men. Ten *berserkir*. This day, my deeds here, men would remember it.

I allowed myself to believe that. To believe it a good thing.

To think that maybe even Odin watched now. Maybe valkyries were circling, awaiting my fall.

The last berserk spit, then stalked forward, sword before

him. Didn't fling himself wildly. He had learned something from the deaths of his brothers. At long last, they faced a foe where sheer ferocity was not enough. And still, the man wanted to charge. To let rage take him. That much was apparent in his face.

I beckoned him with the axe. "Come now. Do you not wish to rejoin your brothers in Valhalla? Do you not share their courage?" The berserk stiffened. That had hit something. "Perhaps you were the youngest ... never quite their equal. Not worthy to sit at their table among the honored dead? Do not feel bad. You can still go home and embrace your mother, boy."

I had not even finished speaking when the man charged at me, shrieking like an animal. I didn't have the stamina to fight him. I had almost naught left.

Naught save a trick I'd already used. One that, hopefully, the berserk was too mad to prepare for. As the man swung, I too attacked, making no effort at defense. The berserk's blade swept up over my alfar shirt, scraping on it as though it were armor, before shrieking loose and drawing a cleft from my chin—you can still see the scar.

Of course, my axe buried in the berserk's skull.

I stumbled away, fell over, and lay in the sand.

I don't know how much time passed. Less than an hour, probably. The sun had risen but not high. I pushed myself and crawled forward.

Angantyr and Hjalmar both lay nearby.

My ... brother ... my blood brother was ...

I rose, stumbled over to where Hjalmar lay. The man looked to me, alive, but his eyes had grown weak. His helm was cleft down the middle, a vicious wound over his face. Even his chain had been rent. Tyrfing had cut clean through the mail like it were cloth.

The berserk was dead; Hjalmar's sword had cut half his face off. And Hjalmar ... more than a dozen wounds oozed blood.

Gasping, I pressed the wounds. Hard. Blood oozed through my fingers. It did not slow. I could not tear my alfar shirt but ... I yanked off Angantyr's armor, then his tunic, and tore it in straps. Each, I bound against Hjalmar. The blood just kept oozing. It was slowing but not thanks to my efforts.

My blood brother fumbled with his ruined helm.

I helped him, easing the thing off. "Brother. I cannot staunch the bleeding. I fear you have seen the end of your days."

"Ugn. No, I can't see ... except maybe my father. He is drinking at Valhalla. And valkyries ..."

Death visions had taken the man. Or perhaps a valkyrie truly did come for his soul. I saw naught. "I'm sorry, brother."

"My arm ring ... for Ingibjorg. Do not let her wonder ..."

I grimaced, then slipped the red-gold ring from my brother's wrist. Yngvi's father Alrik had given him that on achieving manhood. And he was right. Ingibjorg would know it, know what it meant.

"There is a raven ... his meal on my blood ..."

Hjalmar's breath left him.

Trembling, I shut my brother's eyes.

And then I ...

I was mad with grief ...

Samsey was thick with barrows of the Old Kingdoms, from days when men entombed their dead rather than freed them on pyres. I did not know or care why the old men did such things. I did know why my people burned bodies though. While the body lingered, so too might the soul, unable to escape Midgard. Bound to waste away the ages in half sleep, locked in eternal damnation.

A fitting urd for the berserk brothers who had wrought countless evil deeds in their lives. Not least among them the slaughter of Hjalmar and all his crew on a day sanctioned for a duel. These men had violated law and custom and did not deserve to feast in Valhalla. They deserved to linger in torment for their crimes.

So I thought then, so bereaved.

And so I laid them in one such barrow. The torch gave the only light in that thick, suffocating place of shadow and death. Fitting. On ancient slabs, I laid them beside their cursed weapons. Let them comfort each other down through the ages. Or not. Samsey was a place of nightmare, an island best left lost in time.

And Tyrfing ... fell power coursed through me as I held it. I could take this sword and with it become the most famed warrior in all the North Realms. I could become a king and raise up such an army I might challenge any nation of men, perhaps even the dvergar of Nidavellir.

And more like than not, meet such an accursed urd as these berserkir. Like all the works of the dvergar, the blade cut in more than one way. It did not belong in the world of men. The runeblades were works of ancient evil, driven by curses to destroy all who crossed their paths.

And so I laid it upon the slab. The sword seemed to glimmer with hidden flame, begging me not to abandon it. It *wanted* to go, to be free. To kill, murder, and sow discord across the land. It *wanted* to work its evil.

And I sealed them in that barrow.

I would keep my promise and return to Ingibjorg, give her Hjalmar's blessing. And give them all the warning that Starkad had been right.

And no living man ought to ever again tread upon Samsey's shores.

And that done, I walked away from Sviarland. Walked away from even being Arrow's Point.

I fled my grief ...

46

HERVOR

*O*h.

But he had left out the part where he laid a curse upon the brothers. Nor had he simply lain Tyrfing beside Hervor's father's corpse. No, Orvar had lain the blade beneath the man, and bid him burn forever upon his once-trusted weapon.

And too, he had hoped to deny Tyrfing the World. To never again let it taste the blood of men.

Even from across the boat, the sword called to Hervor. Its anger mirrored her own.

She could lunge across the boat, grab the blade, and cut down the man.

But her oath ...

All of this, Hervor had done for an oath.

So she would wait.

But there was no forgiveness.

On the shore, three men worked their way along the coast, heading south. One bore a torch, allowing Hervor to spot the group soon, though not as quickly as Naliajuk. She had already told her brother, who steered the boat toward them, intent on intercepting them. The party on the shore must have seen them too, for they also drew up short and pulled weapons.

A man with two swords. A welcome sight in this case.

"Starkad!" Orvar shouted through the mist.

"Orvar?"

The three men approached the boat as it banked on the frozen beach. Alongside Starkad walked his servant as well as Tiny. That was it. Where was everyone else? All dead?

Bragi?

Hervor glowered. Poor old bastard. Never should have come here. None of them should have.

Kiviuq pulled a bone knife as soon as he dropped the paddles, and Naliajuk jumped ashore, knife in one hand, cord weapon in the other. Despite their oaths, perhaps the finfolk did not trust them. Certainly not with such numbers.

"You don't look so surprised to see me," Orvar said to Starkad.

The shaggy man cocked his head at his servant before sheathing his blades. "This one knows things."

"So I've heard."

Starkad looked to Hervor now. "I thought you both dead. I searched for you in the gorge."

Hervor grunted. "Long and hard, I'm sure."

Tiny clapped Orvar on the shoulder while eyeing the finfolk.

"New friends," Orvar said.

Friends—a severe stretch of the term. "We have an

understanding. It seems you people went and woke the dead."

Starkad nodded. "Quite a lot of them. Including one with strange powers. A prince of one of the Old Kingdoms, I think. He bears a runeblade."

Hervor grimaced at that. Another runeblade. An equal to Tyrfing? This did not bode well.

Orvar grunted. "The finfolk know of him, know him as a prince, so I gather you're correct. And I ... made an oath to slay him."

"You what?" Tiny said.

"I swore to bring down the draug prince in exchange for my freedom." The man looked to Hervor. Would he betray her now? Tell them of her treachery and thus order her death? The thought seemed to cross his mind. "And hers as well. She has also sworn to kill the prince."

Starkad folded his arms across his chest. "And you came to us thinking we'd want in on the glory?"

"Don't you?"

"We barely got out of Nordri the first time," Tiny said. "Still. I want that blade."

Orvar spread his hands. "Either way, we gave our oaths, and those oaths bind us. You can help us or not."

Starkad looked to his Serkland servant, who shook his head. "It will end in death," the foreigner said.

Orvar scoffed at that. "Life always ends in death, boy. But you people went and woke up something better left alone. So set aside my oath and forget about the treasures of Nordri. Consider—under direction of a singular power— the draugar may not be the mindless forces of death we know. Imagine what would happen if such an army marched on any of our homes."

Starkad spat. "We have no reason to believe they could get off this island."

"The finfolk have boats," Hervor said.

"Besides," Orvar said. "Sooner or later others will come here, trying to claim what we did. And the draugar will kill them and take their ships."

Starkad waved it away. "You don't know that. That's pure speculation. You want to scare us into thinking we have no choice but to fight this monstrosity. But you don't need such tactics, Orvar. I welcome the challenge. If we do this, we can return home as *legends*. And now, with you two back, we actually have weapons that can hope to slay the fiend."

Orvar nodded. "You're talking about my arrows. But I have only one left."

"And the runeblade."

He frowned. "I'd consider the runeblade a last resort."

Hervor glared at him—how dare he speak ill of Tyrfing —then turned to Starkad. "Tyrfing has never failed me."

"Didn't save you from being thrown off a cliff."

Orvar rubbed his face and looked over the group. "You lot get me close enough, keep the others off of my back. And I'll put my last arrow through the prince's skull."

"I will go," Starkad said. "Afzal?"

The Serklander sighed and hung his head. "I go where you go, Master."

Orvar looked to Tiny.

The big man shrugged. "We do this ... I want the prince's runeblade."

Starkad groaned and shook his head.

"Such things come with a hefty price," Orvar said.

"Yes, perhaps. They also bring honor and fame to a man and his line."

Orvar looked over at Hervor. "The dvergar did not forge

the runeblades for the good of Mankind. They do naught for the good of men."

She spat in the snow, offering no answer.

Starkad folded his arms. "In any event, it's decided. We'll make for the city again. It will take us long to trek back to the main entrance."

At that, Naliajuk stepped forward. "No. No main. Take river." She pointed to the boats.

Starkad sneered at her and pointedly looked past her at Orvar. "You trust this shifter? Those rapids could break a man in half. We already lost Bragi on that river."

So that was what had happened to the poor bastard. Shame.

Hervor glanced at Naliajuk. "I trust her enough. She wants the prince gone, Starkad. The finfolk stand to lose Thule completely otherwise." Maybe they deserved to die for their barbaric actions. But if so, so too did Hervor.

So too did they all.

Starkad groaned, but nodded, and started for the boats. Eager to be done with it, Hervor supposed. Although Starkad always seemed reckless, fey, and rushing toward his dark destiny, whatever it might be.

Orvar grabbed Hervor's arm as she passed. "Listen. Your father, your brothers were led astray. Maybe by the very sword you carry. It probably brought the ruin on your house in the first place. It makes a man—or woman—hunger for blood. I can see by your eyes you know it's true. But still we need it. If I fail, you have to use Tyrfing to slay the prince."

"I have never broken an oath," she said. "I don't intend to start now."

She jerked her arm free and headed for the boat.

She had two oaths to uphold on this island.

47

STARKAD

*I*cy waters splashed over the lip of the boats as Naliajuk and Kiviuq threaded between rocks. The rapids ran through ice caves lit only by the flicker of Afzal and Tiny's torches, one in each boat. Perhaps the shifters could see, but to Starkad, the rocks rushed by faster than he could pick them out. Wind whipped his hair out behind him, tugged on his soaked clothes, stung his face. And he loved it.

His curse had made him a madman, but he loved it.

The boat almost careened into the ice wall, despite Kiviuq's frantic attempts to turn it.

Afzal shouted something in his own language. All their years together and Starkad had never managed to pick up more than a few words of that strange tongue. Starkad glanced at the Serklander, who had turned ashen-faced.

Starkad grinned and looked forward again. Yes. He'd gone mad.

Round the bend, and the dvergar huts began to draw nigh, rising up from the ground like square hills. One hand on the boat's edge, Starkad reached for his sword. The draugar would see the torches.

Fire is life.

They might catch the dead by surprise, coming in this way. But that advantage would not last. They had to move fast—very fast. The fastest man was the only one who counted. As the bank neared, Starkad leaped from the boat onto it, landed in a crouch, and took off toward the nearest building.

With the light behind him, he could not see much, but Afzal would follow. He always followed. The others too, though the finfolk planned to watch the boats.

A pair of draugar rose up from the rooftops, bows raised. Not good. Starkad increased his pace, readied his sword.

Twang.

He whipped his sword forward, and it hit the arrow midair, knocking it aside. Damn. He couldn't believe that worked.

He rushed forward. An instant later, one of those cord weapons flew over his head and crashed into a draug. The dead man pitched forward off the roof, tangled in the finfolk projectile. Starkad leapt on the fallen draug, swinging his sword and twisting. His blade sheared through the creature's skull, and it collapsed.

Firelight raced closer toward him, illuminating the alley. The other draug still stood on the rooftops and would shoot down his companions. Starkad glanced around the alley. The buildings were close together and not too high.

Maybe ...

Starkad ran at one building, kicked off it, and caught the lip of the other building under his armpits. As he pulled himself atop the building, the draug turned to him.

Met his gaze with those gleaming eyes.

It knew it didn't have time to nock an arrow, so it tossed the bow aside and pulled a knife. Starkad thrust his sword up as he gained his feet, using the draug's own momentum to impale itself. With a twist, he flung the creature down off the roof. Tiny charged into the alley and set to chopping the creature to pieces with his broadsword.

With the torches below him, he couldn't make out much. But glowing red eyes were converging on their location. Many pairs of eyes. He drew his other sword. They'd get swarmed. Unless he could find a choke point. Like the palace itself. Only one way in, and they'd have to face him a few at a time.

He jumped off the roof and landed in the alley. "Orvar! You and the shieldmaiden make for the palace." He pointed with his sword. "You're the only ones that might down their leader. The rest of us will hold them at the entrance. Afzal, follow!"

Not waiting for an answer, he rushed through the city, cutting down three draugar as he went. One stood before the palace gate. Ugly bastard with its face half rotted off, exposing bone. Starkad charged him, one sword high, one low. The draug held its shield out before itself, spear raised high. Starkad leapt to the side at the last moment, causing the draug to thrust uselessly in the space he had just occupied. He chopped down with one sword, knocking the spear wide, while scoring a hit on the thing's legs with the other. The draug wobbled, and Starkad kicked its shield, sending it toppling to the ground.

An instant later, Tiny was on it, cleaving into the fallen creature.

Orvar raced to his side, bow readied. "You're sure about this?"

"Go and make us legends." Starkad turned, both swords readied.

Hervor charged in first, followed by Orvar.

Starkad looked over to Afzal and Tiny and nodded at them. One by one, they retreated into the palace foyer.

The big man tossed his torch to the ground so he could pull his shield. Afzal stood there, breath shaky, torch in one hand, curved sword in the other. "Stay to the left side of the gate," Starkad said to him. "They can only make it through a few at a time. We have to keep them from overwhelming us."

"We will die this day," Afzal said.

Tiny grunted. "Die bravely, then. Maybe Odin will take even a Serklander like you."

"Tiny," Starkad said. "Take the right side. I'll hold the center."

The big man shrugged and took up position. "The dead do not tire, but even a man like you has limits."

Starkad smiled, flexed his wrists. "I've been searching for those."

The first draug surged through the door, sword high over its head.

Starkad whipped both his swords forward, hewing through the creature's abdomen and halting its momentum. It fell forward, and he stepped around it, hacking at its back. No time to see if it were truly dead. Another draug came in, charging with a spear. Starkad knocked it aside with one blade and hacked into the thing's face with the other.

Afzal slashed at the creature's hamstring with his shamshir, and it fell forward.

Starkad left the Serklander to finish that one, facing the next.

A draug with a slight limp in one leg, hefting a mighty

axe. Torn and battered flesh had lost much of its color, but as the draug met his gaze, he knew it. The Axe.

"No ..." Tiny said.

"Fucking mist," Starkad said.

He moved in on his former companion. The way it stared at him, with hatred even beyond that of other draugar. It knew him. Some part of the Axe remained, corrupted by the mist and consumed with rage. Like all draugar, he wanted revenge against every living thing.

"Stop," Tiny said. "I will face him."

The Axe sneered and turned toward Tiny, shield high. The big man faced him the same, his jaw trembling, shaking his head.

More draugar raced into the gate. Starkad surged forward to meet them. No time for caution. No time for tactics. All that mattered now was speed. Just move faster. So fast they could not keep up. He parried, twisted, thrust, hacked. Parry, riposte, parry. Slash. Instinct raging to give ground, but he could not.

Could not afford it.

Four of them, five. Keep them tied up here, buy Orvar time. Everything would fall to Orvar, in the end. If the draug prince died, maybe the rest would panic. Or maybe they would all share the Axe's twisted urd.

Vile urd.

Starkad grunted and roared in defiance.

Parry, parry, parry.

Slash. He lopped off the head of one draug.

Afzal used every chance Starkad bought him, too. The Serklander severed arms, legs, necks. Starkad forced every draug's attention to remain on him. One or two tried to turn away for a moment, face Afzal. Those fools found Starkad's blades cutting them down from behind.

The bodies had begun to pile up. Nowhere to move, to turn. Now they *had* to fall back. The draugar scrambled over their own fallen to engage him.

Seven, eight of them at once. No more chance to attack. Just parry, parry. Keep their attention. Force them to stay on him. None could pass. Not a single one could be allowed to distract Orvar.

From the corner of his eye, he saw Tiny approaching, one hand clutching his side. Shield discarded. And the Axe had now died twice on Thule.

Starkad roared at the draugar. They had taken so many of his people.

And they just kept coming.

48

HERVOR

*H*ervor charged ahead of Orvar, Tyrfing's glow lighting the palace. A pair of draugar guarded the great hall, and she flung herself at them in a fury, engaging both. She'd claimed a shield from a fallen draug outside. This she used to block one draug while driving the other back with Tyrfing.

Even the draugar seemed cowed by the runeblade's gleam, and its fear worked against it. Hervor scored a hit on its arm, and it hissed as though it felt true pain. She whipped the sword around, cleaving through the other draug's shield and shield arm both.

A knife-wielding draug surged out of the shadows, launching itself at Hervor. She turned, already knowing she was too slow.

And then a black arrow punched through its mail and flesh, knocked it out of the air and it fell, lay still.

Hervor glanced back at Orvar, who was already nocking another arrow. She spun back to dispatch the last draug.

She scrambled over their fallen foe without a word, charging into the throne room.

Tyrfing's light did not reach the recesses of the room, nor the ceiling, but it did illuminate those thrones. Dverg thrones, from before they abandoned this place. Glorious work and terrible.

Hervor took a few faltering steps, angling Tyrfing this way and that in the vain hope its light might reveal her foe.

Behind her, Orvar reclaimed the black arrow from the draug he'd slain.

So where was the prince? Had he already left, gone hunting them across the mountains of Thule? How ironic if they had come all this way to kill him and would now die having never found him.

Sword before her, Hervor stalked closer to the thrones, casting glances around the room. "Where is this trollfucker?"

As if summoned, a draug flung itself over the thrones, its own gleaming blade in hand.

The draug prince slashed again and again. Hervor stumbled backward, giving ground, struggling to parry. The draug's runeblade sheared through her shield.

She tossed it aside and slashed downward with Tyrfing. The draug parried on his blade, stopping her momentum dead. And before her eyes, it began to grow, the blade expanding with it. It grew to tower over Hervor, pushing its runeblade against hers with one hand. Its strength drove her back, caused her feet to skid along the floor.

More than twice her height. Eyes lit with the glow of Hel.

Hervor grunted under the strain and slipped to one knee.

A bow twanged behind her. Orvar's arrow slammed into the draug's helm. The creature stumbled backward, hissing, shrieking mind-rending sounds.

Hervor scrambled away from it, but it lunged forward, caught her with its free hand, and raised her up off the ground.

It hadn't died. He'd shot it with a magic arrow and still it walked. Still it—

The draug flung Hervor at Orvar. She slammed into his chest, and they both collapsed to floor, skidding along it. His bow careened away. All the wind blew out of her lungs, and her head struck the stone floor.

The room spun, darkened.

She groaned, trying to rise but not quite able.

Panting, Hervor stumbled to her feet and ambled back toward the prince, Tyrfing out before her. Ears were ringing. Vision blurry.

"Fuck you ..." she mumbled.

She hacked at the creature. It parried her with ease using that giant sword, gave her no opening to reach its body.

The draug looked past her then. At Orvar. Then it jumped over Hervor and landed between the man and his bow.

Trollfucker. Orvar stared dumbly at the fiend.

Damn it.

Finally, Orvar pulled his own sword, moving like a man dazed. An ordinary iron blade, naught but human strength behind it.

They were doomed.

He bellowed a war cry and charged the draug.

It leaned down, roaring at him, exposing fangs and the hellish abyss of its maw. The ground shook as it raced forward to meet him. Sword high.

Orvar dove forward, rolling between its legs. Its blade

scored the ground where he had stood, shearing through stone and sending up a cascade of rubble.

Hervor faltered an instant. Orvar was damned fast with a sword, too. She raced to his bow and snatched it up off the ground. "Orvar!"

He glanced her way, and she flung the bow through the air. It spun, and he dropped his sword to catch it. The man rolled over and scrambled to his feet, even as the draug prince turned.

Hervor raced past him hewing into the prince's leg. *That* got its attention. Its leg gave out, and it fell to one knee, wailing that soul-twisting shriek of its. Hervor had to dive away from its own counter with that runeblade.

Orvar half ran, half crawled to put distance between himself and the prince. Bows were not nigh as fast as swords, after all.

Hervor had to let the man get some space to nock an arrow ... but an ordinary arrow would do naught when the bastard's magic arrows had failed. So now what?

"Prince trollfucker!" Orvar shouted at it.

Hervor and the draug both glanced at the madman. So the dead thing had understood the Northern tongue?

"I'm going to ram that runeblade right up your arse, trollfucker!" Orvar shouted.

The prince raced forward, half limping, half jumping. Its sword scraped along the floor for an instant before surging into the air. The prince whirled it around in a wide arc.

The draug was about to steal Hervor's vengeance away from her.

Hervor ran at the prince at an angle, leapt onto the throne and stepped on the back of it. Then she flung herself onto the prince's back as he passed her.

The prince spun, flailed. Hervor shrieked, cleaving

Tyrfing down on its skull. The runeblade cleaved through the helm and tore into the skull. The helm fell away in pieces, but the prince did not fall. The flailing draug sent Hervor flying through the air before slamming into the ground.

The impact blew the wind out of her lungs and sent darkness clambering in at the edges of her vision. She gasped, trying to rise. Trying to even get a breath.

Tyrfing had skittered away from her.

She tried to push herself up. Her arms gave out, and she collapsed back to the floor.

The ground trembled as the monstrous draug ambled toward her.

The draug bellowed at Hervor as she tried to rise. Black ichor spewed from its mouth. It cursed her in the Old Tongue. Hervor did not need to understand the words to feel the wrath of Hel behind them.

"Prince trollfucker," Orvar shouted again.

The draug turned toward him. Roared.

He had reclaimed the black arrow from the fallen helm. He loosed.

Orvar's arrow struck the draug on the bridge of what remained of its nose. The shaft punched through the unarmored skull and exploded out the other side, spraying ichor. The draug stood, trembling for an instant, before pitching over backward. It fell with a tremendous crash that shook the throne room.

Orvar panted. "Go back to Hel."

Gasping, Hervor forced herself to her feet and stalked to the prince. Then she slammed Tyrfing into its chest.

Had to be certain.

"We make a good team," Orvar said, clutching his sides as he walked toward her. "Let us bury the past, yes?"

Still struggling to breathe, she jerked Tyrfing free and cast a glance between the dead draug and Orvar. Then at Tyrfing. Its light shone beneath the black ichor now coating it. She blew out a long breath.

So her oath was fulfilled.

One of them.

Orvar had saved her life at least twice in here. But her oath ...

An oath could not be broken. Vengeance, declared, must be sated.

And so she lunged at Orvar.

The man tried to step back, to twist aside. The runeblade punched through even his alfar shirt with ease. It scraped along his ribs and exploded out of his back.

He looked down at it. At her. He tried to speak, but only blood gurgled out of his mouth.

"I held my oath ..." Hervor said. "I ... forestalled vengeance. Now the prince is dead. And I offer you the same mercy you offered my father." She struggled to even keep her voice from breaking. "Burn in eternal torment, Arrow's Point."

She yanked the blade free, and he fell to his knees without her supporting him.

And then he pitched forward and died.

Her oath was fulfilled.

HERVOR SHEATHED Tyrfing and stared at Orvar's corpse. "My father and uncles are avenged." She spat on him. "Rot in the embrace of Hel."

She knelt beside the other runeblade. When it had left the prince's grasp, it returned to the size of a normal blade.

Her hand hesitated over the hilt. Tyrfing was her family's legacy, and still. Still it had brought about death, suffering, woe—as her father's ghost had warned.

What curse would hold this runeblade? It didn't matter, she supposed. They had promised it to Tiny, and he could have it, for good or ill.

She snatched it up and headed out of the throne room.

Beyond, draugar corpses littered the foyer. Still more of the fiends swarmed in. Starkad whirled from one to the next with uncanny speed and ferocity. But his chest heaved. The man could not have much left in him.

And they had no way out of this palace.

But the draugar all served their prince, and he was dead. Did they know that?

She ducked back into the throne room. Pieces of the shattered crown lay strewn about the floor. She grabbed the largest chunk, the one displaying the great ruby. With this, she rushed out among the growing horde.

"The prince is dead!" she shouted. And she flung the crown among the draugar.

The undead creatures paused, many turning to stare at the crown.

An opportunity, if a brief one. She ran for the door.

Tiny met her halfway. "Where is Orvar?"

"He helped bring down the prince but fell to his injuries." She thrust the prince's runeblade at the big man. "Take it. We have no time."

Tiny grunted, looked to Starkad. "Best be off, Eightarms!"

Several of the draugar lunged at the crown. They fell to fighting amongst each other in an explosion of chaos and hellish shrieks. Starkad shoved past them to join her and Tiny at the door. Afzal was already there, struggling to find a way out, but more and more of the undead tried to jam themselves into the doorway.

Tiny bellowed, charging into their midst runeblade first. The mass gave way before his flashing blade. Hervor drew Tyrfing off her shoulder and joined him, cutting her way free. Starkad and Afzal would follow as best they could. She had to trust in that.

The draugar shouted at each other in their forgotten language, more now trying for the crown than any of their human prey. Still, other draugar—perhaps unaware of the prize—continued to move in on them. Hervor raced back toward the river, cutting down three different draugar as she did so.

The occasional shout behind her was the only indication the others followed.

An arrow whooshed past her head. Reflex twisted her around to look. It had hit a draug archer in the chest, caused it to drop its bow. She turned back and ran. Kiviuq, her would-be husband, held a bow, nocking another arrow.

Her arm felt like lead, her chest like ice.

Just a little farther.

A draug leapt from the shadows at her. She tried to turn, to bring Tyrfing to bear. Not fast enough.

The undead creature bore her down, the sword slipping from her grasp. Ice-cold fingers closed around her throat. She grabbed its wrist but could not pull the creature off her.

Its grip closed. Breath refused to pass into her lungs.

Her vision began to dim at the edges. She slapped at the thing, but her strength already ebbed. The weak blows didn't even faze the creature. Its glowing eyes bored into her mind.

Like it knew. Her crimes, her murders. Betrayals.

Even now, she had betrayed Orvar-Oddr. Honored only the letter of her oath.

And she deserved to be dragged down to Hel by this creature.

The draug burst into flames and fell back off her. Afzal thrust his torch into its face again, then slashed it with his curved sword. It fell, shrieking.

Gasping. Pain. Trying to breathe. Air wheezed through her bruised throat.

Someone was dragging her to her feet. Shoving her toward the boat. Kiviuq?

She tried to speak, not even certain what she wanted to say. It didn't matter since her words came out a garbled mess. Naliajuk grabbed her from her brother, guided her into one of the boats. Afzal jumped in a moment later, and Naliajuk kicked the boat off.

Leaning on the rail, she could make out Tiny and Starkad fighting their way toward where Kiviuq stood at the other boat. The sudden twisting of the boat made her slip down, and she clutched on both rails for support. The boat smacked against ice, throwing a shower of it down on her.

"Starkad!" Afzal shouted. "We cannot leave him."

"No. No leave." Naliajuk glanced back. "Kiviuq bring."

Not that they could have stopped if they wanted to. The rapids had them now, yanked them forward. Draugar arrows clattered against the ice walls as the boat whipped around a corner. Out of their line of shot.

Water splashed over the side, drenching her. So cold. Couldn't breathe.

Murderer.

She clenched her eyes shut. She'd always been a murderer. Ever since she'd run with Red-Eye's Boys.

Now she was something better. She had avenged a wrong. The first vengeance.

She had slain mighty Arrow's Point.

And no one knew.

No one save her father, who maybe now, could at last find respite from his pain.

49

STARKAD

The river let out from the ice cave and cast them under a sky lit by the blue-green lights once more. As the rapids passed, their rate slowed, and finally, so did Starkad's raging heart. He slumped down in the boat. The most profound fatigue of his life had settled over him, left his limbs feeling like unresponsive water. Keeping track of time on Thule had become impossible, but certainly he'd had little sleep in many days. An entire moon, maybe.

And they had done it. Orvar—rest his wandering soul— had slain a prince of the Old Kingdoms. Starkad would not have minded that glory for himself, but holding off a draugar army would win him his share, he supposed.

Even Tyr ought to be impressed with such a feat. And maybe Starkad had found his limits after all.

Had Hervor taken a few moments more in coming, he'd have given out. He could not now swing his swords against the meekest of foes.

He had seen Thule, had walked in Nordri, and now lived to tell of it. Whatever else Odin may have wanted from this island, Starkad was done with it. Thule had cost them all more than they had counted on. Maybe the Aesir had known what they would find and failed to warn them. Probably, in fact.

So he shut his eyes, let the rhythm of the paddles soothe him.

THE BOAT JERKED as it ran aground, waking him. Starkad opened his eyes to see numerous finfolk gathered on the shore, all watching the two boats. Kiviuq climbed out of their boat and joined his sister, who stood nearby. Some of the finfolk held bows, some knives, some those cord weapons. None had raised them threateningly, but neither did their eyes speak of friendship.

He groaned. So that was how it was. Sitting up hurt. Having to fight off an army of wereseals would hurt more.

Rubbing her throat, Hervor approached Naliajuk and nodded at the other woman.

"You. Prince you killed."

Hervor nodded again.

Starkad stumbled over to where the two women stood, leaving Tiny and Afzal behind. "We upheld Orvar's bargain. He paid for it with his life."

Naliajuk gnawed her lip. "You. Mmmm. Good you. Prince dead."

Encouraging. Starkad stretched his neck. "So? Take us to our ship, and we'll leave Thule to you."

"Island. Mmmm. Mmmm. Danger, still."

"They'll choose another prince." Hervor's voice sounded raspy.

He almost pitied her. But Hel, she had brought her woes on herself, lying to join this expedition. And ... and she had helped save them all. Were she not there, had she not brought the crown, they'd have all died in Nordri.

Maybe she was worth more than he had given her credit for.

Maybe.

Starkad shrugged. "Yes, a new prince. Probably not so strong as the last. We have his sword. Either way, we upheld our deal."

Naliajuk looked to her brother, then at the other finfolk. "Deal. You deal. Good. Fix prince." Now she pointed at Hervor. "Still. Still first thing. Wedding."

Hervor snorted or tried to. Sounded strained. "I am not marrying. Not anyone."

Naliajuk frowned and worked her mouth. "Human. Human marry. One human. Least."

"Go to Hel," Tiny said. "None of us are staying here." The big man drew the stolen runeblade.

Starkad frowned at it. That should have been his. With Orvar dead ... Starkad grit his jaw. The treasures of Thule were his to claim. Tiny—Ecgtheow—had insisted on claiming what did not belong to him.

"No!" Naliajuk stomped her foot and took several threatening steps toward Tiny.

The big man threatened her with the runeblade, but Hervor stepped between the pair.

"They don't like it if you invoke that name," she said.

Tiny cocked his head. "And I don't like being told to marry a fucking seal. So we beat the draugar. We can cut our way through these bastards too. Let the dead claim Thule."

"We are in no shape to fight again," Afzal said. "Much less against such odds."

Starkad found himself forced to agree, though he let his hands drift toward his sword hilts. If it was the end, he would go down fighting. The finfolk would pay very dearly for this treachery. That, at least, he could promise them. Kiviuq met his gaze now. The wereseal's hand went to the bone knife at his belt.

"Wait, wait!" Afzal said. "Master ... I will stay."

Starkad spun on the Serklander. "No you won't. You don't have to do this."

"I promised to repay my debt to you."

"Troll shit. Where I go, you go. Remember?" It had been that way for years now. Afzal was his constant companion. Whatever dire adventure he found himself on, the Serklander was there to hold the torch, offer wisdom, and occasionally talk him out of his worst ideas.

"I could never have repaid my debt with a blade. But this will save your life, Master. I would have Naliajuk ... if she wishes me."

The finfolk woman looked to Hervor, then to Starkad.

"Don't do this," Starkad protested.

Afzal smiled. "You know it is the way. You call it urd."

"Fuck Fate. Come back to Sviarland. We have some treasure from Nordri, gold, Afzal. You want a woman, we'll find you a real one."

"You," Naliajuk said. "You insult?"

"No," Hervor said before he could respond. "He doesn't mean it."

The finfolk woman gnawed her lip. Looked to Afzal. "You. You choose me?"

Afzal nodded.

"Mmmm." Naliajuk looked at Hervor, then frowned. "Oath. Weapon oath."

Afzal hesitated a bare moment. "I swear upon my father's sword."

The shifter nodded then and pointed to the boat. "You. We take you ship."

Starkad ground his teeth. This wasn't supposed to happen like this. Afzal Ibn Hakim. As a boy, he'd lost everything. Dragged to the North Realms by his father only to have the man slain. Starkad had never asked him to follow as a servant, but he had. He always had.

He could not be gone now.

He felt numb as he settled back into the boat. Afzal nodded at him again. This was what he wanted, his choice, his sacrifice. His honor. And Starkad had no right to steal it from him.

And yet.

A long time ago, Starkad had lost his little brother. And then, somehow, without seeking it, he had found another. And now that brother was being taken from him as well.

On a bench before him, Tiny sheathed the runeblade.

Starkad's hands twitched at his sickening desire to strike down the man and claim his prize. Instead, he gripped the boat's side. This was his curse. This was his curse making him think this. He ought not to ... ought not to even consider betraying Tiny.

The man had fought bravely ...

And still. Still, Starkad had to have the blade. He had to. It was a physical ache in his gut, demanding he claim the greatest treasures for himself. Even *knowing* his curse might cause him to lose that in turn.

Afzal's hand fell upon Starkad's shoulder.

Maybe the boy knew. He'd been with Starkad for so long, he understood the curse. And he understood courage ... maybe more than even Starkad. He was staying here, making his life here, so that Starkad, Hervor, and Ecgtheow could be the few to escape Thule.

And the only way to honor that was to maintain peace between them.

So fuck the blade and fuck the curse. Starkad would not dishonor another brother. He breathed out a long sigh and cast a nod of acknowledgment at the boy.

In the end, the Serklander *had* saved him.

50

HERVOR

*H*ervor sat in the boat, across from Naliajuk. Beyond her sat Afzal and Starkad. Of course, Hervor could draw Tyrfing, lunge across the boat, and kill Naliajuk. The young man probably wouldn't appreciate being saved that way—and it would break his oath.

There were people out there who had earned her wrath, and she would focus it on them. Naliajuk was ... just different. Very different, Hervor supposed. But the woman had shown a hint of a smile when Afzal had asked for her. Maybe the finfolk had grown so used to having to abduct human spouses, they did not know how to react, how to feel, should one choose them.

And since then, the woman kept smiling, casting glances at the Serklander over her shoulder.

"Part of me will almost miss you," Hervor said.

In the distance, their ship rose up out of the mist. Still waiting for them. A more loyal crew than the one she'd sailed to Samsey with.

"You. You miss me?"

"Hmm, yes."

"Why?"

Hervor chuckled. "Odin alone knows."

"Odin?"

"King of the Gods?"

Naliajuk shrugged, and Hervor laughed. How could she even explain that?

Maybe she didn't need to. "This island will not be safe for you, for your kind."

Naliajuk gnawed on her lip, nodded. She stuck her hand inside her fur coat, fished around for something, then came out holding an ivory carving of a walrus. She thrust it at Hervor. "You. You don't miss me."

Hervor took the carving and ran her fingers over the smooth surface, not quite certain what to say. No one had ever given her aught like that before. A gift without an ulterior motive, without bargain. All because Naliajuk wanted her to remember her and not miss her. "I ..." She sighed and tucked the statuette into her own coat. "Thank you."

Naliajuk continued to row until the boat drew up along their ship.

The remaining crew shouted greetings and helped Hervor, Starkad, and Tiny on board.

She looked back to where Afzal remained sitting beside Naliajuk. The Serklander had probably saved all their lives. She raised a hand in acknowledgment. No words could do justice to the sacrifice. She hoped he could understand that.

"You are the bravest of us," Tiny said.

Afzal chuckled. "All I have to do is marry a beautiful woman. That's not courage—it's wisdom."

"Boy, you plan to live on an island filled with draugar. A frozen pit of misery shat out of Hel's own arse."

Starkad cuffed the big man, and Hervor frowned. "Afzal," Starkad said. "Just say the word."

"I already gave my word, Master."

"Don't call me that."

The Serklander nodded. "Then goodbye ... Starkad."

"Farewell. Little brother."

Afzal smiled at the term, and then Naliajuk shoved the boat away from their ship.

Starkad stood watching them go, glowering. Finally, Hervor left him.

"Get us away from this cursed place," Tiny ordered the crew. "Toward Faeroerne with all haste."

Over the sea, the sun had begun to rise, banishing the mist and glaring off the waters. Hervor shuddered and followed Tiny to where he collapsed on a bench. The wind was up and in their favor, so the men set the sails. Just as well since she suspected none of the three of them could have manned an oar.

She had to pray the wind stayed in their favor until Faeroerne. Sailing in winter was a horrific risk ... just not as bad as staying on Thule.

Hervor sunk down in front of Tiny. "So. You have a runeblade."

"So do you. Nine runeblades in all the World, and two are on this ship. How strange is urd."

She shrugged. Fate was a concern for gods. She had to make her own course. She had always done so, though little good had come from it thus far. Arrow's Point—Orvar-Oddr —was dead. That was a good thing. It *was* good. Though his face, his eyes had held the shock of betrayal. As if he could not imagine she would have avenged her kin.

Which made him a fool.

"You are deep in thought," Tiny said.

"Huh? Oh. Wondering what you will do now."

Tiny grunted. "I must return to King Gylfi. He will want

to know what we found and that no colony is like to thrive on Thule."

Hervor snorted. "Thrive? Not unless they plan to cut down an army of draugar first. And send several men and women to marry seals."

"Indeed. Brave boy."

Yes, Afzal. Back to Afzal. Starkad remained by the gunwale, knuckles white from clutching it so hard. "They knew each other a long time."

"I think so."

She sighed and rose, then drifted to where Starkad stood. "I'm sorry about your ... little brother."

He didn't look at her. "All men make their own choices."

"Women too."

"Indeed. And you ... well, you fought bravely."

She leaned on the rail beside him, trying not to smile. "Must have been hard for you to say."

The man mumbled something under his breath.

Hervor sighed. "So. You will tell King Yngvi we failed here."

"Failed?"

"We didn't take Thule."

"Perhaps. But reclaiming that runeblade might well have been all Odin ever cared about. I find it doubtful the Ás wanted the island itself. Especially if he had an idea what lurked in Nordri."

"Hmph." She stared at the glittering waters. Aught beyond her ken might dwell in those unknown depths. Much as such hidden dangers had lurked beneath Thule's surface. And maybe Odin could predict such things. But Starkad spoke as if he could understand any of the Aesir. "You find it easy to guess the mind of a god, do you?"

Starkad spit in the ocean, then turned away from it and sank down onto a bench.

Not going to answer then. Fair enough. They all had their secrets, didn't they? Especially her.

"What will you do now, woman?"

A difficult question, after all. Because of her many secrets. Her many enemies. Her reckless oath to bring down the whole Yngling dynasty. And that meant destroying Yngvi and his brother Alf, whom Starkad may or may not have held special loyalty to. She blew out a breath and sank down beside him.

Not a man she wanted as an enemy. And not only because of his prowess, great though it was.

He had saved her life on several occasions. The man may have had the personality of a troll's arse, but she couldn't hate him. Could almost even ... what? Want his approval? After all, to hear him say she had fought bravely was high praise. And who didn't like praise?

"After this winter? I guess I'll be seeking more glory. Wealth. You and Tiny claimed treasures from Nordri, but I didn't. I have naught to show for this whole endeavor." Naught save for one dead enemy. The first, clearest step on her journey, accomplished.

Now she faced the more difficult task. How to destroy a kingdom, one well loved and strong. She lacked the wealth to raise an army against them. But there were other ways to kill men than war. As Orvar-Oddr had learned, sometimes growing close to an enemy offered greater advantage.

"You earned a share," Starkad said. "You'll not return home empty-handed."

She nodded in thanks without really looking at Starkad.

Orvar had learned a hard lesson from her. But he had learned it. That she had seen in his eyes, the glare of hatred.

Of betrayal. Not a look she relished. And yet, he had earned it. Now he would know the suffering he had heaped upon her kin. And in the end, she hoped she'd see that look on Yngvi and Alf's faces too.

But not on Starkad's.

Not if she could avoid it.

51

ORVAR

*P*ain lapped at his flesh like waves upon the shore. No, not just his flesh. His mind and soul were swept up in that current, tossed apart and flung raw and bleeding back into a corpse.

Lifeless but not still.

Denied stillness, denied quiet. No respite. No peace.

Not without revenge.

Orvar opened his eyes. They seemed clouded with a haze, tinted red. Though he could see in the dark, see shifting hues of hot and cold, moving about. Draugar fighting with one another over the prince's crown. A large draug held it now, marching into the throne room with the crown held high above its head.

Betrayed.

Oh, she had betrayed him with such ardor, such zeal as could be repaid only in kind. A writhing hatred slithered through his mind like a serpent, venomous and hissing, coiling about his heart.

Whispering, ever.

Vengeance.

Orvar rose and hefted a sword from the floor. All his flesh protested his unnatural life, seized up in pain. And yet, despite that agony—or because of it—unholy strength drove him. Always, toward singular purpose.

Vengeance.

He flung himself forward, roaring. The sound unlike any he had ever made in life. A shriek of pain only the damned could utter. Only the damned could understand true, unbridled suffering. His blade bit deep into the neck of the draug holding the crown. The undead creature fell forward, dropping his prize.

Orvar spun, hacked into another draug that ran forward. He twisted, cleaved a third.

A fourth.

All pain. But not fatigue. Not exhaustion.

Just the endless well of rage and agony.

Vengeance.

Yes. All of those who had betrayed him. The bitch shieldmaiden, of course. He would rend her limbs from her body. Tear her spine out through her mouth. Drive spikes through her eyes.

Vengeance.

He swept up the fallen crown. The prince's oversized helm would not have fit him, but this piece. It could be forged into something that would. It would take time.

First, he'd have to unite the wretched. The writhing, suffering horde out in those streets. Leaderless. Themselves betrayed just as he was. Betrayed by life, by the living. Trapped in eternal torment, unable to sate this burning thirst to be revenged.

Oh, but he would. Vengeance upon Hervor, for the bitter, traitorous stroke that had felled him in his moment of glory. Upon Starkad and Tiny for leaving him to rot. Upon

Yngvi and Alf and Gylfi and every last kingdom of man. Upon the gods themselves for failing him, casting him out. For failing the World.

As all gods had.

All save Hel.

Vengeance.

The goddess moved in him now. He felt her. Her breath keeping the ultimate decay abated.

Well then. First, to claim a throne.

And then.

And then.

Vengeance.

EPILOGUE

*T*he Döglinar prince had long lain buried in the ruins of Nordri, hand clutched around the runeblade Naegling. There, it had offered scant boon to any. Odin's visions had revealed a wakening among the draugar, a stirring that would cost lives of men in Midgard. Such a price seemed acceptable to bring Naegling back into the World.

Back into the hands of men Odin might use come Ragnarok.

Disguised as another old man, Odin sat in a feast hall in Sviarland. The revelers might think him drunk, asleep at the table, but Odin cared naught for their assumptions. He let his mind drift into Starkad's dreams. As far as Odin knew, Starkad had never made any use of his latent gift for the Sight. The man would have had dreams of the past and future, cryptic and maddening. Unaware of his gift, he might only think it part of his curse.

Tormented by his losses, by his crimes, and by dark visions of the future.

Not unlike Odin himself.

Yes, Odin could see his own mirror in Tyr's son.

Had Starkad proved a more willing servant, Odin might have done more to obviate his suffering. But the man was obstinate and deliberately chose to distance himself from the Aesir and their graces. Such an attitude hardly earned him any more aid than Odin had already granted him.

Willing or not, Starkad did present a *useful* tool. A man Odin could reach and steer, one who oft seemed unaware of the prodding. And one who proved exceptionally good at inciting the chaos Odin needed to enact his greater plans.

Having found Naegling—and not even claimed it for himself—Starkad would already be well primed to seek his next challenge. He could never stand to stay long in one place, nor let any potential wealth lie unclaimed. His wanderlust and greed ate away at his soul with each passing day. The more he tried to fight those urges, the more wickedly they consumed him.

Yes, Odin would have pitied the man. Had Midgard been able to afford pity. But the World had no room for it.

If Odin faltered, if he failed, Mankind died.

With such stakes, the happiness of a single man meant naught at all. And so, as with Gylfi, Odin would use Starkad as long as he could, as hard as could, until naught but ash remained of the man. If he pushed hard enough, Odin just might buy Mankind a little more time.

All Odin had to do was ensure Starkad would seek out the next of the lost runeblades. It would take Odin time to determine *where* to send the man, of course. But until then … a gentle prod from time to time, and he might engender an obsession in the man.

Starkad, after all, was wont to be taken by obsession.

And before they were done, Odin would see a great many more deeds done by the man.

Deeds great and glorious. And dark.

For such was Starkad's urd.

THE CYCLE CONTINUES ...

Dear Reader,

Thanks for reading!

Hervor has avenged her family.

But what price will she pay for that vengeance?

Her own victim now hunts her, even as she becomes embroiled in a war for the throne.

As things grow bloodier, she is forced to ask ...

Does a darker force lurk behind the chaos?

If you loved book 1, get ready for even higher stakes as the saga continues.

Get it now.

The Saga continues in *Days of Bloody Thrones:*
books2read.com/daysofbloodythronesbook

hanks,
Matt

Join the Skalds' Tribe and get access to exclusive insider information, conversations with the author, and updates about new releases and sales.

https://www.mattlarkinbooks.com/join-the-skalds-tribe/

For Juhi. Thank you.

ABOUT THE AUTHOR

Matt Larkin writes retellings of mythology as dark, gritty fantasy. His passions of myths, philosophy, and history inform his series. He strives to combine gut-wrenching action with thought-provoking ideas and culturally resonant stories.

Matt's mythic fantasy takes place in the Eschaton Cycle universe, a world—as the name implies—of cyclical apocalypses. Each series can be read alone in any order, but they weave together to form a greater tapestry. Want a place to start? Check out *Darkness Forged*.

Learn more at mattlarkinbooks.com or connect with Matt through his fan group, the Skalds' Tribe: https://www.mattlarkinbooks.com/join-the-skalds-tribe/

Printed in Great Britain
by Amazon